Against the Ruins

Also by
Linda Lightsey Rice

Southern Exposure

Contents

The action takes place in Columbia, South Carolina.
Liberties have been taken with various historical places and events.

Lyra's Prologue

◈

2004

I grew up between a cemetery and a madhouse. I played in ancestral Civil War ruins. Our family car was a yellow Checker taxicab, my best friend's mother a prostitute. A neighbor believed she'd trapped her husband's soul in a green glass jar and our house sat atop a potter's field. My childhood was leafy oak trees, craziness, and ghosts.

This was the South Carolina I knew. That upstart state, rabble-rousing bunch, swept-yard poor and Cadillac-rich all hot and sticky together and plumb overrun with crimson flowers, slow afternoon syllables hanging in the soft scented air like fluttering wing-weary butterflies. Cape jasmine, gardenia, magnolia, mimosa—even the words droop heavy with scent. So much color and so much sunlight so tormented by the old gray memory. This is the tattoo on my psyche, inked deep, lasting beyond death.

Troubled history, scars both public and private, everywhere you look.

My family's past is like the place we come from, a mirrored hall of memory, mythology, mirage. Dizzying images appear and recede, combine and separate. The real picture is as wavy as old glass. That rippled reality began the December I was six, when afterward everyone acted as though

1

none of it had happened. A penchant for sorcery travels true in our veins. But I know what happened, a few bits and pieces anyway, even if I don't know what—in the long run—these fragments mean.

I can't see the scar, but I know it's there.

Part I: Lyra

❖

2004

Chapter One

In the air, I remember a day in Uta's house. I'd only been in her house a few times: I was leery of the imposing granite mansion with its two-foot-thick walls, its turret, even a carriage ramp. A low stone fence ran alongside her sidewalk, a rusty iron gate—the cemetery kind—admitting visitors into the yard. Not that many came to call. The whole place felt like a perfect spot for the undead to hang out. And Uta herself—always in dark rustling clothes like you'd imagine in a Brontë novel, white ringlets, one sleeve pinned back where her left arm should have been. I had yet to discover that she could make flowers grow just by whistling at them.

Ours was a weary street of leaning, lazy clapboards, old wood houses that breathed and shifted and whined in the wind, making Uta's imperious dark castle mysterious, a fortification not to be messed with. Everything in her house was fusty, old-fashioned, spooky. The air felt filmy with dust motes, the hallway smelled like lavender sachets people were always giving old ladies, and in the "parlor" a double-globe lamp with roses painted on the glass sat beside a high-back velvet sofa obviously stuffed with lead. That day, though, my mother and I were in the less formal "sitting room" (in my house we sat in all the rooms) when Uta put a raw egg on a dish and said we needed to hear the Legend of the Egg. I figured on a tale about how baby chickens poked their way through the shell. Maybe Uta'd make those baby chicks fly or change color or do something interesting.

"This story is from the Ashanti people," she said, lowering her voice as though speaking of secrets or sacraments, "but they got it from the ancient Egyptians. I heard it from an African man down to Charleston. He was a magic man—why, he could make a woman pregnant just by touching her stomach. Women would go to see him, never tell their husbands. He was seven feet tall, always wore a purple turban. All he had to do was walk down the street in Charleston and all the white people got the jitters."

Uta asked my mother to pick up the egg. When my mother grasped it by one end, Uta made a fuss, said she'd drop it that way. My mother curled her whole hand around it but got scolded again. I was hoping Uta would make the egg disappear up the sleeve of her good arm.

"The egg is the symbol of life," she said, looking at my mother but nodding toward me. "Your egg made this amazing child, did it not?"

She reached for the egg and balanced it on her upturned palm. "Like this, not too tight, not too loose. Or life will be destroyed."

Apparently no baby chicks were going to do anything. I began wishing somebody would just cook the thing.

It's clear that nobody in my clan ever really got it.

I cried almost the entire flight, soared over the Rocky Mountains in an emotional and uncharacteristically public free-for-all. The pinstriped, lizard-skin-booted Texan sitting next to me was so uncomfortable he went to the bathroom three times. When he noticed I was holding a biography of Lucrezia Borgia, he ordered a double Scotch and didn't stop drinking until we landed. This is a story my mother would like, except for how enthusiastically I joined the freaked-out Texan in swilling Scottish single malt.

The stroke has left her unable to speak or open her eyes. I lean over her hospital bed and run my fingers through her thick white hair—I sense that she's still here yet somewhere else too. Actually, that's always been the case. I picture her deep-set blue-gray eyes, eyes of rueful sadness, and recall a black-and-white photograph from her twenties—her eyes when young, with their well of amazement, their dazzled joy.

If I ever saw that joy, I don't remember it.

The ventilator hisses, she moves her head slightly.

Gently I take her swollen hand and whisper, "I'm here."

I could swear to God—an expression she'd disapprove of—that she's talking to herself, or thinking hard, or something. I brush back new tears. I can't bear the thought of her death, yet for years I've not been able to bear the thought of her life either.

Suddenly I drop her hand and pace across the room, stare at the wall. She didn't speak or open her eyes when she could have. Did she?

I whirl back around. *Why the hell didn't you* do *something?*

When I arrived at the hospital, my father sidestepped our wooden ritual embrace. "I've got a contagious disease," he announced, backing away. He's been dying of something or other for forty years. He once told me he had lung cancer, but he didn't seem to need a doctor for it.

He does not look me in the eye—he never does—nor ask how I am. At eighty-one, he seems a decade younger, still a tall and slender figure with thick silver-blond hair. Healthy, mentally sharp, handsome even. Although he keeps his lovely hair too short to do it justice, his slightly dashing mustache always startles me, especially since it's wedded to a timid voice and demeanor. Timid with everyone but family, that is. He can remind me, down to the subject and letter, how bad my grades were my freshman year in college, before I discovered there were classes one might do well to attend. He can still name which of my high-school boyfriends were "dumber than toads." Apparently they all were. Of course, my father also believes that a telephone solicitor, without his permission, can charge a new Buick to his Visa account. Never mind that he wouldn't give his account number to the Holy Ghost.

Updating me on my mother's condition, he steps closer to me than feels comfortable. "I haven't had a day to myself in four years for taking care of your mother," he says. Then he stops, as though suddenly realizing who I am. "You gain some weight? Better watch out, you'll end up as fat as your mother was way back."

Welcome home.

For days now, he and I have watched machines pump life in and out of my mother's tired body, but we exchange only as many words as necessary. Every night he sleeps in the armchair beside my mother's bed but he does not speak to her, nor touch his wife of fifty-seven years. When he's out of the room, I chatter to her about anything and everything. I sound like a robot on speed. Sometimes I offer up a silent prayer that she's not in pain. She's never complained about the considerable difficulties of her old age. I, on the other hand, probably came down the birth canal pointing out that there wasn't enough room.

I stare at my father across the room. His large, artistic hands are spreadeagled across his khaki-clad knees—he favors informal military dress, a starched white shirt and pressed khakis, as though he has to report to Fort Jackson at any minute. He still wears his gold military academy class ring, its surface worn smooth now. He stretches his fingers nervously. Those are my long fingers too. Piano fingers. As a child, did I ever hold mine against his to compare the length? What would it be like to have a father who'd reach for my hand today?

While my father keeps overnight vigil at the hospital, I retire to my parents' suburban rancher in West Columbia, where I lived only a few years before leaving home. Pulling the rental car into the driveway, I wonder—did they move here to get away from the Lincoln Street neighbors who pointed at us for years? This bland, rectangular brick box, flimsy detritus of the 1950s, sits at the dead end of a busy road: a car running the stop sign could leap right into the living room. It still amazes me that my father chose this location. He did plant a row of pine trees along the front property line, his barrier against wayward cars, and the world. I sit staring at the house for a moment, waiting for the familiar knot in my stomach. In the past I often had to force myself to go inside. *Would it be okay this time or gut-wrenching awful?*

I spent countless lonely nights here wanting to break dishes, sometimes doing so. I walk toward the carport, stop beside oddly pruned azaleas outlined by heavy three-cornered bricks from the columns of a house burned to the ground in 1865. On the carport, eight small fire extinguishers are lined up like ladder rungs on a moth-eaten wool blanket. This is new. Has he joined the fire department? I pass the padlocked white freezer—who steals frozen chicken around here?—and unlock the side door and go inside. I almost knock over the homemade sawhorse my father uses to barricade the door at night—apparently the two dead bolts will not suffice.

The bright blue tablecloth I gave my mother one Christmas is still on the oak breakfast table. I close my eyes—I can *feel* her here. I lean against the wall and remember her voice when I was a child. "You're special, sweetheart," she whispers to me. "You can do anything."

Except find peace or stay in one place or with one person.

I breathe in again. Houses, homes, their aroma comes from the woman who lives there, the woman whose sweat seeps into the woodwork and drapes. This smell is my maternal grandparents' house in Brantley too, their musty furniture overlaid with my mother's Estée Lauder perfume and Avon body lotion (where did she still get that?) and the deep female scent of her aging. In the knotty-pine paneled den, I sit on the plaid sofa and stare at the painting across from me. My maternal grandmother completed forty paintings before dying at age thirty in the Spanish flu epidemic. This one, four feet by five, is a raging forest fire—Indian red, burnt sienna, brown madder palette. Did oil paints have those names in 1919? Several trees are falling over, a massive plume of gray smoke behind them—yellow ocher and ivory black is my guess, maybe some Payne's gray. A very dark painting, smoky tonality, acceptance of destruction, no pity.

My mother's favorite of her mother's paintings is this scene of loss. True to the English landscape tradition, all my grandmother's pictures are dark and moody; she died too early to discover modernism's bright colors. Suddenly I get up and do the irresponsible—run a forefinger across the texture of hundred-year-old paint, wondering over the relative I know almost nothing about but nonetheless feel connected to. I come away with the mute dust of the past on my fingertip.

I call and leave a message for the dean of the small Denver college where I teach. I phone several friends, eat my Chinese take-out and watch television mindlessly for an hour, then lie down in my mother's room, which was once my room. Facing me is my Mother's Day gift at age twelve, my inept portrait of my mother's childhood home. That same Mother's Day she gave me a heartfelt letter telling me how much she'd always wanted a child and thanking me for being so mature that she could depend on me to take care of myself. The letter also contained instructions for my education should something "happen" to her. Even then, I knew that my father lived on another planet and my mother was in a state of retreat. All because of a December over forty years ago? Why couldn't they recover?

I decide to shower but can't abide the threadbare towels in the bathroom—a Depression teenager, my mother still kept "company towels" in a cedar chest. We spent a lot of time preparing an appearance for the company that rarely came after my father installed security cameras on the carport—a burglar could start a film career here. I rummage through the cedar chest. The company towels, which smell wonderful, look a decade old. *What are we saving them for?* As I plunder, I'm also hoping—I admit it—to find letters or other clues to my mother's psyche. Louise Copeland has left no opportunity for scavenging her inner life. I admire this. I'm also disappointed. I'd like to know what she's most hidden from me—who she really *is*.

Underneath the towels is a box stuffed with newspaper clippings: reviews of my first gallery show and of others that followed, interviews, an article in a national arts magazine that included me. Photos of my paintings with information about who bought them. My mother's archives of my work are better than mine. Which surprises me given that she once suggested I be "practical" and become a dental hygienist. At the time I wondered if her message "You can do anything" only meant *anything safe*. Absently I smooth out a crease in a newspaper photo of a younger me. Fiery eyes. Eyes determined to rip through the shroud of despair tenting my childhood by becoming *someone*. I'd escape. Cheat fate. The clippings are brittle and yellowed now. A decade ago my Bonnard-influenced palette went black and muddy, Goya meeting El Greco on a bad day. My cooler abstracts looked confused, and the museum curator who mentored and sustained my career abruptly dropped dead. I began painting portraits in which human skin looked shredded; even my friends thought I was on drugs. Eventually I became too restless—or *something*—to paint at all.

After my shower, seeing it's not locked as usual, I peek inside my father's bedroom. On every surface papers and files are stacked halfway to the ceiling. He has bank statements from 1955, maybe even earlier. A small television, circa 1982. Old transistor radios and brass lamps waiting to be fixed, a metal detector no doubt bought at a yard sale. A Goodwill store has been taking root in here for decades. Two windows are still sealed with clear plastic to keep out the post 9/11 poison gas that's going to be shot into South Carolina. On one wall hangs his World War II Bronze Star certificate in a rickety, scratched frame, his metal dog tags slung over it. He never mentioned his wartime service until he was sixty-four, and then out of the blue he dusted off his uniform and joined a veteran's group. The Air Medal awarded his younger brother, a pilot who died over the Mediterranean the day before the war ended, also hangs on the wall. His is the only photo in the room. I'm the pacifist descendant of warriors: both my great-grandfathers served in the Confederate army, my grandfather fought in Mexico at age sixteen, my mother's brother drowned himself in alcohol upon returning from North Africa. But my father's history has particularly haunted my family, the twenty-year-old slogging through the cold sea toward Omaha Beach, jumping off a life raft into history.

I return to my mother's orderly bedroom, which is inundated with pictures of her parents, her brothers, me, my father as a child. I peek inside her jewelry box at her most prized possession—the Victorian cameo set in delicate gold filigree that belonged to my painter grandmother. I hold it over my heart for a moment. Prowling back into the living room—I've not been alone in this house since my twenties, I feel like I'm trespassing—I sit down and stare at the glass-front oak bookcase, its old-fashioned finish ebony, and at the ornate 1820s tarnished-black silver coffeepot atop it. All that's left of my paternal ancestry, buried in the well when Sherman came to call. I don't know which South I belong to, the dead old one or the tacky new version; I was raised in the latter by parents groomed in the former.

Often it's felt as though their lives, and this house, most properly belong to the 1940s and to world war, like all our clocks stopped then.

Suddenly I hate how beaten-up and tired the furniture looks. The 1950s coffee table was bought with Green Stamps, cheap wood with a plastic shine, incongruously juxtaposed to my grandmother's 1920s Empire rocker, whose cracked leg is crudely repaired with duct tape. My father has always controlled my parents' lives. Did my mother ever buy anything simply because it was beautiful and she wanted it? Did she love this house she's lived in for forty years?

Finally, like a good modern girl, I take a Xanax and go to bed.

Morning after morning in the ICU waiting room turns into softer evening, and I often stand at the metal-frame window to look out over the city of my youth. Absently I run a hand along the slick marble ledge—a modern window, no history, even less myth. Once upon a time I wanted to be an architect but soon discovered I only love *old* buildings. Perhaps I should have been a conservator. Several years after art school, I spent a year on studies of windows and doors; I was in love with O'Keeffe and Diebenkorn at the time. Some doors and windows were partially open, many closed tight, means of egress from my travels in Europe, the historic South, the Southwest. I still prefer making love beside a window and can't sleep in a room without one.

From this characterless opening—no, being hermetically sealed, it isn't an opening at all—I can just make out the distant dome of the State Capitol. In an old photo, an eleven-year-old me hangs onto Washington's statue on the front steps, his presidential cane snapped off by Union soldiers, repaired and rewelded, then broken again by locals so no one would forget who originally broke it. And we wonder why people still think Southerners are *weird*. This is, after all, the state where a lieutenant governor murdered a well-known newspaper editor on the capitol grounds. Doesn't pay to disagree politically in South Carolina, though I guess everyone knows that by now.

It's also my vein of madness, this place is. Can't stay, can't ever really leave. *Home* is a word in a language I apparently don't speak. Yet part of me is always here. Literally. My very proper schoolteacher mother, she was about thirty then, her silky black hair parted in the middle, and … what does she have it in? What does afterbirth look like days later? She and the Gullah woman must have gone somewhere after dark—surely not a cemetery, maybe a remote spot in the swamps along the Charleston road—and I guess they dug a hole and put the "stuff" in it. My mother the Matriarch of Reason out in the dark burying the slimy placenta? When she told me she'd done this—I was twenty-seven and indifferent to folk myths, I certainly didn't believe this would bring a child good luck—she said she did it because having a child come out of her body felt like a miracle and she wanted us to stay connected for always. Even now, lodged deep in Carolina mud, is the decayed tissue she and I once shared.

Across the room my father sits in an upholstered beige armchair; occasionally he reminds me to use the wall hand sanitizer before going into ICU. The man who was once completely silent around strangers chats amiably with the woman nearest him, makes jokes about being eighty-one. I don't think I ever saw him smile until I was forty; even at Christmas dinner he could be dour and mute until my mother desperately asked him inane questions. To pass the time, I thumb through the Columbia newspaper, abruptly pull it nearer. The massive state mental hospital, about ten blocks from where I grew up and closed for years, is for sale. The city hopes a developer will turn it into condos: "a perfect spot for downtown living." *Jesus*—I try to imagine kicking back in rooms once used for electric shock and lobotomy. And I think I sleep poorly now. At thirteen, to earn a Girl Scout badge, I did volunteer work in the hospital's arts and crafts center. Without telling my parents. I can barely remember being there. My recall of my childhood is often facts devoid of context. Sometimes I long for emotional memory.

My father jumps up as my mother's doctor walks in. Dr. Dumaine—big and burly and gray, rumpled suit, tired eyes, a distant cousin—has been my mother's doctor for decades. He sits down and says that my mother seems a little better today but full recovery isn't likely.

I stare at the man I've met only twice. "Is there any chance she'll wake up, be able to speak or open her eyes?"

"There's no way to know. I'm sorry. Your mother is a favorite patient. I've known her for a long time. She's—very special."

His voice is melodic, sorrowful. My mother adores him, has vowed to die before he retires. I've often had the feeling he knows more about us than I know about him.

After he leaves, I go and tell my mother she's doing better. She mumbles and winces. I lean close and ask if she's in pain; she seems to shake her head no. Or that may be involuntary movement. Hearing is the last sense to go, the nurses say, so I talk about Easters in Brantley when I was a child, azaleas ten feet tall and the sunny Easter dresses she always made us. All the women in big hats—"Remember Grandmother's hat with the silk daylilies on it? How they flopped when she walked?"

I laugh to keep from weeping. I feel cheated that I can't say good-bye properly. I yearn to hear my mother's lyrical Low Country voice one last time. Perhaps I even hope, absurdly, that she'll finally *talk* to me.

❧⊙❧

I belong to a much older house than my parents' rancher. Families are architecture—*home* is a place, a structure. A stage of rooms and walls against which live theater takes place. Often my family feels like the abandoned shack in remote Southern woodlands—creepy with kudzu, doors left open, bedstead still in place, razor-lonely, redolent with disillusioned expectation. Or we could be the once-venerable two-story sitting beside small-town railroad tracks, leaning and deserted, flint gray from years bereft of paint, which the relatives—who wouldn't be caught dead living there and won't pay to tear it down—allow to slowly fall to its knees, brick by brick, board by board. The houses I understand best are empty.

As I always do when in Columbia, I need to see the actual house of my childhood. I read old houses like tea leaves—in a way, I've had to. Even if I can't remember what was done and said inside them, I can recall the look of certain rooms down to a protruding nail in a floorboard.

Architectural memory. I believe that old houses have souls—not ghosts, *souls*. So at dusk one evening I drive into the city. Soon I'm across the Broad River and passing the city cemetery where I once counted Confederate graves, as the interstate dumps me onto the wide boulevard of Elmwood Avenue. The Elmwood mansions I remember are gone, defeated by the squatty huts and incomparable cuisine of The Lizard's Thicket and Piggie Park Barbeque. I'm sure people go there for the salads. A huge red dome, inflamed by the coral sunset, looms in the distance. This beacon of the South Carolina State Mental Hospital, a city-state of ancient buildings with barred windows, always guides me home.

I turn onto Lincoln Street. In my old neighborhood the clapboard houses saved by the National Historic Register have been dipped in exuberant pastels. I pass several rambling Craftsman bungalows, a Queen Anne or two, mostly rows of two-story foursquare houses with balconies shaded by old oak trees. I hesitate beside a yellow bungalow with a wraparound porch and steeply pitched roof; a girl who lived there was a favorite friend until her mother would no longer allow her to play with me. These houses are as elegant now as when they were built a hundred years ago, mythically Southern, where on companion front porches black families sit in the twilight talking to their white neighbors about last night's ball game. A way of life reinvented by these newly entwined, sibilant voices.

Uta's stone house, on the other hand, looks exactly as it did in my childhood, solid, impressive. I park at our old house, a 1913 clapboard foursquare. In the 1970s this neighborhood was a slum, a victim of white flight. Several houses were razed but someone saved ours at the eleventh hour. I'm thankful it's still here. The house is now French blue with white shutters; a bay window has been added to the kitchen and the open-air porch sports carved balustrades, a wooden swing, and hanging baskets of red geraniums. But as I sit there staring, the gentrification fades. I see the house as I knew it—sagging on a weakened foundation, dirty white walls, torn window screens, broken shingles, crumbling concrete steps. Ditto the nearby houses: one sheltered a group of people whose relationship to each other was as questionable as their housekeeping—the city inspector routinely condemned part of their house, and they closed those rooms off and kept living in the rest. In those days our porch was a screened-in square of rotting gray-painted floorboards, its furniture two metal nylon-strap beach loungers, one with bent legs. In the backyard the ramshackle garage leaned to the left, and two towering pecan trees framed my rusted swing set. I can still hear nuts *kerplunking* onto the ground like wooden rain.

How many times have I come here like a lost dog who finds his way home only to discover his family has moved?

I get out of the car and lean against it, gazing at the renovated house canopied by luxuriant leaves that glisten in the twilight. The humid air knocks me breathless—I've barely been outside since arriving in Columbia. The evening air is soft as only air in the South can be—gentle yet heavy, full of texture, presence. From some backyard wafts the musk of ripening tomatoes, a nascent trill of gardenia, the day's heat lifting from the cement sidewalks and floating away. All around me the loamy aroma that is old and decayed, organic, full of melancholy portent. Full of the past.

Our first day here—I think I was five, maybe wearing a ruffled sundress my mother made, running through the large square kitchen of torn blue-flowered linoleum, past the scarred refrigerator and the pitted ceramic sink with a cracked mirror tacked to the plaster wall above it. The kitchen leads into a central bedroom, a tall brown oil stove fronting its blocked fireplace. In my small bedroom four windows overlook the backyard. My closet is a makeshift plywood cube covered by a curtain; the plank floor, unsupported by the main foundation, slopes downward. Children who grow up in added-on rooms lack balance. My dropped marbles always rolled toward the windows leading outside.

I dash into the rectangular bathroom: white pedestal sink, toilet, squatty iron bathtub on claw feet. The side of the tub is plastered with a decal of blonde women—creamy white skin, flawless blue eyes, slender tapered legs. Perfect women, bright yellow curls bouncing as they prance about on dainty feet, strategically placed bubbles barely covering the full breasts and each abdomen below the belly button. I drop down beside the tub and study them, and then pop up and twirl around. They'll be my friends in this new place. Good-luck fairies.

Just then my mother—she has black hair that shines like it has stars in it—appears and I ask, "Are the ladies so happy because they're wearing bubbles, not clothes?"

"Sweetie, I'm not sure. Maybe."

Hand in hand, we walk back through the empty rooms and down the front steps. She turns to look back at the house. "The screen porch will be nice in summer," she says. "All the old trees, hardwoods, they'll give beautiful autumn color, and I'll plant hydrangeas beside the steps, and azaleas too."

My daddy—all the relatives said he was good to look at, all that thick blond hair and robin's-egg eyes, a war hero to boot, they said it was still hard to believe shy Louise snagged such a good-looking *younger* man—is in the driveway staring at the roof, checking the condition of the chimney. Everybody says we're charmed, no money but my parents have college degrees and "opportunity." Watching my father, my mother whispers, "Sometimes I close my eyes and remember your daddy taking the stairs two at a time at the Summerville Teachery—that's where the single schoolteachers lived—with flowers in his hands, or a beautiful bird feather he'd found. He seemed to discover life anew every day."

She points to a dogwood tree in the side yard. "Look—my favorite tree." We skip over and she reaches up to caress the brown scars on the petals. "Tree of rebirth," she says. "Can you believe I once tried to press dogwood blooms to preserve them like we do rose petals? I wanted to have them all year. Guess what: dogwood petals turn brown and ugly." She gazes down at me. "Sometimes, Lyra, you just have to *trust*. Yes sir, I'll sweep the dust out of this old house and everything will be wonderful."

The past fades as I gaze again at the reinvented Lincoln Street house. Like people, buildings either recover from their wounds or they disintegrate. History's been remade here. My mother's blue hydrangeas are still there, almost ready to bloom. There it all is, a lovely old house and flowers and love. All that should have come to pass—it happened, but only for the house.

Part II: Louise

1957

Chapter Two

❖

It's Friday and I'm walking down Park Street, 4 p.m. The air snaps and crackles, unusually cold but just right for December. Small patches of white remain on the grass from the amazing snowfall of a few days ago. I love this neighborhood of clapboard houses with sprawling front porches, wise old houses, ancestral texts filled with secrets. Life is amazing—there are occasional glitches, of course. I know I'm a Pollyanna but I don't care. Really, when you think about it, what's a Cold War compared to the awful world war we lived through? I feel like skipping. I'm not thirty-six today, more like ten, and Christmas is two weeks away, and my stepmother and brothers and their families will soon be here. It won't matter that we don't have much room. We'll rent roll-away beds, and it'll be like the old days when on hot summer nights the whole family slept on the sleeping porch. I can still hear insects buzzing against the metallic screens and my father's gentle snoring.

Sometimes—it sounds silly—I feel as though, when no one was looking, I sneaked in the back door of the life I always dreamed of.

As I turn onto Aiken Street, I see a child on a bicycle, peddling with her arms crossed across her chest. *My* child. It scares me when Lyra rides like this, and thrills me too, I who never learned to ride a bike. Suddenly she grabs the handlebars as the front wheel jackknifes. She sees me and waves—can she really be six already? My dream come true, this child, this clay pot I'm hand-building to be as sturdy as possible. She peddles over and rides along beside me, silky blonde hair escaping a tortoiseshell barrette, pants dirty at the knees. I ask about her day at school and while she babbles, I walk in sync with her sidewalk shadow. I don't want her slipping away.

We turn onto Lincoln Street. Down the block I see our car in the driveway. "Your daddy's home early. That's nice, isn't it?"

As we go inside, I make a mental note to wash the living-room curtains before Christmas. I step over Fluffy sprawled on the hall carpet runner—that cat lies everywhere except out of the way. As usual, I almost trip over the torn edge of the kitchen's blue-flowered linoleum.

"Darling?" I call toward the closed bedroom door as I set my things down on the marbled-yellow table. Formica may be easy to keep up, but give me a wood table any day. I call again, "How was your day, sweetheart?"

No answer. Maybe he's taking a nap, though that's odd at this hour.

Fluffy wanders in and makes inquiries about dinner while Lyra sits at the table with a coloring book; then Lyra crawls down and buries her face in cat fur and of course starts sneezing. I open the scarred refrigerator door—there isn't much for supper. A can of salmon and grits will have to do.

A sudden slam from the bedroom. William's voice.

I push the swinging bedroom door open, Lyra behind me. William's lying on our lumpy bed, his eyes closed, saying something I can't make out.

He doesn't usually talk in his sleep. "Darling, are you awake?"

He doesn't open his eyes. He must really be sleeping. I walk over to the bed and run my hand through the wild wavy hair I love. Lyra's hair.

Dark stains on my good white sheets. Where did they come from? It almost looks like blood.

William jumps up—eyes unnaturally white, he's wearing only his pajama bottoms, they're stained red too. He whispers in a harsh rasp, "Get down here." He drops to his knees beside the bed. "We've blasphemed God," he shouts. "We must *beg* for forgiveness. Hell is coming."

"William, what's *wrong*?"

He yells, "Get down here, I said." His eyes are unfocused, wobbly. His voice booms, "Get down here so we can pray."

He grabs my arm and forces me onto the floor as Lyra scurries backward.

"William, please. Please let me up. Tell me what's wrong." I turn slightly, cry out, "There's blood on your arm—you're bleeding."

He pushes me face down against the bed, holds me there. Lyra runs to the corner of the room, hides in the shadows.

"We've sinned against *God*," William yells into my ear. "Those circles, those circles of hell, that's where you're going, where all of us will go if we don't beg for our lives. I've heard them."

I'm shaking as I whisper, "Lyra, go to your room, everything will be all right, go in your room and close the door. Please do this for Mama."

She begins inching away, but William rears up from the bed and grabs her by the arm. *Oh God.* There's blood on his chest, stains on both arms. Lyra screams as he pushes her down beside me. I grab her into my arms as William yells, "I said *pray*, you wicked child. You've sinned, you must pay for your sins."

My terrified voice: "Run to your room, honey. Go on. *Now.*" I push her to her feet. She starts crying and holds onto me.

William leaps up and runs around the room, cries that he has to find his mother's Bible; he turns and bellows, "What did you do with it, Louise? What have you done with my mother's Bible?"

"William, please tell me what's wrong!"

He runs toward the living room, there's a crash, he runs back into the bedroom, looks at Lyra and me as though just realizing we're there, and snarls, "If you two move, I'll have to shoot you."

He begins talking to someone who isn't there. He runs back to the living room, stumbles into the hall, the dining room—another crash, things are falling. I grab Lyra and pull her through her room and into the bathroom; I'm trembling and crying as I tell her to lock the bathroom door and do *not* come out—

Then William's suddenly there, he grabs me and drags me back to the bedroom and shoves me to my knees again. I try to get up but he—he's crying now—knocks me to the floor; my knees hitting the wood sounds like bones breaking, and I cry, "What's wrong, William, why do we have to pray?" and then he yells again—

Now I see more blood on the bed. I feel sick looking at it, I can't seem to move. Blood all down William's left arm—oh God, there's so much blood—

❦❦❦

No—I'm not back there. No. It was a long time ago. Thank God.

I'm in a bed that feels strange, someone is whispering. I can't tell who it is. I feel—disorganized, a jumbled closet no one's opened for years.

Can't get my eyes to open. I start to say something but no sound comes out. Perhaps I'm gone, maybe I only think I'm still here. Yet I feel—younger.

I know my name. Louise. My name is Louise. I must still be here. I wish I knew what day it is.

I'm so tired—

❦❦❦

Something woke me—I'm in a hospital again, I can tell by the smells. Very noisy too. Was that a nurse or dear Dr. Dumaine?

Wait—that's my child's voice. My baby girl's. Isn't it? Lyra! Lyra, you're here. That must be your hand touching mine, which is so swollen and pinned down by tubes. What torture that I can't look into your eyes.

I must really be sick this time.

Darling Lyra. Even now it's hard for your old mother not to call you "darling baby girl"—like I did when you were little. You're whispering—I can't quite make it out. A minute ago I felt like I was in Brantley again, back when my three brothers and I were children and we rushed outside whenever an airplane flew by—airplanes being rare and exotic then. We'd look up and wave like mad. I didn't always see the plane but I said I did.

I didn't want to be left out. *Some things are there even when you can't see them,* I'd say when telling you this story. My mantra, for more reasons than one.

Now you're here, I feel so clear, Lyra. Yes, talk to me. I can hear you. What was that? You went back to Lincoln Street?

Well … of course. Of course you would.

I seem to be alone now. I couldn't tell my child that since I've been lying in this bed I've been reliving Lincoln Street too, reliving the worst day there. I try not to remember it, I've kept it at bay for years, but now it keeps returning. It won't let me alone. Why after all this time—

Why on earth didn't I phone an ambulance that night? Can shock be that bad? I didn't even think of it, perhaps because we couldn't afford such things.

I don't want to go back there—still clinging to the bloodied bedspread. Still wondering how life can change so abruptly. It's the next morning. I'm still kneeling by the bed when I open my eyes. I remember the night, the blood, the praying, and I put my head back down—*I will not wake up to today, I'll wake up to yesterday, to how much there is to look forward to when we get a house of our own and have a second baby.* Then I look at William mumbling in his sleep and it comes back again, the terrible screaming senseless night, and I jerk across the bed, check the bandage I put on his arm and sigh, relieved—no fresh blood. I slump back down. One moment the world was one thing and now it's another. A dial was spun, and I'm in a foreign country.

What *happened*?

Oh, God—where is my baby?

I stumble to my feet and run into Lyra's room—

I hear you talking to me—right now, in this hospital room. But no, you're under your sheets. You're only six years old. Too young for this. I pull the covers back but you don't open your eyes as I kiss you on the cheek. I wonder how much you saw and heard and lean over, head in my hands—I want yesterday back, I'll make sure you don't see what happens. There I am, taking care of my beautiful child, hustling you out of the room before William grabs me, taking your hand and speeding you over to Uta's house. I tell her William is sick and could she look after you for a while and Uta says *why of course* and you stay there and when it gets dark she puts you down in her spare bedroom, reads you a story, and you never know.

My tears spill, hard slow exhaustion confusion dismay tears.

I stare through the doorway at William, at the blood on the bed, a scene from a war—

What is *wrong* with him?

I walk over and gaze down at him—he looks like himself now, his slender face peaceful, like the smiling shy boy in that old jeep. "Who goes on a Florida honeymoon in an army jeep?" my stepmother asked, and I laughed: "We do, we do!"

As I lay my head down on William's thigh, on the blue pajamas streaked with blood, I begin to cry. No, I can't, I can't fall apart. I lean back up. It'll be all right, it has to be all right, if only I could get some sleep, in a few minutes I'll call school and say I'm sick and then call a doctor—

William stirs. He glances at me and then stares at the ceiling.

"Sweetheart, how do you feel this morning?"

Nothing but that fixed stare at the ceiling. I reach over and touch his forearm. Rigid, like steel.

"Sweetheart, do you have classes today?"

It's like he's not there. But he seems to be thinking something, perhaps hearing something.

I stare at the clock. Get Lyra to school. He'll just rest this morning. I can't think beyond that.

In the bathroom I sponge blood off my school dress and brush my teeth while staring at the wicker clothes hamper. It could use a coat of paint, it would look much better green, I'll paint it soon. Then my face crumbles like an old cookie. What does a clothes hamper matter *now*? I comb my hair, staring into the medicine-chest mirror. I'm older than I was yesterday.

Why so much praying, so much talk of sin? My God, he—

Get Lyra to school. I head for your room, hesitate. Where is William's service pistol?

Get my child out of the house. *Now.* In your room, I close the door and sit down beside you and whisper, "Time to get up, sweetie."

You open your eyes and I just hold on to you for a minute and say I'm sorry that things were so—*odd*—last night, and do you remember that your daddy kept practicing saying prayers? That's to help him become a minister. I hurry you into the bathroom and peek at William; it unnerves me how he seems to be asleep with his eyes open. I know nothing about … nervous conditions. I'll fix breakfast, maybe he'd like something to eat. Just get Lyra to school first.

In record time I get you dressed and for once I don't care if you make your bed. I explain that your father isn't feeling well and he's resting, and I take your hand as we walk past him into the kitchen. You don't look at him. I fix your cereal, remember the milk out front and tell you to drink your juice and stay in the kitchen. Opening the front door, I peer left and right, cross the porch and open its door for the milk bottles and the newspaper.

When I return, you say, "Daddy was bleeding."

I lean down and hug you. "It's okay, everything's going to be all right. Your daddy is tired today."

You ask if I'm tired too and suggest that we spend the day making fudge. I laugh so hard tears roll down my cheeks. I barely notice that you don't touch your cornflakes; I do notice that from time to time you look over your shoulder toward the bedroom door.

Back in your room, I get out your navy blue coat with the red cuffs I attached when the sleeves got too short. I say I hope you have a good day at school.

"We don't have school on Saturday."

Saturday. It's Saturday.

"Put on your play clothes, Lyra."

I hustle you into corduroy pants, a sweater, and your car coat. When we pass by him, William is still staring into space, and again I say that your father is very tired. But you're no fool, you see that he has his eyes open while the rest of him looks asleep. Walking you out into the yard, I prattle that everything is going to be fine and force my lips into an imitation smile.

"What a nice December day—look at the sunshine, sweetie—soon old Santa will be coming."

"Is my daddy real sick?"

I say no, not exactly, and well no, everything is okay, and you be sure and tell anyone who asks that things are fine. I lean down and give you a hug. "I have to take care of Daddy and I need you to be a big girl and stay out here and play. But don't worry, I'm right inside if you need me."

Across the street, Johnny Truesdale is playing hopscotch. I wave him over and say why don't you two play together this morning. His mother, Rosa, wearing her scarlet bathrobe and big foam hair curlers, appears on her porch and calls out, "They can play over here if you like. I'll just be wrapping up gifts this morning. Alone. All alone."

She knows.

"Thank you. William is—he's—sick this morning. I don't want Lyra to catch anything."

Johnny, in his Roy Rogers shirt, walks across the street, asks you, "Who was hollering at your house last night?"

You say, "My daddy can sleep with his eyes open."

"I heard tell onc't of a horse that could do that," Johnny says. "Kept him from falling down when he was sleeping standing up. Can your daddy sleep standing up?"

As you two head toward Johnny's house, you say you don't know. I wait for you to tell him about the blood, the praying, seeing your mother thrown to her knees. I almost hope you do tell him.

I wish this would go away, this going back to *then*—it does no good to think about it. Are you still here, Lyra? I know it's idiotic that I'm talking to someone who can't hear me.

You know, I think I sensed something odd—some invisible

emanation—from the moment we set foot on Lincoln Street. Maybe I taught the pathetic fallacy too well. I wonder if you remember that first day. A Friday, all April azaleas and soft Carolina sunshine, and we're standing in front of that ramshackle two-story in Elmwood Park. Next door is Uta's granite house. Up and down the street more clapboards like ours, all on the come-down. Well-off German and Irish immigrants, many working for the Seaboard Coastline Railroad, began building these houses in 1904 on the former site of the state fairgrounds; the neighborhood was fashionable then, full of evening strollers heading up to the governor's mansion to view the gardens. But as the century aged, as wars and depressions and changes in faith settled in, the well-off ferried themselves across the Broad River to the tract ranchers in sparkling new suburbs. By the time we arrived in Columbia, Elmwood Park's stately homes had been carved into haphazard apartments for stragglers and strangers. For people like us.

The house looked tired to me that first day; it was sliced into two apartments—the upstairs empty, the downstairs ours. The carved oak front door to our five rooms is caked with careless paint layers, the metal doorknob rusty. In the entryway I smell mildew, mothballs, old cooking grease. The rooms are damp, cold. The living room lies behind double glass doors, its fireplace choked by an ugly brown oil stove. Through another door of glass panes is a tiny dining room. The dining room makes me feel better, and I put an arm around your shoulder.

"Now we can get a real table, Lyra. It'll be a little like home in Brantley, the dining room with the long oak table and brick fireplace, my brothers and the ghost of dear Daddy perching their feet on the hearth to light their pipes or Lucky Strikes. I'm going to clean up this house and we'll be happy like that here."

I remember the tinny uncertainty in my voice. I'd never lived in a city, never lived so far from relatives. I was still reeling from William's abrupt decision to uproot us so he could study for the ministry—he didn't even go to church until we got married.

I don't know if my uncertainty was made better or worse when Uta Moazen came over to introduce herself. I soon learned that neighborhood children believed Uta was a witch; her dark stone house *was* intimidating.

Flowers that would flourish in no other soil leapt from the ground in her garden. Uta herself was tall and stately. Long straight back, black eyes, a black dress with white collar most days, one sleeve pinned up. Her left arm had been amputated just above the elbow. At our front door she introduced herself and, with her intact arm, proffered a casserole dish covered by a tea towel embroidered with Dutch girls in braids. She gave me a penetrating look and said, "I'm glad you've moved here. This is the right place."

I led the way to the kitchen—our living-room furniture wasn't there yet, not that it amounted to much. Uta sat at the breakfast table and I poured her coffee, said how glad I was to meet my first neighbor. I gazed into her piercing eyes, which never seem to blink, and then at the single long slender hand. Two or three rings on each finger, as though compensating for the missing hand. Her silver-white hair hung to her shoulders in ringlets; oddly, they made her look regal rather than ridiculous.

You come into the room and I introduce you to Uta, and you look at the empty sleeve and are about to say *Where's your arm?* when—thank the dear Lord—my look stops you dead. After you crawl under the table with a coloring book, Uta explains that she's of Irish descent, that her relatives fled the famine and her grandfather eventually took a job with the railroad in Columbia.

"My grandparents landed in America right before you people started cooking up civil war. If you'd been hungry, you'd not have got the bloody energy for fighting. Not that that ever stopped an Irishman, mind you."

"It's in the water," I say. "My brothers asked the tooth fairy for rifles."

Uta laughs. "Got a sense of humor, you do. I like that."

I think our lives entwined right then, as though someone knew what would happen later.

You poke your head out and ask Uta if she was a Yankee in The War. She gives you a withering glance. "My dear child, I'm Irish. I can't *ever* be anything else."

She gets up, motions me to the kitchen window, and points at her house. "See that stone on the left side of the porch post—people call that a column but it's *square* for mercy's sake—see how at the bottom there's one stone that's slightly different? Over on the left? It's smaller, darker. My grandfather brought that stone from County Galway. It's our returning stone."

In a second she adds, *"Corr baille*, we call it in Gaelic. The need for home. I'm waiting for when that stone grabs me up and carts me back to my country."

You poke your head out again and give me a wide-eyed stare. I suspect you're picturing our one-armed neighbor riding down the street on a rock.

Uta is still staring out the window. "There goes that crazy one." She turns back to me. "Have you seen her?"

I stare out the window again—a bedraggled woman in a brown dress, head down, talking to herself, is pulling a child's red wagon down the street. The woman's gait is odd, she stumbles often.

"Loony as a bat," Uta says. "Spent five years in the insane asylum on Bull Street. The place is only a few blocks away, you know. Horrible place, people in chains. The husband put her in there, some say he did it just to get rid of her. When she got out she was completely mad, and he took the children and moved. People tried to force her out of the neighborhood. Poor wretch."

Uta backs away from the window. "My father said if you looked the mad in the eye, you'd go off your own head. The banshee."

As we sit back down, she adds, "My da, now there was a superstitious man. He truly took to South Carolina, fancied all those burned-out ruins in the country. Loved scary stories too—he fit in here splendidly."

She lowers her voice.

"Elmwood Park is haunted, don't you know? They once held the state fair here, circuses came—we live where the snake charmers plied their trade. Sometimes I think I hear a carousel. Before that, this was a potter's field: we're living over the dead too. Imagine the ghosts. During the Civil War they trained soldiers in the fairgrounds buildings, then made ammunition there, then turned the buildings into a hospital for the wounded, they did. I studied on the history some time back. An elephant mauled a man to death here too. Circus people were bringing the giant creature across the bridge, and he balked and threw a man and a horse into the river, and they calmed the elephant down, but when they got over here he suddenly picked up another trainer and dashed him against the ground over and over. Tore the man to pieces."

She pauses for effect—

"And do you know—I looked it up—it happened right where your house sits."

You crawl out from under the table and lean against me, and I shiver despite myself. You ask to go back to tell the elephant story to the bathtub ladies. You're so fascinated with that bathtub decal you now kiss the ladies goodnight before going to bed.

Uta and I talk a while more. Later, walking back to our front door, she glances into the living room. "You have a piano, I take it."

I say no. I don't say that my stepmother offered the one from Brantley but William said it would cost too much to move it.

"Well, you must have music, my dear. Please come to my house and play mine. I heard you singing. A very fine voice you've got."

I blush again. When was I singing that she could hear me?

"That's another thing—my husband Henry didn't like music. Reason enough by itself."

She hesitates, eyes me soberly. "You have to be careful about what husbands do." With that, she shakes her ringlets off her neck, waves, heads out the door.

❧◯❧

You're back, Lyra. I can tell by your scent—always a little whiff of linseed oil in your hair. I love that. I always imagine my mother in you. You're asking if I'm in pain. For the most part I'm not. I feel like I'm floating, like when my parents took my brothers and me to Folly Beach and I'd lie on a rubber raft in the ocean when the tide was coming in and let the sea send me back home. Only now the tide is going out. A tired metaphor, but true.

A minute ago I was thinking about our first months in Columbia. That first summer was lovely. You're flopping about in your blow-up swimming pool and it's hot but not too hot yet, and the world seems reinvented. Joseph McCarthy of the scare tactics died a week ago, and yesterday Martin Luther King stood on the Washington Mall to tell the world that "there is something in the soul that cries out for freedom." It's your sixth birthday, you in the ruffled one-piece bathing suit with the pint-size hula hoop, and your father is playfully squirting rings of water around you. He's wearing the unaccustomed Bermuda shorts, and you run over and jump up and almost knock him down, and he drops the garden hose and it snakes around and soon he's soaked and laughing. I'm happy to see him playing with you, he seems so serious lately. I get the Brownie camera and shoot a picture of the two of you, which years later you will stare at as if you don't believe it's real.

We looked so—well, *normal.*

Later that day you and I plant azaleas in the backyard and gather honeysuckle—I love those tiny aromatic flowers. They're the smell of my childhood, they grow wild and unruly in the cemetery where my parents are buried. Suddenly overwhelmed, I kick off my shoes and grab you into my arms—I'm wearing a flowered spring dress and holding my baby close, your golden hair twining through a mother's darker locks, whirling you around in the soft grass, barefoot under the pecan trees, singing to my child, this living light. This cup always running over, this dream where to give love is so much better than receiving it. In my perfect alto (if I do say so myself) I sing a hymn of thanksgiving, waltz my darling into the light of old trees, waiting for the best of all possible worlds to come for us. Soon we'll have a home of our own, our own garden. It's just around the corner, fruition, pinnacle, all the hills of Olympus. A smart, handsome husband and this gorgeous child—how did I get so lucky?

When we're both giggling and dizzy, I put you down gently and place a bouquet of blooming honeysuckle in your hand. This child, I vow silently, will always know she is loved and beautiful. As long as I breathe, nothing awful will happen to this child.

～⌒◯⌒～

Nurses come and go. I hear an intercom. I think it's nearly lunchtime.

No, around eleven a.m. I'm sitting in the living room, sewing. Really just holding the shirt with the loose button. My hands are shaking too badly to sew. I'm trying to decide what I should do. *What is wrong with him? Why would he do such an awful thing?* When he wakes up, I'll call—

A crash reverberates through the house. I throw William's shirt down and hurry into our bedroom.

He's rummaging in his bureau drawer, tossing socks, undershirts, handkerchiefs onto the floor. He dumps out the contents of another drawer. Seven transistor radios in unopened boxes fall out. I've never seen them before. He bought seven radios when he's out of work and we barely have enough money for Christmas?

William fumbles in the compartment filled with ironed shirts.

"Darling, what are you looking for? How do you feel?"

His voice is surly. "I've got to find it."

"Would you like some breakfast? Hadn't we better put on a clean bandage?"

He stops and stares at the bandage. "What did you do to me?"

I flinch. "You had an accident, remember?

"I don't remember any accident."

He turns and runs into the living room, calling, "I've got to find it." He ransacks the hall bookshelves, spills books onto the floor, hurls three across the room. He runs back to the bedroom, tears open dresser drawers again, runs into the living room, searches the secretary desk and jerks bills and letters out of the wooden cubbyholes and throws them on the floor. He lopes back to the kitchen and heads toward the side door. I think, *Oh dear, he's still in his pajamas,* as he flings open the door and runs down the steps to the driveway.

I sprint outside as he heads toward the car. When he gets in, I cry, "Darling, come in the house, you're in your pajamas, you'll get a chill."

"Stay away. I know what you're doing."

He starts the car and throws it into gear. I jump out of the way—he's backing up way too fast, isn't looking where he's going. A loud *craccck.* The ten-foot dogwood falls over, just misses the side stairs.

He gets out, stares through me and walks away as though nothing has happened. At the steps he turns back to me.

"I'd like breakfast now," he says calmly and disappears inside.

Uta is on her side porch staring—I barely hear her as she calls to ask if I need help. I stare at the dented fender, then at the upended dogwood. There'll be no white blooms at Easter; this tree is beyond salvation. I go over and kneel beside it, wondering what to do.

∾⊙∾

Over the years I've asked myself—what was the first sign that something was wrong, what did I miss? That crazy car? We'd only been in Columbia for a few weeks when William became obsessed with whether our 1949 hump-fendered Chevy was safe in the city. He's pacing through the house, fuming over this for hours, heavy leather shoes striking heart-pine floors. Then he announces he's taking a bus to New York City to buy a new car.

This seemed odd—we had a few used cars in the South—but William had always been eccentric. He explained that he'd have a better selection in a big city, so three days later you and I drive him to the bus station. In those days a woman dressed up to go downtown—Sunday dress, stockings with seams, heels, gloves. Can you imagine? No matter how I dressed, though, I was self-conscious. And this was before I gained so much weight. My oldest brother, who knew I was insecure, often told me I was beautiful, which I didn't believe, but when I look back at old photos I realize I did look better than I thought I did. My brother called my deep-set eyes (yours are bluer) "mystical" and my hair "black satin"—such a charmer he was, a lot like our father.

Once seated on the bus, William—who never wore a hat—smiles at us through the window. His perpetually hesitant, uncertain smile: its vulnerability always went straight to my heart. After the bus pulls away, you and I amble past the historic First Baptist Church where the Confederate Secession Convention met. I gaze at the white portico, the thick round columns—your father could recite arcane details about South Carolina's history, which I liked before I realized it could become a liability.

Driving us home, I think about the first time I saw him—at a funeral, in his dress uniform, firing a rifle into the air for a fellow soldier whose body had just come back from Europe. Watching him across a flag-draped coffin, I sensed that this handsome stranger was different in some way. Of course I never told anyone I picked out my husband at a funeral—they might think it bad luck.

That night, with William away, our new house feels lonely. You're sprawled on your bed studying the tongue-and-groove walls. Yesterday you'd counted the boards—age five was your counting phase. Also the year you began writing regular letters to Rin Tin Tin. Your other great joy remained the bathtub ladies; you'd given them all names now. The next morning I missed your father whistling as he shaved, his footsteps thudding against the wood floors. People are sound, everyone has an auditory thumbprint, a personal pitch, a melody—harsh or harmonious—that follows them around like an aura. Your father is a fast-paced staccato.

Two mornings later, while we're eating breakfast, a car pulls into the driveway. I peer out a window. A boxlike taxi has stopped at the wrong house. I go outside to tell the driver he's made a mistake when William emerges.

Sunlight glistening in his shaggy forelock, he smiles and points at the vehicle. "Look what I got us."

The car is yellow, a fat breadbox on wheels, with checkerboard squares and a dent in the back fender. A black and white roof sign blares: *Off Duty.*

"It's a *genuine* New York Checker cab," he says. He hauls open a heavy back door, which groans. "Bet you haven't seen a jump seat in years. It's like the one in my old roadster, before the war."

"You bought us a taxicab?"

He's walking around kicking the tires. "Taxis are specially made to withstand all road conditions. I got a great deal."

"Our family car is going to be a taxicab? A taxicab?" My voice is in the upper registers. "People will think we've lost our minds. It's so—yellow."

"Maybe I'll get a yellow suit to go with it."

"I don't think this is funny."

He shakes his head back and forth. "You don't understand cars or what the highways are like, you can hit this thing with a tank and it'll come out the winner. It came with snow tires too—remember that dangerous ice storm a few years ago?"

I remember that it snows twice a decade. Maybe we should get a sleigh too.

He's smiling like he's won a Cadillac. "The neighbors will be jealous of this beauty."

"Then let's give it to them" slipped out before I realized I'd spoken.

"What's got into you—don't I take good care of you and the child?"

"The *child?*"

I look around, hoping our new neighbors won't see us arguing. As I head to the front door, his voice trails me: "I'll have it painted."

He has the cab painted burgundy and gets the roof sign cut off, though a tell-tale bump remains. A car with a brain tumor, not exactly what I'd been dreaming of. He waxes the thing, shines the chrome, presents the reincarnation to me. A week later, yellow paint begins leaching through the burgundy—soon the cab is a striped, polka-dot affair. I can assure you that no one ever missed us coming down the street.

⁓◦⊙◦⁓

Lyra, I know you've wondered—especially given how things became later—why I stayed with your father through so much. Why I so often kept still. You can't imagine what women were taught when I was young. You've grown up in a completely different world, but I was born into one where women couldn't even vote. When your father and I got engaged, divorce was still illegal in South Carolina. Not just frowned upon, but *illegal.* Women like Elizabeth Cady Stanton had stood up for our rights fifty years earlier, but these voices—with no media yet—scarcely got to the South, where the idea of the proper "Southern Lady" held on like an ink stain. After the 1940s war, when women built airplanes in factories but were tossed out when the men returned, a terrible backlash was aimed at us, magazine articles that compared our maturity to that of preadolescents.

Books calling us weak—I remember one, *The Lost Sex*. Many men were apparently afraid of how capable women proved to be in those factories. Now women were instructed—often by a minister wielding a Bible—that we were subordinate to our husbands and that if something was wrong in a marriage it was our fault and our *duty* to fix it.

Though embarrassed, I dismissed the taxi episode as harmless eccentricity.

Several weeks later I'm humming along with "I Could Have Danced All Night" and "Que Sera, Sera" on the radio and emptying the last moving box, which I'd deliberately saved for when the house was organized. I take out a delicate glass bud vase and hold it up to a lamp. Swirls of blue glass, which I press to my throat like perfume. It belonged to my real mother. My mother Elizabeth, who died when I was a toddler. Next I unearth a large vase, ugly really, a patchwork of broken china shards glued to a heavy pitcher. I study the haphazard pieces—old patterns, mostly roses, Havilland, some blue Delft.

You walk in and ask why the vase looks like that.

"It's what happened to our neighbors when I was a little girl. Their house burned down and Mrs. Llewellyn, bless her heart, was walking through the ruins crying. The house had been in the family for three generations. She started picking up the broken china—people had two or three sets of dishes then. She glued the broken pieces to the only vase that survived."

"It's not pretty like the blue one."

"I know, sweetie. But it's—it's special too. She was my piano teacher and all that family is dead. I'm their memory now." I run a hand through your silky hair. "I'm gluing myself to you, you're my memory. Want to help me unpack?"

You help for all of five minutes, go say hello to the bathtub ladies, then escape into the yard. I put the vase on the oak sideboard and straighten myself up, check to make sure your father is around, and head for the local store. It was so nice when you could *walk* to buy groceries. On the way I pass a young woman with dull brown eyes sweeping her front porch; the right porch column is missing, a two-by-four holds the roof up, and four children—one in a sagging diaper—are squealing in a wooden sandbox. I wave to her, feel for how hard her life must be. At the store I ask the owner, Mrs. Flo, who seems younger than the silver hair pinned up in a bun, about the two neighborhood schools—you'll soon go to one, I to the other.

I buy supplies and head home. A few minutes later, when I come through our front door, I stop sharply. A child screaming. *My* child—I've never heard you cry like that before—never. I drop the groceries and run to your room. You're in the bathroom, in the green sundress I made last summer, alternately wailing and sucking your thumb, which you've not done in two years.

William is leaning over the tub. "Obscene," he cries in a high unnatural voice. In his hand gleams a silver razor blade. He slashes at the decal, edges the razor under a dancing woman and tears through her until she's halved, until her breasts and disembodied smile fall onto the floor. Shredded pieces of other women already lie there, severed necks, broken legs, torn and mangled arms.

"Don't hurt them," you scream, sobbing, stamping your feet. "Please please don't hurt them!"

I grab you, pull you to me, say, "There, there, sweetie." You tremble, cry against my stomach. William holds the razor blade aloft; a triangle of plastic blonde woman still hangs from it. I turn sharply and lead you into the kitchen and say it's time to make dinner. I take a fryer out of the refrigerator. As you sit at the table sobbing, I tell you everything will be all right.

William has never even used the word "obscene" before. Doesn't he realize Lyra loves those dancing women?

I hum nervously as I fry the chicken. Realize I'm off-key.

You bolt out of the house and run down the back steps and flail into the backyard. I stand transfixed at the kitchen window, watching. Why am I not following you, comforting you? Why am I not telling you it was unkind of your father to take away something you loved? Why don't I march back there and tell him the decal was a little cheap but wasn't hurting anyone?

My feet want to move. I stop them with a trained head. A good wife does not contradict or criticize her husband, especially in front of the children.

I turn on the radio, listen to someone talk about the Cold War as I move the chicken around in sizzling grease. The radio chatter grates on my nerves—I have to get a record player. Maybe there'll be enough Green Stamps before long. I turn the dial and Frank Sinatra croons as I keep picturing a razor blade.

I've never seen him quite that—angry. Over a bathtub decoration?

Hot grease splatters onto my skirt. I burn the chicken.

It's so many years later now, Lyra—lifetimes and decades—as you sit in this hospital room and listen to me struggle for each breath. Even though I knew something was wrong that day, I didn't know what, or what to do about it.

You're touching my hair—I'm proud of my thick white crown, downy soft, not a hint of yellow. I hope you know how much I love you. We take so much for granted: time, a voice, breathing itself. The air of life enters and departs my body urgently now, preparing for the only unpaired breath a human being ever takes. The last time we exhale is the last moment we feel the love we've known. Our history stands still after that.

Can love, can happiness, with the finality of a last breath, disappear like a decal scraped from porcelain? Can one moment shred a lifetime?

It can. Did. On the day I learned the difference between chance and choice. Choice is what you get if chance leaves you alone.

Chapter Three

❧

I've often wondered what would have happened had we stayed in Summerville. I loved that small town, especially the yellow shoebox cottage where we lived when you were a baby. I didn't want to move to Columbia. I had a good job in Summerville and the romantic in me loved the town's sprawling old houses on stilts, the garlands of Spanish moss on crepe myrtle trees, the nearby meandering marshes. You've painted those dusty roads canopied by live oak branches as claustrophobic, but I felt safe beneath the ancient oaks, protected. Geography, I've come to believe, can be destiny.

William and I were part of the first generation of Southerners—I should say of white Southerners, as many blacks fled the South decades before this—to seek our fortunes beyond our small hometowns and never return to them. But although I've spent my adult life in a city, my heart will always belong to the coastal plain northwest of Charleston. To Brantley. As often as I could, I took you to my native village of wide porches and tall tales, of summer afternoon naps and sultry evenings. Maybe you remember that the Brantley railroad tracks ran right behind the house my father built for his artistic bride. My grandfather lived down the street, and before my time the local conductor stopped at his house every morning to give him a ride to his office three miles away. That seems unbelievable now, given that no passenger train goes near Brantley.

Your father's hometown was larger and more modern, closer to the Piedmont, a farming and commerce center. More businesslike, less summer-lazed, than Brantley. Hundreds like William left its railroad station to go to war—your father didn't volunteer, but he was drafted in 1944. Just in time for the worst of it. Our two hometowns were but one county apart, a distance breached by crossing the dark, moody Salkehatchie River swamps. When we two joined hands, as all couples do, we set out across that dangerous water.

Now Columbia—not a whiff of live oak or Spanish moss—seems inevitable for us, as if an unseen force sent us there to be tested. To walk the plank of rootlessness in a city still insecure in those days, still psychologically and financially damaged by the Civil War. I like that Columbia's a river city, that it sits at the confluence of the Saluda and Broad rivers, which join to form the mightier Congaree. This mirrors South Carolina's sectionalist landscape—its three geographic and philosophical zones, Low Country and Up Country, with the Midlands, the narrow strip of Piedmont sand hills, in between. Your hometown never possessed the leisured style of Low Country aristocrats, or the be-up-and-doing of Upstate farmers. It's middle ground, on the fall line, chosen to govern for that very fact. A mediator. But a fulcrum of balance can be a lonely place. Like we were, Columbia is defined by where it does not fit in.

Our city does have one famous characteristic, which would obsess your father: it was brutally and intentionally destroyed in 1865. On one February night, one-third of the city disappeared. Imagine over four hundred buildings in flames, the newly homeless wandering and wailing, graves opened and robbed, libraries and art collections ransacked. What child, in my generation or yours, was not told in the cradle of Sherman's men, eyes fired by drink, wreaking vengeance on the secession state? Carolinians can go into spasms of Lost Cause mythology: When a people have been singled out for punishment, left in fiery ruin and abject poverty, this humiliation seeps into the earth and into the blood. You don't hear many African Americans singing this tune. Yet for us, despite the terrible racial sins of generations, it does have the ring of prophecy—my grandfather and William's both fought for the Confederacy, and each lost a son and his home and never fully recovered.

But to my mind, what Columbia lost in that fire was something more significant than its houses and prosperity. It lost the record of itself—a century of journals, diaries, letters, and civic records. I understand this loss because nothing written by my mother survives; when she died so young, I lost the family stories she might have told me and that I might have passed on to you. Our narrative chain was broken. Imagine the poetry someone in Columbia had hidden in a bureau drawer in 1865, the annotated family Bible, the drawings of an unknown artist. Thank heavens Mary Chestnut's journal survived. Losing the words of the past is the death of particularity. Often I think of immigrants forced to flee their homes and history because of Hitler. How can we be sure who we are—especially in the traditional South—when we have few clues to who we were? To what can we aspire when the loss of our past is our claim to history?

I suspect this was how your father eventually felt, thanks in part to me.

Places matter. History matters. You threw our history into a backpack and took off. Checked that backpack in the lockers of a hundred airports. Where we come from—no matter where it is—silts under the fingernails, whether we notice it or not. Grains of earth scatter across the shoulders of the children and the grandchildren, whether they notice it or not. I'll tell you, as your grandfather once told me: You cannot truly know yourself without understanding your relation to this earth and this history, without attending the whispers of the ground beneath your feet, without retelling the legends breathed over your cradle. Ours is not easy history, this is not an easy land, not a place for the faint of heart, not a homeland or a tale of simple answers. It's easy to love a place that's perfect, more courageous to love one that isn't.

I've heard it said that passionate alienation is nothing if not a sign of attachment.

∽⊶⊙⊷∾

He became mean—I've never said that before, but it's the truth. Mean and irresponsible. Abruptly that summer he quit his part-time registrar job at a small Columbia business school, which had helped pay his seminary tuition. Leaving us with only one income, which he didn't tell me until a week later—

"I think they were planning to fire me," he said, "so it was best I resign first."

This seemed strange—William had never been fired from any job. He was smart and diligent. As we know now, though, abruptly leaving a job because he imagined someone had it in for him would become a pattern—a far more complex issue later on—that lasted for decades. One afternoon soon after this, I paused in the hallway beside his oak desk. The book *Morality in Christian Life* lay open on the blotter. Library books about the Civil War sat piled on the floor—he could read faster than anyone I knew. Often he didn't sleep well and got up and read until morning. But these days he was reading more Southern history than theology. While I was still looking at his books, he came through the front door. I asked how his day was; he gave me a quick kiss and said it was fine.

"We'll have liver and onions and green beans for supper," I say as I go back to the kitchen. I've cheered up the dingy kitchen walls with French-blue dishtowels and curtains, and while I cook I sing silly ditties, then old hymns. Do you remember when—years later—you said my voice was as mellow as an old wine saved for years? I loved your saying that. Sometimes song flowed out of me like a trapped bird set free. That evening I thrilled to the majesty of "A Mighty Fortress," and then to the quieter "Faith of Our Fathers." Hymns are so beautifully sad, and suddenly I was beside my father again in the white clapboard church in Brantley and he's singing his heart out, and nothing is dearer to me than his hearty off-key voice, and as I sing hymn after hymn in that Lincoln Street kitchen, everything I know I can never do and won't ever do loses import in the shape of melody, in its rise and fall. When I sing, I am beautiful as I've never felt, and in song my husband is taking me in his arms—

William appears in the kitchen doorway and I smile, am about to say that supper's almost ready.

"Louise, please stop singing. You're not a real singer. It's getting on my nerves."

I freeze. His eyes are so remote. All through supper—I'm dieting and eat only Melba toast and green beans—a day from the past perches across the table. William and I are standing on the porch the evening of our first date, and after friends urge me into singing "What'll I Do," your father leans over in the wan, flower-scented moonlight and whispers, "Louise, I could listen to your sweet voice forever."

∾◦◦◯◦◦∾

It's surprising that mostly I see pictures while I lie in this hospital bed. Somehow I'd imagined these hours would be accompanied by music. I've been waiting for that heavenly choir. Apparently no one showed up for rehearsal.

What a flood of images. Sometimes the past feels like it's still happening, other times it's way off in the distance. Time is a camera: long shots, close-ups, the long ago, the right now. Some memories are never really in the past. Mostly awful ones, but a minute ago I could see your father on our first anniversary. We're in the Summerville house, no baby yet, and I've saved up my grocery money and bought a roast for our anniversary. The house smells heavenly, I've filled it with greenery and holly berries, and I've bought William a silver stand for his pipe. Soon he waltzes in the door with a huge box and sets it on the kitchen table.

"Come over here," he says, smiling. "Close your eyes."

I hear him pull something out of the box—I admit I peeked—it's a cage with a towel over it. "Okay, Louise, open your eyes."

He stands very tall and with a flourish flips the towel off the cage. Two beautiful canaries, one yellow-green, one yellow-blue.

"Happy anniversary—meet our Bill and Coo."

That was so like him then. I never told you how we met—after a while, it was hard to talk about. A teaching job landed me in his hometown, and shortly after the military funeral where I first saw him, I inveigled a friend to introduce us. At twenty-eight, I was haunted by the specter of spinsterhood—that death sentence of loneliness, embarrassment to the family, proof of one's lack of grace and beauty. Sounds archaic to you, I know, but an unmarried woman in my day was dismissed as unwanted, doomed to flutter around other people's hearths for lack of her own. Marriage was also the only legitimate path to the children I longed for.

I also wanted what we all want—to be loved.

It was raining that first day, a fuzzy drizzle casting its misty spell over streets and sidewalks. I dressed with care—a soft blue dress that brought out my eyes. Despite the weather I went hatless. I stared into the scratched mirror in my boardinghouse room. My father—hardly impartial—said my face was a picture-perfect oval, but I despised the slight gap between my two front teeth. A black woman—I know I should say African American now—once told me that a space between the front teeth is the passage through which God speaks. I thought it terribly unattractive, and in high school I tried not to smile much because of it; my oldest brother figured that out and told me that space was put there for good sense and laughter to slip out.

I saw William from the window first. He was leaning back against his 1930s Ford roadster, staring at the boardinghouse, a pipe cupped in his right hand. A tall and slender man in a suit, angular and wiry, a gazelle with thick sun-streaked hair. No hat to hide that lovely blond forelock falling into his eyes. And a mustache! He looked like a movie star. His left hand on the door handle, his left knee bent, he seemed relaxed, elegant. He reminded me of the photo I kept on my desk—my daddy in his thirties, wearing a three-piece pinstriped suit and white scarf, fedora pulled low, his right foot on the running board of a Model T. To the day he died, Daddy dressed like he was going to Washington to talk to FDR. When I came downstairs and William and I were introduced, he smiled at me, looked away, looked back and nodded a little, walked over to the porch railing and looked out, turned back and said something about the rain. Unlike that swell by the car, now he was shy—I loved that shyness, it was so familiar.

We walked to a nearby restaurant and ate fried chicken, butter beans, hot biscuits. William didn't say much but when he crossed his legs, I noticed a worn argyle sock slipping down his ankle. His suit was new, his socks weren't. I loved that too. Perfection unnerved me, still does. This handsome man held the door, walked on the outside, took my arm and looked carefully as we crossed near-empty streets and ambled toward the town square. In the early darkness I imagined us walking all night long, maybe into tomorrow, or to some place I'd never seen before, just walking, the two of us, and maybe sometime he would take my hand. I guess that sounds silly but it wasn't then. As we strolled beneath the dogwoods and magnolias and sycamores, he talked about trees—his family owned a farm, now its crop was loblolly pines. Did I know what ring shake was? I didn't of course, so your father stopped in the halo of a streetlight and told me about the hurricane he'd witnessed as a child, how it came inland and lopped off the tops of all the pines.

"Trees can survive a hurricane and look all right on the outside," he said, "but when they're taken to a sawmill to be cut, some will crumble into dust. Unseen damage makes the internal layers separate. It looks like a sound tree but on the inside everything's broken down."

I did like a smart man.

I've thought of that conversation so often over the years.

We walked along the boulevard beside the railroad tracks, past stately homes once owned by the town's elite: several had never recovered from the Depression, peeling paint around a front door, a widow's walk missing a railing. Eventually we reached the gabled Methodist church and your father said the bell would ring in a few minutes. When it did, he stood almost at attention. The bell had been paid for by his mother, he explained, in honor of his brother, Jake, who had been killed in the war. William paused, added, "It cost a thousand dollars to bury Jake in Arlington. We thought the army would pay all of it but they didn't."

Before I could respond, he added, "Jake died just two days before the war ended. His plane hit a mountain. Three months earlier my father died. Heart attack. My mother also last year."

I wanted to throw my arms around him. No one deserved that many losses so close together. No one deserved to lose his entire family by age twenty-three.

The drizzle had stopped now and filmy moonlight dusted the sidewalk as we stood listening to the bell tolling.

"I always thought it would be nice to be a bell ringer," he said. He smiled vaguely, as though remembering a distant place. "In large European cathedrals, where there are many bells, ringers are specially chosen and the bells are rung in mathematical order. Change-ringing. They use ropes or wheels to move the bells. But air currents can affect the way a bell sounds—air can curve and deflect sound waves."

In that dreamy moonlight I noticed nothing except how interesting he was. And—he loved music. We returned to the boardinghouse and joined my friends on the porch, who talked me into a song. My voice that night—forgive my bragging—was a luminous cascade of stars. When afterward your father said, "It's *so* beautiful, Louise," well, I guess I was already in love by then. After he left, I raced upstairs and flopped on my bed and impulsively grabbed the book on my nightstand—happened to be Yeats's poetry. I wrote on the flyleaf: "He said he could listen to me *forever.*"

So you see, the beginning for your father and me was truly lovely. I adored him. Sure, I wanted to get married and have a family, but I'd had other boyfriends. I'd been popular in college—I loved to hear people tell their stories and I had my father's playfulness. Friends called me "Fannybelle" because before a date I once shook my rear end in the dorm and said, "I'm trying to get my Southern belle going." Truth was, to achieve belle-dom, I'd have needed plastic surgery, a fatter wallet, and a lobotomy.

That's not very nice, is it? For the first time in my life, I'm not all that concerned with being polite. What a *relief.*

William was different from other boys I'd known—even though he could be boyishly enthusiastic about one thing or another, he wasn't a boy at all. An army sergeant who'd won a Bronze Star Medal was clearly a man. When a friend revealed that William had been pulled from the front lines twice suffering from shell shock, I understood why he rarely spoke of his combat experience. Maybe I shouldn't say this, but I liked it that war hadn't agreed with William. I was no Victory Girl: I'd lost three cousins I loved, and my brother had not returned the same man. The treatment for shell shock was only two days away from the screaming and bombing and dying, but even so, at the Battle of the Bulge your father saved the lives of several fellow soldiers. I admired him for that too, that even though war had literally made him sick, he'd still been brave. It was romantic that William was a decorated veteran; except for the terrible loss of life, the 1940s were romantic in many ways. Ironically, the war that stemmed the Depression made life at home better. Love, life, had an intoxicating intensity that was lost when the 1940s *we're-all-in-this-together* turned into the 1950s *I'm-gonna-get-me-mine*.

Little was known about wartime trauma in those days, and we were all so horrified by the discovery of the Nazi death camps and relieved that the war was over that few considered what that war had done to our own. It never occurred to me, even when he locked it up out of sight, that my husband might find his Bronze Star embarrassing, might find his valor—because of the killing no doubt—painful. That he might be suffering from terrible guilt.

But I saw your father's war damage in July of our first summer on Lincoln Street. During a bad thunderstorm, lightning struck our chimney and coated the entire house—everything we owned—with black soot. That Saturday the weather had turned strangely chilly and dark in the afternoon. I'm washing dishes, listening to the radio; you're lying on the threadbare living-room carpet looking at your dog-eared *Littlest Angel* book. Lightning slashes across the sky, lights up the sodden sidewalks. Angry white light, roaring thunder. Again, again. The radio goes dead. Suddenly the house shakes, as though elephants are jumping up and down on the roof. I run to the living room—books are flying off shelves, pictures crashing to the floor. Another roar of thunder. Then—*whammm*! Like the house has been shot. Furniture careens sideways, a table falls over, and the oil stove blasts into the middle of the room just as you scramble out of the way.

I'm screaming as I grab you into my arms. Soot rains down on us, my eyes sting, I taste dirt as clouds of dark smoke swirl through the house.

Your father is standing in the living-room doorway—completely still, eyes unnaturally wide. He looks through us as I hold you tight and whisper,

"It's okay, Lyra. Lightning must have hit the chimney. Everything's all right."

William remains in the doorway—frozen. I call to him, "Are you all right, William? Are you hurt?"

He stares at me blankly. He yells, "Where is my *brother*?"

By that night, as we survey the damage, he seems himself again. The walls are black, the furniture, curtains, rugs, even clothes in bureau drawers. The next day—dark and cloudy, still cooler than normal—a massive clean-up begins. Firemen arrive and climb up ladders to inspect the chimney; they say the creosote needs to be burned off before the oil stoves can be reinstalled. They build a fire in the living-room fireplace. See that room flooding with light? We're terribly hot, but the contradiction of winter heat on a summer day sloughs off a chrysalis, and for a moment your father and I sit talking companionably, as we haven't in quite a while, remembering when most homes were heated with open fires. I recall how my father got up early and lit all the fires in our house—when I awoke, my bedroom always glowed with dancing flames.

I ask William, "Couldn't we leave this fireplace open, have real fires here this winter? It's so cozy."

He says no. His eyes narrow. Fire is nothing to play around with, he adds. Wood houses can burn down in an hour. There was a reason Sherman won the war by burning a sixty-mile-wide path through South Carolina. "William R. Huntt borrowed private wagons and took all the government records to railroad cars sent from Charleston. He hired more wagons at Chester. His wife hid the state seal in her clothes. Eight days of occupation. Wind, whiskey, and cotton. Soldiers, rifles, bayonets."

I'm still wondering what the Civil War has to do with our fireplace when William flings a bucket of water onto the dying embers.

Maybe I didn't pay enough attention to changes in your father because I was so in love with your sweet and sensual early childhood, in that lost era before child-theft when children played freely in open space, when the point of an afternoon was to roll around in the dirt and take the smell of the earth inside your small body, when you were safe lying in damp evening grass and watching stars twinkle on like rows of lighted paper dolls, when every flower on earth blew thick aromas through our open windows and bees buzzed around the blooms before first light. Often I stood at the kitchen window watching you, bearing witness to the beginning of your senses. As I watched you stare into skies so bright they hurt the cornea, I'd forget how fussy you'd been that morning, how tired I was, what a job it was taking care of you and the house while William was studying or at the seminary. I'd forget all the talk about "the Bomb" that some said might be dropped on us at any moment. All that would float away as I watched you and washed dishes, singing "For the beauty of the earth, for the beauty of the skies." My voice would float out into the yard and curl around you in embrace. Sometimes I'd stop singing and come out and sit beside you in the grass. I wanted to share with you all the marvels I'd never shared with my own mother.

One afternoon I asked, "Do you remember Mrs. Moazen telling us there used to be a fairground with a merry-go-round here?" Your electric-blue eyes took my breath away, glittering with eagerness for life, burning with a child's effervescent faith.

I said, "We're on that carousel right now. You're riding a purple pony."

We were, you know. Our world then *was* magic. Sunshine dappling through leafy old trees, the air stunned-lazy and droop-heavy with the aroma of the gardenia bushes blooming beside the porch. Always a thrum-thrumming in the air, insects buzzing at screens and cooking grease sizzling through kitchen windows, automobile tires throp-thropping onto hot steamy pavement. So many colors and patterns to see, so much rain and sun and sky and green grass to taste and smell that some nights neither of us could sleep for the weight of all that experience. Often we both lay awake—in different rooms but umbilical—and listened to the circle of night becoming day again.

∽◦⊙◦∾

I've spent a lot of years thinking about, and trying not to think about, what happened to us. In many ways, besides war, our undoing was religion. Before that, before we moved to Columbia, William was a forestry agent for a timber company in Charleston, where he helped make decisions about when and where forests were harvested and replanted. He'd majored in biology in college and cared deeply about South Carolina's woodlands, about how the longleaf pine, which took a century to mature, had been destroyed by overcutting. Do you know that your father wrote a history for every single tree on his family's farm? How old it was, its condition, I don't know what all. Imagine the time that took for 462 acres.

Then one day in Summerville he came home and announced he wanted to become a minister. He wanted to go to divinity school and he wanted to go *now*. He told me his mother had been very religious and had wanted him to become a pastor. First I'd heard of that. Why, then, hadn't he been baptized? He showed me her Bible and said, "It was her most prized possession, and I'd like you to have it. She read it every day of her life. From when she was a little girl to the day she died."

Moved, I embraced the tattered Bible and admired the hand-colored illustrations, so like a Bible my father gave me when I was twelve. I flipped to the copyright page to see if this was the same edition. It wasn't—nor did it seem likely that William's mother's read "every day of her life" a Bible published six years before her death.

I seem to have lost my train of thought—hospitals are so noisy—

Oh—I was telling you about the lightning strike—it took forever to clean up afterward. While I was busy with this, though I didn't know it, you were often on the front porch watching live theater across the street. Our neighbor Rosa Truesdale had the lead: she lived in a house where love (or a loose facsimile) was working hard that summer. You watched love walk up onto the porch of her house and go inside, and then in an hour, or maybe two, come out again. Love went back to its car and drove away. When I found you at this, we watched love chug down the street and disappear.

As I would learn later, Rosa had lived on Lincoln Street for a decade, since the day she'd scooped up her son, Johnny—a skinny kid with a mop of brown hair and a cleft-palate scar, you uncharitably said he looked like a mole—and fled her violent husband. Since "nice" women didn't leave a husband then, no matter what, Rosa's family never spoke to her again. Later Rosa did the unthinkable—she sued for divorce, which had just been legalized. She told a judge she'd committed adultery, which she later said wasn't true but she knew she'd get her freedom if she claimed to be a "fallen woman." She was the only divorcée I knew then, but she didn't seem a bit disturbed about diminished social status. She looked quite happy when she appeared on her second-floor balcony and leaned over the wooden railing in her tight pants and gold hoop earrings and bright scarves to wave at a man getting out of his car below. Rosa had the voice of canyons and caverns, a loud hearty invitation: "What took you so long, Frank?" (Or Tom or Lester or Bill.) I know you remember how she'd toss her head back and laugh and throw a kiss to the man rushing up the steps. Rosa had flaming red hair, huge green eyes, big breasts, big shoulders, and she always wore dark red polish on her fingernails and toenails. Sometimes when a "caller" arrived, she'd hold out her hand for a kiss on those red fingernails. She was the kind of woman South Carolina pretended it didn't have, even when she defiantly brought her "men friends" to the elementary-school PTA meetings.

About a week after the lightning strike, Rosa showed up on our porch one morning. As I shook her hand, staring at the six silver charm bracelets, she said, "Our young'uns are pals, so I thought I should come over to say hello. I know it's late for housewarming gifts, but I brought you some cookies. It's terrible about lightning hittin' your place."

Her bracelets jangled as she handed over a plastic bowl. I stared at the pale blue plastic and tried to imagine Rosa at a Tupperware party.

I thanked her awkwardly. "Will you come in for some iced tea?"

Rosa studied me for a long moment. "Not just now, but thank you for askin'." She paused, added, "I take note your husband won't let Lyra play in the street with Johnny no more—this isn't a highway. M'self, I try not to listen all that much to what a man has to *say*."

She raised her eyebrows slyly and then said, "By the way, I give dancing lessons up to Arsenal Hill Park. For little kids. If Lyra wants to come, I can fix it without you having to pay."

"I don't—I think Lyra's a bit young yet." She teaches *children*?

"Oh we got 'em tiny." Rosa smiled her huge smile, revealing a gold tooth. "Never too early to learn 'em to swish and sway." She turned to leave. "Suit yourself."

I wondered if I had ever in my life *swished*. I thought probably not.

"Thank you again for the cookies, Mrs. Truesdale." Or was it Miss?

"Rosa, honey. I'm just Rosa."

She waved and headed down the steps. I watched as she—what was the right word—*sashayed* across the street. Rosa was a feast of alliteration. Later, when I popped open the Tupperware bowl, I found very round chocolate-chip cookies, a single Hershey's kiss sitting atop each generous mound, pouty brown tips pointing toward heaven.

❧⊙❧

As I lie here thinking about those days, feeling nurses come and go, especially the one who smells of eucalyptus and massages my feet, I find myself wondering what you did when your father called about my stroke. You keep whispering that you wish you'd come home more often. I know you had your own life, but I missed you terribly. You left me here with your father.

❧⊙❧

It's the next day, after the praying. I wake up and think maybe it never happened. Maybe I'm dead. The *blood*. Maybe it's two days later, after the hand in the air for twenty-four hours. He's backing the car out of the garage, it's heading down the driveway, and I'm running toward him—

I will *not* think about this anymore—

The noises of a hospital, the squeak of rubber soles upon polished floors. That day I was in a hospital, maybe a year later—1958? 1959? What I'm about to do is madness. So I won't hope anymore? The doctor is murmuring, the mask is coming down over my nose. I begin to breathe the sweet oily ether—

Lyra? Are you there?

I think I've been asleep. Did you say something else about Lincoln Street?

I know how obsessed you are with that house, even though I've pretended for years not to know. You keep going there because that's what an expatriate become prodigal does. Remember how often I returned to Brantley? The city of one's birth, the small town, the family farm, the old home place. These are the beams we use to build a suspension bridge across the accumulating waters of change and inconsequence. The place of youth rises as a beacon of hope across that water—there my existence began, might be remembered. *Home* illuminates the darkness of our lives and harkens us back to a dim unremembered consciousness—why were we born there and not in some distant hamlet, why did we blithely sail away or remain rooted in place, what is it about that earth that both attracts and repels, and why can we never escape its persistent yet elusive ghosts?

Your father's psychological mooring was the farm he'd inherited, and during our first summer on Lincoln Street he showed it to you for the first time. It seems such a symbol to me now, the farm does.

That day we all piled into the taxi and as William started the engine, his shimmering blue eyes above his lit pipe regarded you warily. Disconcertingly, he sometimes looked like he'd forgotten who you were.

He drives us down Assembly Street toward the Blossom Street Bridge. "The night Columbia was burned," he says suddenly, "there was so much cotton stacked along Assembly Street and so much wind blowing it around that it looked like snow. Wind, whiskey, and cotton. And fire."

You pipe up from the backseat. "Will it ever, ever snow?"

"Before that night was over," William says, "some people fled to the seminary buildings for safety, others to the lunatic asylum."

Thirty miles south of Columbia he turns onto a narrow dirt road, and we meander past vacant fields and falling-down wood cabins with snaky vines growing out of their chimneys. More fields, more acres of pine trees. A caved-in barn, another old shack with a pine tree pushing through the roof. Finally he stops the car, opens the trunk, and lifts out a lawn mower, and we three walk into the woods. All around us, and in the distance, stand orderly rows of loblolly pines. You breathe in pinesap and say you'd like to live in a tree. Soon we reach a grassy hill where a rusted wrought-iron fence encloses a small family cemetery. Ravaged rounded tombstones, some so weathered the names are worn away, others that look damaged by vandals, lean right and left haphazardly. You tell me they look like old people too tired to stand up straight.

You were an amazing child, if I do say so myself.

William begins mowing around the graves, sweat staining his starched white shirt. After a while he rolls the mower out of the cemetery and we head deeper into the woods. Blue-black clouds appear, a sprinkle of rain falls. Through the damp mist the charred ruins of a small plantation house emerge, bit by bit, as though coming into focus through a camera lens. Deep shadows and crumbling brick walls no more than two feet high appear first, then huge shards of broken and jagged mortar and a burial mound of blackened lumber topped by a single once-white door lintel. The stone chimneys on either end of the original three-story structure have toppled sideways—one is broken in half—and a tangled jungle of weeds and vines crisscross the open space of what was once a formal parlor.

I shiver. Even the air around the ruined house seems old and gray, as if its ashes never fully settled. You walk toward the ruins eagerly.

Your father, staring into the distance with a gone-away look in his eyes, tells you, "This land has been in my family for two hundred years. Destroyed in 1865." He climbs over the jagged brick wall, shovel in hand, and walks toward a mound of upturned dirt.

"The place was called China Grove. We had the largest brick kiln in South Carolina. We never grew cotton, we grew food and made bricks for the columns of the great houses in Charleston and Savannah." William gazes at the nearby woods. "In Civil War times it was six thousand acres. Lost most to pay taxes during Reconstruction, when it sold for a dollar an acre."

Your father starts digging in the bare spot. "My grandfather left here at age fifty-six to join the Confederate Army; he was too old, the war was lost, wasn't anyone left to fight it but old men and boys of twelve or thirteen. I don't think we'd ever had slaves, but it was personal once Sherman made it clear he had it in for South Carolina and started burning us out. He sent looting men into people's homes to steal everything, including food, from women and children. Then they'd torch us. Around here, 1865 was a lot like being in London during the Blitz."

You scramble across the stone wall to join your father but he orders you out, says there are old nails everywhere. So you wander into a nearby stand of trees to play while I lounge in the grass, gazing out at the fields. The farm's spaciousness appeals to me more than its history does. *The woods, the fields. All this land.* Because we're educated, I've never felt poor even though, if cash is the barometer, we are. Now I realize we're "land poor." No money for a piano or a dining-room table, but there are 462 acres. Something valuable and important to leave to our children.

William tosses dirt behind him as he excavates his past. Over the years he exhumed hundreds of the wedge-like handmade bricks that formed columns. The only valuable he found was a blackened sterling coffeepot hidden in the well.

I call out to him, "You truly enjoy this, don't you, darling?"

He doesn't hear me. He moves back and forth across the ruins rhythmically, stops and unearths two more tri-cornered bricks, rough bumpy exterior, inexact sizes. He picks up something—I can't see what—and examines it, then looks toward the nearest trees as though pleased. Here, I realize abruptly and not comfortably, he's happier than he is at home. Why is that? I didn't understand that day why ruins were reassuring to him, why the mystery of disintegration was comforting, why it was a relief to him that there was something no one could fully fathom, change, or control. But as evening falls, my husband is a silhouette against a darkening sky, a desperate Lear straining back and forth before his fallen house. What your father needed, as we now know, could never be found beneath that hallowed dirt. It was never Old South sentimentality, it wasn't even about history. Your father was drawn to ruins and to cemeteries—as you've followed in painting after painting—because nothing is more mysterious, or more normal, than death.

❧❧❧

William continues digging, but the ruins feel less and less peaceful to me, so I round you up and call to him, "Shouldn't we be heading home?"

Despite his warnings, you clamber over the brick wall into the interior of the ruins. William yells for you to be careful. He knocks dirt off his shovel, finally brushes it off with his hand. And does the most startling thing. He walks over and drips a handful of dirt across your shoulders. I watch the grains of Carolina earth—part beige sand, part black loam, part red clay—cascade onto your denim shirt, dirt so old it looks like dried blood. You gaze up at your father, his shaggy blond head hovering over your cornsilk waves, and you smile at him like you rarely do. My breath quickens, as it does when something is happening that you know is important and you want to slow it down. Staring at your father, you kneel down and scoop up dirt and hold out your hand to give the handful to him. He takes the dirt and puts it in the pocket of his khakis, reaches out and tousles your hair, smiling as though seeing you for the first time.

"It'll be yours someday, kiddo."

It was a moment unlike any other in our lives, and adrenalin love for you both hurtled through my veins. I'd been afraid your father hadn't really wanted children, so this baptism filled me with joy.

That night William and I lie in our bed across from the reinstated brown metal oil stove that I've covered with bright purple cloth. The full moon outside the window slips through the filmy white curtains, making the roses in the claustrophobic wallpaper twist and turn. He leans over, gives me a quick kiss, turns away. I wish he'd put his arms around me the way he did on the magical dreamy night you entered my belly. I feel ready for a second child. How often do a husband and wife usually make love? I have no idea. I move closer to him and slip my arm around his back and think about our early days together. He'll love me soon—

While William sleeps, I picture you in the next room nestled into your small child's bed beside the four windows overlooking the backyard.

You with the sand on your shirt: you are the proof of how lucky we are, of how good our life is. Tonight there is no potter's field below our beds. Tonight an ancient carousel sings to us and colored ponies trot in circles all night long.

Chapter Four

I hear you asking again if I'm in pain. Do stop fretting. Who enters or leaves the world without pain? Or lives in it, for that matter. I told you years ago to reconcile yourself to my death—you kept saying you didn't think you could bear it. I made my way through breast cancer, diabetes, and all the rest; I was tired and wanted my death to be about *me*. Maybe I did resent it that you rarely came home. And when you did, you acted like nothing here quite suited you.

When you were in your twenties and—dare I say it—quite judgmental, it was clear I hadn't lived up to your expectations. Wasn't bold enough, enlightened enough, something enough. You acted the same way about your hometown; you couldn't wait to exit stage right to New York. Columbia wasn't evolved enough, liberal enough, interesting enough—you kept saying the city had no "aesthetic intention." What on earth did that mean? Columbia's no visual stunner, I admit that: what the Civil War didn't take, its citizens often have, showing a remarkable penchant for sacrificing historic structures to the gold coins of the twentieth century. But Elmwood Park—with its ghostly old houses and dramatic history— fed the vivid imagination that makes you creative. Think about it. We were bookended by the Seaboard Coastline railroad tracks, the Broad River Canal, Elmwood Cemetery with its sleeping Confederates, and the high brick walls of the state mental hospital. You grew tall crossing rivers, walking train tracks, tramping wide streets and haunted graveyards. Fertile soil for an artist, if you ask me. Only lately have I realized this difference between us: in my way, after years of making so many dear friends, I came to belong to Columbia. You belong—always—to Lincoln Street.

Myself, I don't care much for drama.

Uta Moazen, the only original owner on Lincoln Street, helped anchor me to Columbia that first year; by now I knew she'd lost her arm because she'd not seen a doctor soon enough about an infection. One day I was outside weeding around the hydrangeas when Uta—wearing a flowing blue caftan—appeared and said, "Come with me, Louise." I followed her up her steps; she had a commanding presence it was difficult to say no to. We landed in a living room crowded with glass-globe lamps and Victorian chairs upholstered in gold brocade. Ringlets bobbing, Uta led the way through rooms bulging with heavy furniture. I noticed a pretty green glass jar sitting on the dining-room mantel. Uta paused and nodded toward it. "Now that's a story, all right."

I waited for her to explain, but she didn't.

Soon we were in a storeroom crowded with more ornate furniture. Uta—who didn't look her seventy-five years—pointed and said, "You don't have a dining-room table, and I'm not using this one. I want you to take it over to your house."

I stared. Six feet of quarter-sawn oak burnished to a rich dark sheen, thick turned legs. Some scratches but not bad ones. Smaller but almost identical to the table in Brantley.

"It's lovely," I said, "but I couldn't think of borrowing it."

"Silly goose, I'm not lending it to you, I'm *giving* it to you. It's downright rude not to accept a gift." She paused. "Louise, did it rain on your wedding day?" When I said no, she said, "That's good. You know rain at a funeral means smooth passage to heaven. Not good at weddings."

She talked me into the table, which didn't take much urging, I admit. While we dusted it off, she said, "When you start school, get to know the janitor. Max Wells, a very fine man. He did me a big favor once." She hesitated, looked at me thoughtfully. "If you ever need help of any kind, don't hesitate to ask me."

Later that morning, the milkman and Uta's yard-man moved the oak table into our dining room. I polished it until it glowed. This sounds silly, so much fuss about a table—you know I've never put much stock in material things. At first William didn't want to accept the gift, but I convinced him. To me that table represented both the past and the future. Noisy family meals were the heartbeat of my childhood, and someday you'd have siblings and we would sit here together in the same way. So several times that day I returned to the dining room to run my hand across the smooth oiled surface. Eventually I took out my mother's silver flatware and set the table with the mismatched patterns of lovely aged luster, once touched by hands I longed to remember.

⌖

Soon it was August, the sweltering damp hell of late August. You've been away so long maybe you don't remember what a South Carolina August is like. Imagine too many people locked in a steam room together for weeks. In 1957, legislators going up and down the steep stairs of the State Capitol had their white shirtsleeves pushed up like blackjack dealers; many used folded newspapers to fan themselves as they sat in the stunned heat of the house and senate chambers. At noon they went over to the Capitol News Stand lunch counter, where oscillating metal fans only circulated the hot air people came inside to escape. The Elite Epicurean restaurant ran out of ice. The lunch counter at McGregor's Drugstore had no more ice cream. People floated down city streets like slow-moving barges and plopped down on bus-stop benches, thinking they'd go to the "air-cooled" movie house if only they had the energy.

Despite the heat, I was excited as I walked up Aiken Street wearing a jersey print dress. I took a right at the corner, and the impressive visage of Laidlaw Junior High appeared—an Olympus of learning, a progressive school housed in a square three-story brick palace. The first junior high in South Carolina, which taught new subjects like photography, sat on a five-acre former plantation site studded with thirty massive magnolia trees. Steep granite stairs led to the second-floor bay entrance of pointed arches and Gothic window tracery. A hulking, imposing façade—a face with hooded eyes, almost the frown of nineteenth-century tintypes. I liked the sense of history in its bricks and doors and porticos. Collegiate architecture let the world know that education was serious and important.

My parents couldn't send four children to college during the Depression but found a way to give each boy one year and the only girl—in case I never married—a degree. Walking into Laidlaw, I'm thinking about tomorrow, your first day in the first grade. My footsteps echo on the terrazzo floor and I breathe in the musty old-books smell; schools were living history, they filled me with hope for the future. I thought of them as the House of Life, the wing of the Egyptian temple where books were kept and writing was taught. I was young and idealistic. I opened the windows and sat down at my scratched oak desk with creaky drawers. It was Teachers Work Day and various colleagues dropped by—a fellow English teacher named Clarice, who lived in Elmwood Park, and the short, wiry social-studies teacher whose room was next door, who said I shouldn't worry if I heard a loud crash, that when her students weren't paying attention she stood on her trash can to lecture. She'd fallen off twice.

The principal also comes by, Edward Hindeman, a bald man wearing a narrow tie and wire-rim glasses. A broad-shouldered man—"Do call me Ed"—with a hunter's alert watchfulness. He sits in a student desk and asks if I need anything. After I request two dictionaries, he takes out a checkered handkerchief and wipes his forehead.

"I'd like to tell you a little about our school, Mrs. Copeland. We get our children from Elmwood Park, from Earlewood, and from Black Bottom. The Bottom children are poorest—tin-roof shotgun shacks on dirt roads, not much electricity or plumbing, barbed wire separating the white and colored sides. We have many underprivileged students, but that doesn't mean they aren't good children. The other thing is—well, public schools are in changing times right now. I'm sure you know what I mean."

I did. It hadn't been long since the South Carolina legislature's "Segregation Session"—which made it illegal for state employees, including teachers, to belong to the NAACP or to any pro-desegregation organization. Local government officials were threatening to close the public schools rather than integrate, and in nearby Camden a group of whites had attacked a white school bandmaster who endorsed integration.

Ed Hindeman looks at me carefully. "I have to ask all new teachers. Down the road, how would you feel about teaching Negro students?"

"I've always been a big fan of Mrs. Roosevelt."

He smiles, looks relieved. "We're going to like having you here, Louise." He heads for the door, adds, "Now let's pray the Asian flu doesn't show up."

My hands start shaking. "I saw the newspaper. Is it really serious?"

"I hear it could be."

When the door closes behind him, I get up and focus on preparing my room. Eventually there's another tap at the door, and the smallest adult man I've ever seen limps in and says, "I'm Max, Mrs. Copeland. Max Wells. Janitor and all-around handyman. I've come to see if you're needin' anythin'."

The man's smile, all sparklers, lights up a rough-hewn dark tan face marked by acne scars. Blue-green eyes, a slight variation in the left, turquoise stones that don't quite match. He might be four and a half feet tall, and he wears gray work pants and a spotless white shirt.

"I never grew taller," he says without embarrassment. "But I'm strong. You need something lifted, you call me. I'm always near the hall broom closet."

After Max and I shake hands, he asks, "You like flowers? Of course you would." A shock of curly silvered hair falls into his eyes. "Behind the baseball field, they let me have a garden there. I don't have enough room in the Bottom so I made one here. Sometimes teachers like to walk in my garden on their free period. It's—well, restful. You look like a fine lady that might like a peony or gardenia. No, maybe a camellia. You can tell a lot about somebody by the flowers they likes—like. Or resemble."

He waves and heads toward the door, his gait uneven, calling over his shoulder, "English teachers are my favorites. I only got to eighth grade, but they let me use the library here and I done a fair bit a' readin' over the years." At the door he turns around, points at the books on my desk. "I read that story about the white boy and the colored man on a raft. I studied that English grammar book too, the one you teach outta."

"Have you read the novel *Tale of Two Cities*?" I ask. "It's about a remarkable man. You can tell a lot about people by the books they read."

"Well thank you, ma'am, for that suggestion. I just might look into it."

As the door closes, I hear him murmur, "Hydrangea. Gives so many blooms, lasts all summer. Big old friendly flower, pretty too. Yep, that's it. If the weather holds, it can carry us right through to December. Just don't cut it—wilts in an instant."

∽ঙ◯ও∾

Like I said—or I think I said it, maybe I didn't—it was Max Wells who first mentioned to me your father's visits to Elmwood Cemetery. This was the day you and I were on a bus headed downtown to buy you new shoes. As the bus passed Laidlaw, a woman two rows back called out to no one in particular, "That there's the worst school in the whole city. Half them kids' daddies is locked up in the state pen. No sir, I wouldn't let no child o' mine set foot in that school."

I feel my cheeks burn and whirl around. "Do you know anyone who goes to that school? Have you seen how children behave there? I teach at that school and I'm proud to work there."

The other woman makes a snorting noise. I face forward, embarrassed by my outburst. You stare at me in puzzled, impressed surprise.

Soon we're walking down Main Street, past Belks and Tapps department stores, passing khaki-clad soldiers from Fort Jackson who flood downtown every weekend. Just short of the Capitol News Stand, we turn into a stone building and walk down an arcade of polished granite floors; I sigh over the cost of your Buster Brown oxfords, you of the narrow feet. Soon we're sitting at Woolworth's lunch counter. You're slurping a chocolate milkshake and I'm gazing, a little longingly, at bright scarves on a nearby rack, when a group of black men in suits and ties walks in and sits down on the padded metal stools. A thin waitress in a hairnet runs to the back of the store. Soon the manager marches forward, his face purplish, and says, "This counter is not open today." He puts a white sign on the counter, black letters: *Closed*.

A man wearing a red tie says, "I'm sorry to hear that, sir. I'm sure you won't mind if my brothers and I wait until you reopen. We're very hungry."

Each of the men takes out a newspaper and begins to read.

It's hard to believe the demeaning racial "rules" in place then. Nonetheless, fearing an altercation, I drag you to the front door. Out on the street a silent parade passes—men in suits and fedoras, women in Sunday dresses wearing shiny high heels and carrying Bibles. They march down Main Street looking straight ahead, moving as one; they seem to know a tempo that unites them. Traffic has stopped in all directions, irritated white people get out of their cars and stare, some shout at the procession. I stand still, watching, holding your hand, searching the faces of the women beneath their best hats. Brave women.

Near McGregor's Drugstore a short man steps out of the procession. Max Wells in a neatly pressed 1940s suit. With a white rosebud in his lapel.

"Mrs. Copeland, it's good to see you."

"I admire all of you," I say, and nod toward you. "I'd like you to meet my daughter Lyra."

Max leans down in courtly fashion and shakes your hand. "I am pleased to make your acquaintance, Miss Lyra. You have a lovely name. Names are important. I'm Maxmillian H. Wells. I am the janitor at your mother's school."

You study Max's suit. "You clean the school?"

"I do. I'm also the gravedigger at Elmwood Cemetery. If you'll pardon my sayin' so, I'm a man of prodigious talent."

You're processing what a gravedigger might be as Max straightens back up and says to me, "I met your husband by accident last week. At the cemetery. A man came by and asked about the Confederate graves, and he was wearing an army medal. Star on a ribbon. I knew I'd seen the man before—he picked you up after school one day and had this pretty little girl with him."

It takes me a moment to answer. *Wearing his war medal?* "My husband is interested in—in history."

"I find history right meaningful myself," Max says. "For instance—'It was the best of times, it was the worst of times.' " He smiles broadly, then his voice grows more serious. "I hope you'll forgive the effrontery—nice word, isn't it—I just added it to the word notebook I keep—but I had the feeling your Mr. Copeland was, well, not quite all right that day."

"He's been studying very hard. He's a student at the seminary."

"Well, isn't that fine." Max nods. "I'll be going now." He limps down the street to catch up with the group.

"Mama, is Mr. Max a colored man?"

"I don't know, sweetheart. Maybe part of him is."

What does he mean "not quite all right"?

"He looks funny. He's too short."

"Would you want him to say you look funny? He might think blonde hair is not quite right."

You ponder this as we walk to the bus stop. As the bus heads toward Elmwood Avenue, I wonder—was William really wearing his Bronze Star?

∾◠◯◡∿

Intensive-care units are too busy—sometimes I can't sleep for all the attention, nurses coming in at all hours of the night. Occasionally I can feel your father standing beside my bed. I imagine he's staring at the monitors. Sometimes you and he murmur to each other; even now, your estrangement is obvious—I wish that wasn't so. I tried for years to keep the peace.

I just remembered this other thing that happened on Lincoln Street. Funny how the mind jumps around. It was an Indian summer night that first year—September maybe—and I was lying in bed beside your father, he was sound asleep for once, and I could hear the wind whispering outside the window. I knew the moon was full even though William now insisted on pulling the shade tight at night. I couldn't sleep so I got up, put on my housecoat, and tiptoed to the front door. And there it was, the moon on our steps, beckoning me. So even though it was late and I'd be exhausted the next day, trying to teach those preteens the difference between *who* and *whom*, I opened the front door and slipped out onto the porch and sat down on the steps beside the hydrangeas—they were cobalt in the moonlight—and I held one to my face. It was soft and beautiful, and I was doing this when I happened to look up and lo and behold there was Rosa Truesdale sitting on her steps directly across from me, smoking a cigarette. She waved, I waved back, and she sauntered across the street, cigarette between her teeth. She was not afraid of looking any kind of way, Rosa wasn't, and she said howdy, wasn't it a right magnificent night, and I said yes it was, and she gazed at me for a moment and I saw she'd been crying. I never did know why, though I can imagine. Then she said in a very non-Rosa voice, "Louise, I'm right sorry for us both." Before I could say a word—I wasn't sure if I was insulted or not—just like that she turned and went back across the street and opened her door and disappeared.

Three weeks after the civil-rights demonstration, the Asian flu roared into Columbia. Two Low Country high schools were closed, the Columbia College infirmary was full, and soldiers at Fort Jackson were confined to the base. Several young people in New England had died. By mid-October three students from Camp Fornance were sick, and then six more, eight students at Logan Grammar School, and then fifteen more. Soon sixty-five students from Laidlaw were sick and the school closed briefly. The seminary stayed open, it had only a few cases, and for once I was glad your father didn't often touch you. This flu took particular aim at schoolchildren, and I felt frantic. I barely let you go outside. Hadn't my mother died from a flu that took particular aim at her age group? Over two hundred Americans were now dead—twenty thousand would eventually succumb. I'd been so relieved to see you get the new polio vaccine. Now this?

Sometimes I'd remember my childhood, remember the women moving silently through the house my father built for my mother, with its dormers and wrap-around porch, an aunt and a cousin who wear billowy white muslin dresses with high collars and look worried and speak in quiet voices. I'm sitting in a tiny wicker rocking chair, unnoticed, cradling a limp cloth doll with a china head that has a crack through the face where I dropped it on the brick hearth. No one has asked if I would like to have supper. Instead, white skirts float by and the aunt carries a pan of water, and a man in a suit comes to the front door and speaks with my daddy—my daddy picks me up all the time and says he intends to name a rose after me as soon as he has a chance to breed one. He and the man in the dark suit sit in the parlor and speak in whispery voices, and I know Daddy has forgotten the rose.

The man in the suit goes to the bedroom where my mother is sleeping; he leans down and picks up her arm and holds her wrist. He speaks to the aunt who has been staying with us for a week—Daddy told her to go home, which is odd because he loves visitors. My brothers were sent to another aunt's house a week ago, before my mother took sick. Now the man in the suit talks to Daddy again, and Daddy walks the man to the door. I'm hungry, I would like some milk. I slip into my mother's room, tiptoe up to the bed and ask to have a biscuit, tell her my stomach hurts. I gaze at her stomach, which is *Big*. God has sent a baby in there—I've asked him to send a girl. Aren't three brothers *enough*? My mother's eyes are closed. Her skin has turned blue over the past two days, and sometimes there's blood under her dark feathery eyelashes.

Up and down our street crepe door sashes abound. I've not been allowed outdoors, but I've seen them from our windows. As I'll learn later, white for the young, black for the middle-aged, gray for the old. There's a war across the ocean and there's another war at home, and it's severe cyanosis, I'll also learn later, that turns some victims nearly black. The Brantley undertaker has run short of coffins. Someone stole two newly made coffins from his shed during the night. Daddy, head in his hands, cried, "Where is the Almighty when a man has to steal a casket to bury his son?"

After the doctor leaves, Daddy paces back and forth across the dining room, slams his fist down on the oak table. "She had to go out and nurse the neighbors who were sick. Why didn't I stop her?" He stares at the forest-fire painting above the mantel, shakes his head as though angry with the picture.

My aunt has told me not to go in my mother's room, but I keep sneaking in anyway. My daddy comes in the room, tears in his eyes. When he turns my mother over, she crackles like grease on a hot griddle.

It was really air leaking through damaged lungs.

Above the bed is a painting of a girl with a long brown braid down her back, floating in a small wooden boat under a half-shadowed full moon. My favorite painting—well almost, I like the wild reds and blacks of the forest fire, and the one of the peaches, and the deer swimming in the ocean. My mother held me up to the deer while she was painting it so I could smell the woodsy paint. My mother said she hoped heaven smelled like oil paint.

The aunt shoos me out of my mother's room. I'm still hungry. No one brings food like they used to when somebody was sick. No one comes to visit on Sunday afternoons. The milkman wears a handkerchief over his mouth and leaves the milk at the gate, he won't come on the porch. Daddy says it's now illegal to shake hands in a place called Arizona where the Indians live. He takes my mother's hand all the time. But he swears at God a lot, especially when the church bells ring, which they do often now, and not just on Sunday.

✎∽◯∾✎

Uta always said that there was one defining moment in everyone's life that shaped and cemented the psyche forever. *We're nothing if not the hardened clay of our first date with chance*—that was how she put it. *We live there forever.*

Did you know that more people died in the Spanish flu epidemic than in all the wars of the twentieth century? Sudden, virulent, unpredictable death. It's unkind that I almost felt better upon learning Margaret Mitchell's mother had died of it too. I wasn't the only one.

One morning I sneaked out of our house and skipped down the street, a whirling dervish set free. Soon my father came running and grabbed me up. But not before I saw the corpses lying on a neighbor's porch. Five of them wrapped in sheets. An entire family, including a playmate.

Bloodstains on the white sheets—I can still see this in my mind. I was too young to even understand death, but no child sees that and doesn't get an inkling. On some unconscious level, I knew the world had changed.

Some experts, I once read, believe the epidemic started in a small Kansas town, moved to a military base, and traveled from there to other military bases, World War I soldiers taking it on to Europe. But there's no army base near Brantley, and few people ever pass through there. How did we get so unlucky? Do you remember when we'd sleep together in the back bedroom in my parents' house? We're lying in that huge brass bed, you don't know it's the bed your real grandmother died in, and it's a hot night so I push the silk-covered comforter onto the floor, where it always slides anyway, it's slick like a grape. The moon—it's so bright, a stark white moon—shines through the window and makes stripes on the sheets. We're sticky, damp, there's no breeze, only the fragrance of summer night, of warm earth and cape jasmine, and at midnight we're awakened by the long low wail of the train.

Brantley is where the Silver Star and the Silver Meteor railroad lines stopped to take on coal and water. Death rode south on iron tracks when three thousand soldiers were mustered onto passenger cars in Rockford, Illinois, for the 950-mile trip to Camp Hancock in Augusta, Georgia, passing through the western coastal plain of South Carolina. See those men crowded in a rail car, men coughing, one with blood pouring from his nose, another feverish and mumbling, others leaning out the windows to avoid breathing the same air? When the train stops to refuel, soldiers are forbidden to leave the cars—two thousand of those men will be hospitalized later—but men scramble outside anyway, to escape the fetid air, and not everyone returns.

My hometown lay directly in the path of the invasion.

January 1919 was unusually cold and it snows one morning, big bubbly white flakes. I've never seen snow and go from window to window exclaiming, then I run to Daddy and ask can we go outside. When he says we can't, I slink off to the pantry and don't come out for an hour, even when the aunt promises to make cookies. Finally I go and look at my mother but her eyes are closed and she doesn't say anything. She isn't coughing up blood now. She's almost smiling for the first time in days, but she's asleep too. I climb up onto the bed and nestle close to her, her long hair so dark against the white sheets. I tell her about the snow, curl my fingers into her curled fingers, for those fingers are special, like rabbits and chickens are special because they live and sleep outside and make noises people don't. My mother's fingers do what other people's fingers don't, she puts them on paintbrushes and pictures appear, and I don't have a word for magic yet but I know what it is.

I crawl down off the bed and walk around to look at her from all angles, wishing she would open her eyes. She has deep gray eyes that seem to come from a long way off. I lean against the bed and do what she used to do—I sing "Mary Had a Little Lamb." She taught me to sing before real words came, and now I sing another—

A loud cry, I'm jerked back from the bed, piercing voices of Daddy and the aunt. I'm shunted out of the room by the aunt, my linen shift ripping down the middle like a heart split in two.

∾ᏽᎬᏽᎴ

My mother disappeared without symbol or ceremony. There was no funeral; church services were rarely held then. My brothers and I weren't taken to the burial. I was distracted by an aunt when the undertaker came for her body. I didn't understand what had happened. How could my mother just be *gone*? And where was that baby in her stomach? I wanted her *back*. A year later I still wondered—why did she go away?

When I turned four, Daddy said I was old enough and hand-in-hand we walked past the leaning old white houses of our neighbors and through the iron gates of the town cemetery. Daddy walked very quietly over to a grassy area with a low wall around it. I'd learned to read a little and I saw my mother's name on a stone. That's where she'd gone to live now. I clutched the roses I'd picked for her and sat down.

Daddy said, "No, Louise. It's not respectful to sit on a grave."

I asked where my baby sister went and Daddy said the baby had gone to heaven with my mother. Everything was so different now. I had a new mother; the new mother cooked and cleaned but she didn't make pictures. I spent hours staring at my dead mother's paintings. The sickness was gone, but my first mother did not come back. Before the new mother came, my daddy sat at the dining-room table smoking his pipe every evening. He didn't look like himself, he wandered around the house as though lost, and he kept forgetting his hat when he went off to his job as town clerk. When he came home he just sat and smoked and stared and smoked and stroked my hair when I climbed into his lap to play with his gold watch chain, and now and then he yelled when the boys got into a scuffle. He smoked and stared at the paintings and mildly noticed that my oldest brother had a bloody nose, and he smoked and stared and told the colored woman who was keeping us not to dust the paintings. He wouldn't let anyone touch them.

I wanted him to be like he used to be, when he would laugh all the time and give me smoochy kisses. Sometimes I stood beside him and held his hand, sometimes we gazed at the paintings together, and inside my head I would hear my mother singing her favorite hymns. When I looked at those pictures, she came into the room again, smiling and humming as she took up a paintbrush. I was back in the cradle sleeping and my mother was sitting at a tall stand putting color on cloth, and Daddy would walk in and smile and take her hand and kiss her fingers, her magic fingers he called them, for who could make a likeness any better?

Often after she was gone, I took my mother's paint box out from under Daddy's bed and opened it and breathed the smell of heaven. One day the paint box was gone; my new mother said she'd thrown it away, as there was no one to use it and the paints had dried up. I ran down the concrete back steps and found the wooden box in the trash can beside the privy. I looked inside and it was true, the paints had turned hard. I dragged the paint box across the backyard, found a garden hoe and dug a shallow grave near the rose bushes, where the soil was soft. I picked up the paintbrushes one by one, ran my fingers along the stiff bristles, and buried the dried-out brushes in the ground, covering them with inert tubes of magic color.

I've spent a lot of my life wondering who my mother really was, what I might have learned about myself had I known her. We never talked about her when I was a child; that would have been disrespectful to my stepmother. Only recently has it occurred to me that my mother did what women have always done. In a disaster, she went out and nursed others, sacrificing her life rather than protecting herself and her own.

Part III: Lyra

2004

Chapter Five

⬥

One afternoon a nurse comes to my mother's cubicle to say someone is looking for me. I pull my paisley shawl around my shoulders—the hospital's air-conditioning must be set on fifty—and head toward the waiting room. There the harsh glare of fluorescent ceiling lights nearly blinds me, the wall-hung television perpetually on, but respectfully, quietly. I'd like to jerk it off its metal support and throw it, with substantive disrespect, onto the carpeted floor. Hospitals are not places where anyone should be watching *Wheel of Fortune*.

Among the "regulars," most looking wrinkled and sleep-deprived, is a man in a suit who stands when I walk in.

"Lyra?" He holds out his hand. "I heard about your mother's stroke, my mother asked me to come by and say how sorry we are."

He looks vaguely familiar, but I'm so tired nearly everyone does. Dark brown hair with silver edges, brown eyes, attractive in a nondescript way.

"Well of course you wouldn't recognize me. It's only been, like, decades." Something about his eyes is familiar. "John," he says. "John Truesdale."

"*Johnny* Truesdale? From Lincoln Street?"

The scar above his lip is gone.

"That'd be me. I know it's been a long time. How is your mother?"

"She's somewhere between here and there. How did you know?"

"My mother knows someone who goes to your parents' church. Your mother kept in touch over the years."

Rosa of the endless men? My mother kept in touch with her? "How is Rosa?"

John Truesdale smiles, exposing the crooked teeth I remember, though many have been improved. "Old age has slowed her down a bit, but she's still feisty. She got married about ten years ago. Your mother didn't tell you?"

"No—no she didn't. What's your story these days?"

"Wife and three boys, one in college, the other two in high school. I'm a sales rep for a medical-supply company out of Charlotte."

Suddenly I see us in the backyard on Lincoln Street, behind a pecan tree playing the "doctor game." He's holding the plastic straw stethoscope—he always wants to heal me—but I'm sick and tired of being the patient. I push him onto his scrawny back and shout, "I'm the doctor now. You have a very bad case of TB. Take off your pants and I'll fix it."

"Did you say *medical* supplies?"

He nods, poker-faced, and adds, "Mom and I have always thought so much of your mother. I bet you don't know she helped us way back." His voice drops to a lower pitch. "A year or two after your family moved, Mom got arrested."

He looks away, then back. "Your mother got Mom out of jail. Posted bond."

My mother bailed Rosa out of the joint?

"I know your parents didn't have much money," he adds. "I don't know if Mom ever paid her back, but she's been grateful to her all these years. It turned Mom around in a way."

Several people rush into the waiting room, excited voices, a new family whose son has just been brought in.

John and I walk out into the hallway. He shifts, looks around as though nervous. "Lyra, I came here partially to see you. To apologize. For the way I acted after your father—after he got sick. It was mean that I dropped you, the way I made fun of you and him. My mother whipped the daylights out of me but I was stupid and cruel, and I know it's late but I'm really sorry."

So long ago and still there. Weeks after my father's breakdown and I'm sitting on our front steps; Johnny and two boys from Aiken Street are on his porch pointing at me and laughing. I can hear them: "Bet she's crazy too. Whole family's loony-tunes. Bet she rolls her eyes back in her stupid head like a dog."

Suddenly I understood the earth science lesson about islands, what it meant to be cut off from a mainland.

John's voice: "It was disgraceful. I don't know why I acted that way."

"Everyone acted that way except your mother and Uta. I hated you for a while, I admit it; you were my first real friend. But you had your own cross to bear. To tell you the truth, I always wished my mother was more like yours—Rosa had guts, daring. I'm sure that was a different experience for you." I look my old playmate in the eye. "It's too bad ostracism didn't make us closer." *But it didn't for my parents either.*

As white-uniformed nurses and doctors pass by, I wonder if Johnny knew about the encyclopedia salesman. A man in a white shirt and black tie is trying to sell my mother a set, but we don't have the money; he asks about neighbors with school-age children and my mother points across the street to Johnny's house. The man's eyes narrow to a condescending gleam—"Oh I heard about them," he says. "No point going over there, that boy's from a broken home, his mother's a divorcée, so that poor kid won't amount to nothing. Shame on her."

As the salesman walks away, my mother whispers in a shocked voice, "It isn't even what Rosa *does*, it's the divorce." She leans down to me. "People are never going to look down their nose at you, Lyra. I promise you that."

John gives me his business card and says to please let him know if there's anything he can do. I ask him to tell Rosa the dancing lessons have stood me in good stead.

"Oh, that reminds me," he says. "I looked up your paintings on the Internet. I bought the one of Mom leaning over the balcony of our old house. She loves it—though of course she maintains she was thinner than that."

"I always wondered who bought that picture. Nice symmetry."

"Do you have new work somewhere in town?"

"Not at the moment. I've been doing other things, teaching, not painting so much." Like not at all.

He says to give his best to my mother. "I always liked how she told stories when we were kids, she was always so kind. I remember her helping me memorize things for school."

"Thank you, Johnny—John. For coming by. And for the apology."

I don't want him to leave, this connection to Lincoln Street. "By the way, whatever happened to Uta Moazen?"

"You don't know? She killed herself in the late 1960s."

It takes me a moment to respond. "Did anyone know why?"

"Not as I recall. Your mother sang at the funeral, amazing song, someone translated an African American spiritual into Irish—didn't she tell you?"

"She never liked talking about sad things."

John says good-bye, gives me a hesitant hug, and heads down the hall. I stare at the closing elevator doors. Why didn't my mother tell me about helping Rosa? About Uta?

I know why. After my parents moved across town, she never mentioned Lincoln Street again.

∾⊙∾

My father almost never leaves the hospital. The nurses, who roll a portable bed into the waiting room for him at midnight, say how lucky his wife is to have a husband who cares so much. I want to say something cynical, bastardize my mother's favorite mantra about the airplane sightings of her childhood—*Some things are there even if you can't see them, but other things aren't there even when it looks like they are.* Instead, I suggest that every other night I stay over. He tells me it's his "duty" to be there and sends me home. A half hour later I pull into my parents' driveway and sit for a moment; I still steel myself upon first seeing the house.

Usually when I'd arrive, I'd barely get out of the car before my father would rush out and start inspecting it. "Your car is in bad shape" were his first words to me. Then came dire stories of people dying in traffic accidents.

My mother would appear, embrace me but turn to him. "Stop being so negative, William. If you can't say something nice, just keep quiet."

"I'll talk about anything I want to," he'd shout, brandishing a parking ticket he'd found on my car seat. "See this?" Gleefully he'd wave the ticket in my face. "If you don't pay this right away, you'll go to jail. If you don't pay it, *I'll* go to jail too."

"William, I'm talking to Lyra now. Leave her *alone*. She doesn't want to talk to you. Nobody goes to jail over a parking ticket. You're ridiculous."

"You do not understand these things, Louise."

Usually I'd go inside at this point; they didn't need me in order to decide what I did and did not want to hear. Their bickering was always civil, though; it never drew blood. No profanity, threats, physical blows. Blood and bad words would have been cleaner. Instead, after they tired of jabbing at each other, they separated to different rooms and combat was replaced by global silence and barely disguised fury.

Inside the rancher I graze on odds and ends in the refrigerator, make wine my main course. If it weren't stupider than spit, I'd buy Benson and Hedges menthol lights. Maybe they don't exist anymore. I sit in the den and try to read Ms. Borgia's uplifting history, but I can't stay with the story. I phone my oldest friend, the only friend I ever brought home when I was a teenager; she offers to come to Columbia. I say I'm fine. I go back to the cedar chest for more company towels—I'm becoming downright wanton with them. Beneath the last ones are old linens: dainty embroidered dresser scarves, lace tablecloths made by hand, the regrettably mute history of my family's women. I also find a shoebox covered with bright contact paper; my mother never discarded old boxes and she always decorated them. This small act by the child of a painter nearly brings me to tears. Inside, carefully wrapped in yellowed linen, is a very old doll. Tiny, delicate unclothed rag body, creamy porcelain face, startling blue glass eyes. A note pinned to it reads: "From around 1900." The swaddling cloth is so thin it could disintegrate, and the china face is cracked, but the fissure between the eyes down to the chin has been carefully glued. I trace the crack with my finger.

At the bottom of the cedar chest, under stacks of empty picture frames, is a photograph of my father. A blond boy of seven or eight, freckles, unruly flaxen forelock slicked back, wearing a coat and a tie that's hopelessly askew. The only photograph of him as a child I've ever seen. Why did no one straighten his tie? I notice a static vacancy in his eyes—he's never spoken of his childhood or told me anything else that's personal. Or ever said anything personal about me that wasn't critical. There's also an envelope of black and white photographs: unfamiliar houses, churches, other buildings; for years he took these for no apparent reason. I also find, in a torn envelope with an APO address, a letter in my father's tiny script addressed to his parents. I read its single fragile page out loud, much of it about the weather, packages his mother has sent him. Mailed from a hospital in England, the last line reads: "They're sending me back to the front tomorrow. Maybe someday I'll get used to it."

After I reread the letter, I put it in the box with the doll.

Some days as I sit by my mother's bed, I sense that she's still present mentally. But who knows if that's true or not? I tell her about John Truesdale's visit, and then I remember how I found out what Rosa did for a living, though I didn't know it was her profession until later. One day in our first year on Lincoln Street, I went looking for Johnny and no one answered his door, but I could hear music inside so I walked along the creaking, sloped porch and peered in the front windows. Rosa was sitting on her flowered couch with a man in a dark suit. He looked like a judge or a bank robber—he was all rolls where my father was angles, and he had a large sparkly ring on his pinkie finger. They were laughing and talking; his legs were slightly parted and Rosa's right thigh dangled across his, which had hiked her dress up. The man's left hand seemed underneath Rosa's dress. Her dress moved around a little and she let out a giggle just as Johnny came down the street on his bike—I knew there were times he was made to play outdoors. I hightailed it down his steps before he could catch me spying on his mother. I ran back to my house and jumped on my bed to ponder the strange habits of adults.

Because there were so few cars on Lincoln Street—our neighbors mostly rode the bus—Johnny and I spent hours roller-skating in the street. I could skate rings around him and lost no opportunity to do so. But eventually my father ordered me to skate only on the sidewalk. "Stay out of the street," he yelled. "You'll get hit by a car and we'll have to take you to the doctor. Doctors cost money. Try to behave better."

While I was sitting on the porch steps unscrewing my skates with the metal key, my mother appeared. She was wearing a shapeless flowered housedress and had blue-black ink stains on her fingers from grading papers. "You do skate well, honey. Like the flying wind. You can do anything."

Soon I became quite proficient at the yo-yo. The up and down of it came natural.

One afternoon I defied my father and was whizzing down the street on my skates when he ran down the front steps, grabbed me and carried me inside, took off his leather belt, and turned me over his knee and began hitting me. Hard.

My screams summoned my mother. "William, hasn't she had enough?"

He hit me once more, then left the room. I dove into the pillows sobbing. My mother leaned over me, rubbing my back. I reared up. "Why doesn't he like me? What did I *do*?"

"Lyra, he's just trying to help you grow up right."

"He's never nice to me, he *hates* me, I know he does."

She burst into tears and jumped up and ran out the door. And not for the last time.

Johnny was my escape from my house. That first summer, ignoring my parents' rules, he herded me over to Elmwood Cemetery where he pointed out tombstones for dead little kids and Confederate soldiers, and then over to the railroad trestle to "look for bums" (we didn't find any fortunately), and finally down the ten blocks of Elmwood Avenue to the state mental hospital. As we peered through the wrought-iron gate, Johnny pointed at the massive Babcock Building, dark and scary with bars on all the windows, and whispered, "That's where the old lady with the red wagon used t'live." He nodded toward the ten-foot walls to our right and left. "Them walls's on account of not lettin' nobody get away. They put Yankees in here way back. Now just loonies. Yes sir, onc't you get put in, ain't no way out."

I didn't want to admit the place spooked me. "*Onc't* is not a word," replied the English teacher's daughter. Since Johnny was two years older, I lorded anything I could come by over him. "Say *once*."

"See that dome yonder?" He pointed at the Babcock cupola. "People up there's chained to the wall. Droolin' and stuff." He turned toward me. "They gonna put you in there when they catch you riding that fool cat around in your baby-doll carriage."

"Yeah? Well, they're gonna lock you up when they see you reading a comic book while jumping on your pogo stick. Your head's loose already."

"Your daddy's loco enough to get in here now."

"Everybody says your mama's a bad lady."

Silenced by larger truths, we both turned and stared into the distance.

Johnny was also obsessed with Uta Moazen. Convinced that her arm had been torn off by another witch in a fight, he wanted to catch her at "witch stuff" and get her locked up in the madhouse. One day at dusk Uta's front door was open, and Johnny and I stood on the sidewalk surveying her stone fortress. We intended a secret spying mission, but Rosa stepped out on her balcony and called Johnny home. I stared at his retreating back; thinking to outdo him, I crept onto Uta's porch alone and peered through the screen door. The old lady was standing in the middle of her fussy living room holding a green jar in her right hand. She slid the jar under the opposite armpit, clamping it with her half-arm, and unscrewed the metal ring and took the lid off. A moment passed. Then she put the lid back on and removed the jar from under her arm.

She was still holding the jar when she appeared at her door. I backed up like crazy as she said, "You see, child, my husband was a mean and stingy man, and when he lay on his deathbed I sat beside him and waited for his last breath. He tossed and turned, kept staring at me like it was my fault he was sick. He thought everything was my fault. If he had let me go to the doctor before the gangrene set in, I'd still have my arm. But he kept saying doctors cost too much, the trouble was just in my crazy head."

I was considering whether to make a run for it. And whether Uta would tell my parents I'd been spying on her.

"When my husband was in the bed dying, I decided what I would do." She paced back and forth by the screen door, white ringlets bobbing, half-arm tight to her side. "On his last day his eyes shot back in his head and he gasped. I put this jar up to his lips and trapped his dying breath, knowing full well this would keep his soul from going to heaven. Provided—and I doubt it—it was headed there. You see, my husband took things from me that no one should ever take. Even before they cut off my arm, he stole my soul."

She stopped at the door, stared at me through the screen. "But sometimes I feel guilty, so I let a little bit of him go on. The rest stays in limbo; he's kept me in a limbo most of my life. I've hated him, but I once loved him too. That's the way life works out sometimes."

I wondered if my mother knew you could put a husband in a jar.

Uta pushed open the screen door. "Come in and visit, dear." She held out her only hand to me. I took it. Uta's strangeness didn't hurt.

My mother improves, she falls back, on it goes for a week. One morning while my father is home showering, a graying African American nurse with matching dimples and the gait of a slow dancer comes into the waiting room and says to me, "I'm Darlene. I work down in pediatrics and when I heard there was a schoolteacher named Copeland in ICU, I had to come on up—your mama taught my daughter Annette. Miz Copeland got that gal to love reading, she kept on telling Annette she could do anything."

I burst into tears.

The nurse slips an arm around me and guides me down the hall. "Did I tell you my girl's a big ole lawyer now, partner and ever'thing? Your mama was a fine teacher, she loved children with a big heart."

I cry harder.

"You poor thing," she says. "How 'bout I come see your mama now and again?"

I nod gratefully as she pats me on the shoulder. "One day Miz Copeland told Annette—'You find yourself something in life you can be *for*. Don't base your life on what you're mad about.'"

Darlene pauses beside the nurses' station. "I had the feeling your mama knew 'bout tough times. And these things come on down—it was Annette who pushed me to go to nursing school when I was forty-seven and my no-count husband took off with all our money."

She heads down the hall. As I stare after her, I realize—she is what I love about the South I've spent a lifetime putting in a rearview mirror. Women like my mother. Women of the hard life remarkably missing the gene of self-pity.

❧❦❧

Later, back at the house, I wonder—what am *I* for? Did my mother and I ever want any of the same things?

I wanted to probe what I didn't understand, examine it; she did not. But when I was in my thirties, married, I guess we had more in common. I'd just begun teaching and we sat in this den and laughed and talked about art and books and old family stories. But almost imperceptibly something changed and a terrible distance set up shop between us. She didn't criticize me—my father was always at the ready for that—but I knew she disapproved of my divorce and the wild years afterward. All the moves and job changes, the affairs. I've had enough variations of "relationship" that I ought to be put in a museum. Exhausting work, so for the last few years I've avoided having a romantic life. I like singleness; I've always known what *solitary* means. My mother definitely didn't like the blatant sexuality of my post-divorce paintings: so she told a relative who gracelessly passed that information on to me. Is that why she didn't show up for my final show in Columbia? She didn't like it that I refused to stay married, to accept unhappiness? That I've never behaved like a proper Southern lady? That I rejected her interest in cooking and gardening, swore off traditional women's interests? That I didn't stay in South Carolina and churn out grandchildren?

She adored children. Why didn't she have more of her own? I don't know when the separate bedrooms began. I hated it. One more thing that marked us. Another sign of the failure to thrive.

Why weren't they happy?

Wandering into the living room, I hesitate beside one of my surreal paintings. Uncharacteristic hot color leaps off the canvas. I never understood why my mother wanted this picture. A stooped old couple is happily burying 1950s halter-tops; beneath the ground, skeletons from a potter's field catch the tops and try them on. An ironically hopeful elegy to lost causes. Our Lincoln Street neighbors the Sweetes, an unmarried brother and sister who looked like Russian nesting dolls—gentle farm people out of place in the city—did indeed buy old clothes they didn't wear but inexplicably buried. No wonder my father didn't initially stand out. I notice the Seth Thomas mantel clock atop the bookcase across from me and smile. My father gave it to my mother twenty years ago, a replica of the chiming clock from Brantley. Six years ago he stopped winding it so, in his words, "I won't get any older." Somehow it didn't surprise me to come home to find that correct time no longer existed there. He also told me he'd invented fitted sheets, adding, "If I'd only taken out a patent, we'd be rich." It was always a coin toss, though not until he mellowed at seventy, whether I'd come home to find the funny man or the man from the funny farm. How did my mother live with this for half a century? With so little affection?

Once when visiting in Columbia in my thirties, I hesitated at the back door and said to her, "I can't bear the thought that someday you'll be gone. I feel like you should have had more." A little *happiness*, for example.

She smiled—she was heavy by then and her hair, which stayed dark until her late sixties, was finally turning gray. But her eyes were gentle, seemed wise and forgiving.

"I've had a good life," she said. "I got to have a child and watch her grow up and make her own way in the world. I've had wonderful friends. I've had a full and happy life. You have made it all worthwhile."

It was the kindest gift she ever gave me. A lie. And a responsibility I knew I'd blown to hell.

I'd grown up around too much of her loneliness to believe her—the vampire of loneliness that hides in dusty corners in daylight and comes out to feed at night. All those nights—I'm ten, maybe eleven—when moonlight shines through the windows by my bed as I listen to the creaking of our unsteady house, which always feels like a houseboat that might go under. Often my mother cries out in her dreams, moans as though trapped in a nightmare. Day or night, whenever my father says something unkind to her, words which sting like poison arrows, she retreats to the bathroom, hiding her tears. I don't know how to help. So in my teenage years I fled her despair by breaking rules; she tightened the rules and said I was rebellious and contentious, that I deliberately rattled the windows and shook the rafters. I did: I was angry as hell. I couldn't bring friends home for fear of what strange thing my father might do or say. I didn't want anyone witnessing the palpable lovelessness in the air. As soon as I could, I left South Carolina for good.

But later I took the leap and brought home the perfectly normal twenty-five-year-old man I wanted to marry. When he told my parents of our plans, my father stared at him as if he didn't understand the words. Then he laughed, a high-pitched hyena squawk, and said, "You know she hasn't paid off her car, don't you? She's no good with money, I can tell you that."

He continued to laugh. My mother left the room. My speechless fiancé looked horrified at the implied transfer of poor-quality chattel.

I was too shocked to respond. *My father thinks it's funny that anyone would want to marry me.* I walked into the dining room and stared at my mother, tears turning mascara into coal veins down my face. I screamed at her inside my head—*For God's sake, say something.*

She asked what I wanted for supper.

∾⚬◯⚬∾

There was never a china doll I could glue back together. And only one moment when I saw *into* my mother. As I gaze around her house in this 2004 light, I see us again on the Brantley porch that last day—sometime in the late eighties. The auction is over: the brass bed and mirrored oak armoire are being carried down the brick steps. My grandfather's armchair, the mantle clock. Mother is standing beside a brick pillar, watching. She'll be taking her father's desk, his smoking stand, her mother's paintings. The house was willed to my mother, with the provision that her stepmother be allowed to remain in it for her lifetime. Now my step-grandmother can no longer live alone and the house must be sold to help pay for her nursing-home care. The house of my mother's childhood, the things her mother touched, will soon belong to strangers.

My own memories crowd into the room. I was sent to stay with my grandmother for part of every summer after age seven. Here, playing with antique dolls beneath huge oil paintings, I learned the lesson of pictures. Pictures were magic. Brantley was magic. My father never came here, but every time my mother did, her sad face remained in Columbia. The longer she stayed here, sleeping in the high brass bed with its slippery comforter, the more she laughed. The house and the paintings changed her; when she dusted the paintings, she always said, in a voice she didn't have anywhere else, *I just like to touch them.* Art made people feel better than their regular selves.

"I'd hoped to pass this house on to you," she says softly, bringing me back to the present. "It would have meant a lot to me to do that. At least you'll have the farm."

She stares at her mother's paintings. "I always thought I'd become an artist because my mother was a painter. Somehow that didn't happen. I guess that's okay."

She had once wanted *more.*

We went into the living room and for a long time she gazed above the dining-room fireplace, where the outline of the forest-fire painting remained.

"Soon a stranger will walk through these rooms," she whispered, to herself more than to me. "Will the memories living in this house still be here then? Does a house retain them?" She leaned against the painted tongue-and-groove wall and murmured—"The man who built this place, his wife was a painter, she died in 1919, in that terrible flu epidemic." She placed her hand on the wall, as though to press history into the wood. "The real story is that the man who built this house loved his wife so much he never recovered from losing her. What love that was, what amazing love."

It was a mantra. A funeral. I thought—*What love some never have.*

Brantley and my mother disappear as I go into my old room and get ready for bed. Maybe I've never understood her life. I didn't lose my mother in infancy, I wasn't born during one world war and had to live through another, I didn't do without during the Depression, I didn't watch my husband lose his mind and have to take care of him alone. Security must matter a lot if you've lived through all that, I think as I get into bed. I gaze across the room at the most unusual of my grandmother's paintings, the one time she escaped the somber English landscape school. This mystical painting of a cliff over a wild sea is the brightest coral and yellow and pink that ever came from her palette. Exuberantly impressionistic. What happened this time? Has there been a time in my life, or in my mother's, when all color turned into its opposite? Dark to light?

We know more about light gone to dark.

Perhaps world-shattering events are quite small. Maybe world events are one man and one woman in one place, and the world spins on its axis around them and nothing is quite the same again. Afterward, a shell-shocked soldier *must* preach the fifth commandment. A woman who loses her mother too early *must* become a mother. Maybe our lives are always an attempt at correction. But if this need is too desperate, if something gets in the way, maybe a whole house can fall down.

One afternoon I go back over to Elmwood Park, ride by my old house, and then drive the five blocks to the brick junior high school, now a retirement home, where my mother taught English. I stroll around the grounds, hesitate under a row of second-floor windows—I think that was her homeroom. Who was she when she held forth there every morning? The building looks exactly as it did in my childhood, and I take a few pictures.

On impulse I drive to the grounds of the closed state hospital. It still shocks me that anyone might choose to live there; the buildings, on the other hand, might make an interesting subject for a painting. Provided I ever paint again. There's no guardhouse anymore and the ten-foot walls, at least at the entrance, were brought down to four feet in the 1970s. I hesitate alongside the Mills Building, an 1820s neoclassical beauty designed by the same South Carolina architect who created the Washington Monument. Protected by the National Historic Register, the building's white Doric columns support a second-floor portico reached by elegant curved twin staircases. Not a barred window to be seen. Because of Robert Mills' fame, 1950s schoolchildren, including my fifth-grade class, toured its public rooms. Did my parents know I was taken there? On the tour we were taught to distinguish between Doric and Corinthian columns, learned how Mills valued natural light, heard stories of captured Yankee officers sequestered on the grounds during the "War Between the States." No leering psychotics in sight. But I had tortured dreams for months afterward.

I drive on and park at the Babcock Building, a mammoth nineteenth-century brick edifice with four stories of row after row of barred windows, huge wings to the right and left, and an interior courtyard outlined with barbed wire, all topped by that omnipresent red cupola. Fifth-graders were not taken inside it. Now I know it's a Kirkbride Plan asylum from the Moral Treatment era, when it was believed that showing kindness to the mentally ill, providing a peaceful and restful environment, was the best cure. Impressive architecture as therapy. The structure is so massive it feels unreal, a small college housed in one building. Empty for many years, it's been left to slowly fall down. Ancient magnolia trees tower around me as I walk toward it, camera slung over my shoulder, my hands trembling. The building is now encircled by an eight-foot-tall chain-link fence bearing signs forbidding trespassing. Windows are smashed behind the rusted iron bars, bricks dislodged, paint peeling. The concrete front steps to the portico are crumbling.

I focus my Nikon and shoot.

In a few minutes I hear a car behind me. A police car, a tall officer alighting, waving at me. I assume he's going to warn me that the building isn't safe. I'm about to say there's no chance I'll trespass this haunted mausoleum when he tells me no one is "allowed" to photograph Babcock—he says it several times. "Special permission" is required.

My blood pressure goes up—his tone annoys me. "I'm an artist," I say. "I paint pictures of old buildings, I use photos for the early studies. I grew up just down the street from here."

"Like I said, you're not allowed to photograph this building." He says I can shoot the Mills Building all I want.

Of course I can, it's pretty. "I can't take pictures of a state-owned building? An historic building?" My voice is shrill; this feels like censorship.

He more or less tells me to get moving, and for a moment I think he's going to demand my memory card. He's a giant with a gun and an attitude so I decide not to argue. But what is this *about?* The state doesn't want photos of ruin around to remind a developer of Babcock's horrific history? No way will I surrender my memory card. Can the policeman arrest me?

He doesn't ask for the card, but stands and watches until I get in my car and drive off.

I know what a Kirkbride building is because as a teenager I briefly wanted to be a psychiatrist. Not that either of my parents ever even alluded to my father's breakdown. And although he never had another, during my adolescence and beyond he was given either to brooding silence or to bizarre, angry outbursts. Even on placid days he'd watch me suspiciously, as though he believed I might be up to no good. Or that I intended him ill will. On bad days he'd erupt over something innocuous and rant at me hysterically, chasing me up and down the hall until I'd lock myself in my room and pull a pillow over my head to escape his voice. He rarely spoke to me except to correct or to condemn, implying that I wasn't smart enough to figure out anything for myself. Day in and day out he aimed verbal pessimism at me, and I took more and more risks. I knew he considered me a nuisance, someone whose insolence for standing up to him, for loudly shooting holes in his paranoid proclamations, needed to be broken like a willful beast. My mother watched the drama silently, sometimes telling me later that it'd be wiser to just go along with him. Easier. I knew this was what *she* wanted, that I had no ally anywhere. Often I'd feel my spirit sinking through the floorboards, where I knew it might disappear for good, and I'd drop to my knees and scratch it back up again.

What was *wrong*? My father looked just fine, though he didn't have the work life—he moved from one job to another to another—of most men with his education. Nor did he act like any father I'd ever heard about— where was the *Daddy* who was supposed to adore his little girl? Because my parents acted as though there'd been no breakdown, I initially wondered if I'd imagined the psychotic episode; it wasn't until my twenties that I began remembering sketchy details. By my thirties, when I found myself painting scenes that surprised and shocked me, pictures with obscure violence beneath their surface, I wanted desperately to know what really happened. By then, a pattern was firmly in place in my life: except on canvas, my wildest thoughts often remain locked in a house whose threshold I allow no one to cross.

When I finally asked my mother for information, she didn't want to talk about it. I appealed to her again a few years later, begged for details. She said it had to do "with the war," and she confirmed the long night of praying, told me about him running up and down the street in his pajamas, the arm straight up in the air.

"What about the blood? Didn't he try to kill himself? Didn't he slash his wrist with a razor blade?"

There was no suicide attempt, she said. No razor. No blood.

I could see her throwing a razor blade under a bed. Seemed like it was Christmas. *Didn't he almost throw me out of a window?*

Maybe I was having false memories. "What month was it?"

"Lyra, please don't bring this up to your father. It'll upset him. You know how he gets, what it'll be like." She stood up, ending the conversation. "It was December.

Part IV: Louise

1957

Chapter Six

I t's 3 p.m. I stand over the bed. William is lying down, glazed eyes staring up. I've replaced the bandage on his left wrist. He didn't seem conscious—it was like touching a corpse. Now his right arm is raised toward the ceiling. He's been like this for two hours, hasn't said a word no matter what I ask. I sit beside him, wonder how anyone can hold an arm up that long. I reach over and touch it. He gives no notice. I pull his arm downward. It falls slightly, then pops back up. Steel.

Suddenly he rears up, hisses, "Get away—get to the station. *Now.*"

I retreat to the kitchen, lean over the kitchen table and cradle my head in my hands, rock back and forth.

Eventually I'll have to call Lyra home from the Truesdales. I must do *something*. If I could just get him to eat something, if he could get some real sleep, if—I go over possibilities, keep my mind busy with details, and when the previous night slips in—no, I can't think about that right now, later maybe, but not now.

I can go to Uta's house and call a doctor, but we don't have a regular family doctor, someone who knows us. I get up and walk through the house and out onto the porch and gaze through the dirty screens. All the houses look different now, familiar cars are foreign, a dark sky despite the sun. Someone is there, then isn't. Things are one way, then gone. I walk through the screen door and down the concrete steps, calling for you.

97

Across the street, I pause and stare at our house as a stranger might. Not a remarkable house, just a tired two-story of white clapboard fronted by the effusive blue-headed hydrangeas, now in crusty December droop, that I planted in the spring. Glorious flowers that hide peeling paint, that soften the square corners and right angles. Lovely cobalt flowers gone to brittle clusters.

Just a moment ago I was young, holding my baby close, whirling her around in the summer grass, singing to my child, this living light.

How did our lives come to this day—to razor-blade blood? How did we turn into these cruel streaks of crimson on my old winter dress?

Groggy. Wonder what drugs they're giving me—maybe drugs are taking me back there. So hard to take a breath sometimes. Dr. Dumaine was just here, the dear man, I wish I could thank him. Someone else's voice. Lyra. Did I think she might not come? Oftentimes I wouldn't have blamed her.

When I imagine I'm talking to her, I want to find excuses for not having seen what was coming back then—I could say a new home and a new job, working full-time and taking care of that home and a child and a husband. The Asian flu epidemic didn't help. Nor did the rigid patriarchal "rules" of 1950s marriages, nowhere more entrenched than in the South. William had always been "unusual," and in many ways I liked that. His passion for trees, for instance. While the Asian flu ran through the schools, he began bringing home a forest. The first was a cedar sapling about three inches high, which he'd noticed in the crack of a concrete bridge and extracted with his penknife. At home he transferred it to a glass jelly jar, placed it in a window, and checked on it every day. I watched the care and attention he gave it and slipped my arm around his waist—this was the man I'd married, my biology major, a man who'd save a living thing he found on a bridge.

A week later he brought home another sapling, this one an oak. It joined the cedar in the windowsill, as did two pines. In time there were more seedlings and several small trees two or three feet tall. Your father never did anything halfway. One day he said that many trees had been burned down in 1865 and someone had to replace them. Since it was still warm outside, he moved them to the front porch. We could barely see the street. Rosa Truesdale reportedly told Bill Faherty, the pot-bellied neighbor who preferred government checks to personal labor and sat on his porch all day smoking cigars, that William had obviously been hit on the head by a big tree.

Your father told you, while we were eating supper, that growing conifers like the loblolly pine was important because they preserved history. "Conifers have undergone little evolutionary development—the trees on my farm are identical to their primeval ancestors."

He never called it *our farm*. I said, "Oaks and maples though—the hardwoods—give us wonderful color. I like the change, variation, the marking of time. Pines are always green, but hardwood leaves are softer than a pine's prickly needles."

You piped up, "Why do the colored leaves go away every year?" You'd told a neighbor that raking leaves hurt them. She'd called to say you were a very *unusual* child.

"The trees can't get the nutrients they need," William said. "The leaves die because the trees go dormant. You're too young to understand these things, but the main sustenance for trees comes from air and sun. They take almost nothing from the ground. They grow deep in the earth but aren't very connected to it."

After supper I sat on the tree-barricaded porch thinking about connections. I could hear someone passing by on the sidewalk, but I couldn't see a thing.

⚬❦❦⚬

A week later I'm sitting at my desk at Laidlaw listening to children's voices in the yard below. I go over and lean on the windowsill, staring down at them. Someday my child will play with brothers and sisters. How many will there be?

I'm waiting for Max Wells to pick up the Underwood typewriter atop my desk. Yesterday he'd stopped by my room looking sheepish, his eyes downcast as he said, "I write a bit of poetry, and I was wonderin' if you'd read it. Tell me how it can be better. It's not anythin' but some things I think about. I get my best ideas when I'm trimmin' the trees, when I'm up on a branch takin' off dead limbs. Life looks different from the sky."

He put a sheaf of papers on my desk. "I apologize for this handwritin'. I'm savin' up for a typin' machine." He was about to leave when he added, "I saw your husband again at the cemetery."

"What does he do there?"

"He just kinda walks around. Seemed that day like he was lookin' for somebody."

Max's voice disappears. I gaze at his poetry on my desk: it's about nature and faith, about a girl he loved who died when he was seventeen.

In a few minutes Principal Hindeman comes in and we talk about the flu epidemic and various school activities. Then he says, "There was a special meeting of the school board last week, don't know if you heard about it or not. We will voluntarily integrate next fall—before some mess like Little Rock has a chance to get started. I have to select the teachers for our first integrated classes. Needs to be our best teachers. I'm here to ask you to be one."

Desegregation was dominating the news. The South Carolina governor had just tried to punish civil-rights activists by ordering the State Board of Education to rescind accreditation of Allen College—a black school then. Allen's students began applying to the all-white University of South Carolina. One week after my conversation with Ed, dark-skinned patrons began lining up at the "Whites Only" ticket windows of downtown movie theaters. Each was refused a ticket and went to the back of the line to try again. No one of any color saw *The Bridge on the River Kwai* that day. Just a few blocks from Laidlaw, at a Main Street café owned by a wealthy Columbia businessman, enlarged newspaper photos appeared on the plate-glass windows: in each, a black demonstrator was being arrested, handcuffed, or dragged across concrete by a policeman. To make matters worse, a sunken Confederate ship was discovered two miles out from

Charleston harbor, with the remains of Confederate soldiers aboard. A Navy vessel hoisted it up and towed it by the Charleston battery, where hundreds of white people stood on the boardwalk and cheered. The governor was planning state burials for the remains.

The world we lived in then seems bizarre now. It wasn't just separate water fountains and bathrooms and seats on the bus, it was also stairs, doorways, pay windows, public benches. All kinds of things you'd never think of. Sometimes I'm amazed that South Carolina's founding fathers didn't build two sets of sidewalks.

Your father objected to my teaching an integrated classroom, which shocked me, given that he was studying to be a man of God "You shouldn't get mixed up in this, putting yourself in the limelight," he said. "You have no idea the trouble you could get into."

"The principal has *asked* me to do this. We'll be specially trained."

"You can tell the principal *your husband* has forbidden it."

He got up and left the table. I stared at the dishes. *Forbidden?* I'm not a child.

While I cleared the table, William went outside to change the oil in the car, which he did every two weeks. No cleaner oil in America, I'll warrant. After I did the dishes, I wandered into the living room and gazed out the front window as evening began shadowing our old houses. William was on his knees in the front yard, several saplings beside him. He was transplanting them along the sidewalk. Someday they would completely hide the house. Separate us from everyone.

Every day in 1957 seemed up and down, an erratic emotional seesaw. One afternoon, unasked, William took sandpaper and wood stain and repaired the scratches on the dining-room table—it looked beautiful afterward. A day later he answered questions in a monotone or not at all. I can't recall much of what I felt—I wasn't accustomed to thinking about *my* feelings. Women of my generation had been taught that emphasis on the self led to no good thing. Relieved that the flu was under control, I ignored my other fears. It was such a lovely time—a glorious autumn. Crimson and yellow stole across green leaves day by day, the air soft and sharp all at once. As chromatic leaves whirled and dipped, I told you that heaven's colors were falling from the sky, maybe from your real grandmother's paint box, and I was about to say that colored leaves were music's lovely accidentals but stopped myself, said well, really, it was science, you'd better understand that so you didn't say something incorrect in school.

Rosa was busier than ever that fall, her patrons getting in their time (Rosa said their *licks*) before winter and family holidays. To return Rosa's Tupperware bowl, I had finally made ladyfingers and after a slight hesitation on our porch, I strode over to Rosa's praying to high heaven that I was not arriving during "working hours." Rosa, to my relief, was fully dressed, chipped coffee cup in hand, bracelets jangling. She invited me in. I said I had wet laundry waiting to be hung out. Which was true.

When she peeked under the dishtowel, she whistled softly, "Uhmm—ladyfingers. Nothing I love better than tasty fingers."

I—for lack of anything better—said Rosa was looking well. She leaned forward and whispered, "Exercise wards off old age, you know."

Did she just like making me uncomfortable? She did have the devil in her.

I said I'd best get to our laundry. Rosa stared at me for a moment. "Listen, Louise, I know you don't approve of me, that's why you won't let Lyra play over here. Nothing happens to kids in this house."

"What you do is your own business," I said stiffly. *What about what children see? Who protects them from that?*

"Yes it *is* my business. So I won't mention that your old man has a screw loose. Maybe two or three. He yells at Lyra too much."

I said I had to go and stalked across the street.

Don't we always bristle over what we fear may be true? On Lincoln Street we all considered ourselves the one normal brick in a wall of misfit mortar.

∽⊙⊙⊙∾

Your father told me almost nothing about his studies that summer and fall. I didn't know he skipped classes, didn't know he believed two professors hated him. Sometimes even now I imagine William sitting on a wooden bench on the seminary grounds—maybe he's staring at the main building, solid granite with arched Gothic entrance, classrooms on the lower level, dormitory on the upper floors. Chapel on the second floor, stained-glass windows glowing greens and gold in the Indian summer sunlight. Beside William might be his books, copious marginal comments in his tiny, slanted hand. Much later I found odd notes in his theology textbook about the burning of Columbia. I forget the exact words but something like: *It's night, suddenly I smell smoke, I see flames in the distance, they hung a man at the mill, women are screaming, people are running past me bleeding, the buildings are falling, people running to the state hospital and onto the seminary grounds—devastation is coming—"*

Things began going downhill for him after the first seminary service he conducted, though I didn't know this until much later. I picture William robing in the hallway, going down the steep stone steps to enter the chapel through its arched wooden doors, up the old oak stairway, walking to the lectern, wearing the gold vestments for the first time, his classmates in reverent quiet, his professors in the back watching. But as he reads the Gospel, almost whispering, he starts coughing. When he looks at the congregation he chokes and can't stop coughing—his nerves can't handle the spotlight. He coughs and coughs, clears his throat and stumbles on, his voice hoarse, nearly inaudible as he labors through his sermon, mumbling the final prayers, swallowing the benediction.

Many days that fall he didn't come straight home after his classes. He went first to Elmwood Cemetery. Likely he paused beside the cemetery's new white brick carillon tower, which didn't yet have its bell installed, then headed to the section containing the graves of Confederate soldiers. I secretly followed him there once, saw him survey the rows of ten-inch concrete markers, many reading "Unknown CSA Soldier." He stared at a small faded Confederate flag lying on the ground and walked over, apparently to replant it, but abruptly froze, gazed around warily, then looked at his feet with relief—remember how dried magnolia leaves crackle sharply when stepped on? William walked on, clearly at home amid rusted wrought-iron fences and leaning tombstones.

I didn't understand *his* civil war.

⮜∘◦○◦∘⮞

When he didn't return home at the usual time one night, I grabbed your hand and said, "Let's go find your daddy," and we skipped down Lincoln Street, whipping up clouds of leaves. Near Logan School we passed the bedraggled woman with the red wagon; as we went by, she shrank sideways and hissed, "Don't come over here!" I pulled you close. After she was gone, I explained that the lady was not well. I gazed over my shoulder to see if she was still making her way down the street. I remembered seeing a frightening picture-show set in a mental hospital—*The Snake Pit*—and wondered what kind of person she'd been before being sent to Bull Street. I kept thinking I should do something for her but I hadn't a clue what. And to be truthful, the wild look of her frightened me.

We turned into the cemetery. You hesitated at a magnolia tree to pick up its oblong pods, and I said something inane about how I'd always thought cemeteries were restful, that was why your father took long walks here. Elmwood Cemetery sat—still sits—on that picturesque bluff above the Broad River; somewhere on its two hundred acres, according to Uta, lies the man mauled to death by an elephant. You and I passed obelisk gravestones, an angel with spread wings, and you ran a hand along the pearly smooth bark of the mimosa trees. Atop a waist-high tombstone sat a stone boy of about seven; he had a plastic yellow rose in his hand. Eventually we headed down a one-lane path and reached the Confederate soldier section. No sign of William, but two other men down the hill stood beside an open grave. One was singing: a clear tenor voice rang out the second verse of the spiritual "He Will Carry You Through."

Arrested by the song, I nonetheless took your hand and headed for the road—an open grave was too much reality for a child.

"Mrs. Copeland?"

I turned around. A short man in overalls was coming up the hill carrying a shovel.

When Max reached us, he said it was a truly fine evening. He looked at you and said, "Hello, Lady Lyra." He mock-bowed and you giggled.

He leaned his shovel against a tree. "You know, I don't mind digging graves because I right enjoy the quiet of a cemetery. Good place to think on things."

I gazed at the concrete markers. He was digging a grave in the *Confederate* cemetery.

He read my look. "It's for the bodies they took off that ship they found down to Charleston. It don't bother me none. Everybody should get a decent burial." A breeze rustled the magnolia leaves and they clacked against each other. "Everybody should get to leave this world with dignity," he said. "Used to be a Columbia insurance man that poor colored folk paid pennies to every year to get a fancy carriage for their funeral. My granddaddy wanted a big funeral in the worst way. Saved for it for years. Pullin' his carriage was the grandest white horses you ever seen in your whole born days."

I smiled, told you it was okay if you picked up colored leaves, just don't go where I couldn't see you. I looked back at Max. "Who was singing?"

"I confess I do that sometimes."

"You have a lovely voice. And what a beautiful song. I remember when gospel music first came on the radio—I was about ten. I loved those songs, I used to go around humming them." *Until an aunt told my stepmother someone should make me stop singing "nigger music."*

"That tune is very special. Saved my soul, you might say."

Max scanned the deepening-purple horizon. "That song came to me in Depression times, when I worked collectin' bills for a furniture store. One day—times were gettin' powerful awful—the man what owned the store told me to go get the money owed him or to take people's things. Or my job was gone. He gave me a list of all these poor folks who didn't have enough to eat them days, and he wants me to go take their settee and dinner table?"

"That's truly terrible."

"Yes ma'am, it were. People was living in the city dump behind this very cemetery then, and this fella had some white folks owing him that had lots more money. But I went on down to the Bottom to tell the poor ones—colored and white—that if they didn't get the money, their things was gone. *Were* gone, I mean. I was a-walkin' down the dirt road and I heard this woman singin', real beautiful, and I saw her in a yard directly, she's wearin' an old rag of a dress and hangin' clothes on the line—them was rags too, you could tell they'd lost everythin', but her voice was as pure and sweet a thing as I'll ever know in this world. She had joy all right, she had joy."

He smiled. "You'll never guess in a thousand years what I did. I waited until a big party was comin' up in a white folks' house, I'd read in the newspaper when one was gonna be, and I'd go to the rich part of town and march up the steps of a big house. I'd show up all spic and span and tell the man of the house we needed him to pay his bills. The big shots, you shoulda' seen their faces, they so embarrassed in front of the ladies and gents they'd right away give me their balance in full. When I did this enough, we didn't need any money from the ones who never knew where their dinner was comin' from."

"Weren't you afraid someone would tell your boss?"

"No ma'am, I was not. Like the song says, 'He will carry you through.'"

"You're a very special man, Max. You remind me of people I grew up with."

"Well thank you for sayin' that." He reached for his shovel again. "If you'll excuse me, I gotta finish up down there."

"I was wondering—you haven't seen my husband here this evening?"

"Yes ma'am, I shore did. He walked through here, looked like he was headin' over to the canal."

"The canal? Why would he go there?"

"If you don't mind my sayin' so—Mr. Copeland, he seems like a troubled man. I guess I shouldn't be sayin' this, but he needs somethin', I don't rightly know what, but somethin'."

My shoulders collapsed, I covered my face with my hands. "I don't know what's happening anymore," I sobbed. "Oh dear, forgive me, I'm sorry, I shouldn't be acting this way."

"Oh that's fine enough. It's a good thing to let your worry go sometimes. My mama—God rest her soul—used to say that when she got an ache in her uneasy place it was best to set to cryin' about it for a spell. She'd say, my heart's fallin' over, Max. But after she cried for a spell, her birdsong always come on back." Max smiled. "She was fair smart woman."

I gazed at him for a second. "She must have been very proud of you."

"I don't know, I can't remember that she said."

"Sometimes people forget to say what they feel. But she was. Trust me."

Max looked down for a second; when he looked back up, his eyes moist, he said, "I do odd jobs in Elmwood Park now and again. You need somethin', no problem for me to stop by. Anytime. No charge, 'cept you tell me what other books I need to read."

I was thanking him just as you came running over brandishing a handful of yellow leaves. Max wiped his hands on his trousers and took your hand and said you were a credit to nature's loveliness. Then he hobbled back down the hill, singing softly into the autumn breeze, slowly fading into the darkening night.

Sometimes late at night the history of Elmwood Park rose like steam into the old floorboards of our house and floated into my dreams. Emanations from another time, perhaps warnings. I heard carousel music and brightly painted wooden ponies went round and round, women in large hats perched atop them, scarlet ribbons like kites trailing behind. And yet. Beneath the colored hats and men in stiff collars languished dead bodies. Then history turned round again in my mind and men in 1860s gray uniforms were learning to kill in fairground buildings. Many returned when the buildings were a hospital, men wounded from learning to kill. Later on, medicine for the soldiers was made in those buildings, and then men made munitions, the acrid smell of niter hanging heavy in the oak trees. Guns explode, my God, the buildings are on fire, men are running from war flames, women are running, children—when that February night ends the city is rubble. More bodies slip beneath this soil, the fairground is finally silent in my night flights. Soil is turned by years, by the slow Reconstructive hell, and in time the fairground is rebuilt. And yet. Hidden bodies everywhere you step.

In my nightmares I saw well-dressed men and women in nineteenth-century clothes walking atop potter's-field bodies, stepping on hands, faces, legs. Night after night I dreamed Elmwood's history and woke up with my heart racing. As the days shortened, it sometimes felt like the earth below the house might open and swallow me.

Many of those darkening fall afternoons you and I visited Uta before William came home. One afternoon I hesitated in her hallway and ran my hand along the closed keyboard of her dusty mahogany piano.

"Louise, I've been waiting for you to play this thing."

"Oh I couldn't."

You piped up, "Please."

I pulled out the piano bench and lifted the keyboard cover. A Stieff piano, known as the poor man's Steinway. "I haven't played in a long time."

Uta said, "I'd love to hear anything at all, dear. Though the thing's probably dreadfully out of tune."

The piano *was* out of tune, but when I touched the keys they sang anyway. I played some Mozart and Bach's "Jesu" and the sentimental love songs from my college days, my fingers tentative at first, but then I began to feel the music as I once had, all those days sitting at the piano underneath my mother's paintings, drawing circles of light in the air with notes. I loved it that music has no right and wrong—bad and good sound, yes, but no rule about what one should do or what was expected. Here was freedom, escape, this rollicking roll down a childhood hill with shards of dead grass all over my skirt and no one to notice or care that maybe I was too old to roll down hills. In music I was again that teenage girl in baggy pants out in the fields picking pole beans with my cousins, or maybe I was in the glorious deep of a cathedral I'd never seen, where I sat amid sculptures of kindly saints, and there were lighted candles in Gothic wall sconces, this was where I went at that piano, everywhere, a surprise every single—

I stopped. "I didn't mean to go on so long."

You begged me to keep playing, so I played another melody, paused, said, "I don't know what that is. My father used to whistle it."

"I know," Uta said thoughtfully. "A mountain song from the 1850s that people started singing in the bad times of the '30s." She looked at me. "It's called 'I'm Sad and I'm Lonely.'"

Soon Uta served us "tea," which in her house was often a small afternoon meal. In her sitting room she placed a tray on a glass-top table, linen cutwork under the glass, and went over to a closet and pulled out a wooden toy. Three-inch figures, a boy and a girl, and a two-foot ladder. When placed atop the ladder, the figures click-clacked and somersaulted to the bottom. Uta told you to please be careful, it was very special.

She established herself in an armchair and poured the tea. "How are things at school, Louise? What's the news on integration?"

"Twelve Negro children will be admitted next year. I've been asked to teach one of the first desegregated classes. William doesn't think I should. He's afraid of—complications—you know, protests."

"What do *you* think?"

"I think it's high time this happened and I ought to do whatever I can to help." I turned as I heard our car in the driveway outside Uta's window. "We should be going, Mrs. Moazen. Thank you for letting me play the piano." I began picking up the toy figures.

Uta stared at the toy for a moment, then turned to me. "Louise dear, please come play the piano again. Music in the house is wonderful. I've been waiting for you and this little girl for a long time." She studied me for a moment. "You must take care of yourselves."

⌒◦꯭◦⌒

William was sleeping less and less. Sometimes he got up two or three times a night and went to his desk to read, or paced the living room. One night I woke up at four a.m. and he had still not come back to bed. I parted the curtains, stared out at the moonlight; all it illuminated was the loneliness of this bed and this room. When did we last make love? What I'd believed was natural to all marriages—perhaps it wasn't. I pulled the curtains and burrowed into the covers. I was so tired and school would come early. This wasn't how we were in Summerville. Whenever he'd pass by me in that house, his fingers trailed briefly along my arm. Casual, lighthearted, wonderful. Our skins loved each other. Where did Summerville go?

I couldn't get back to sleep and at nearly five I pulled on my chenille bathrobe—it was almost time to get up anyway—and tiptoed into the kitchen to make coffee. William was nowhere to be found. I heard something outside and cracked open the back door—it was cold this morning. William—in his pajamas—was in the driveway raking leaves. Raking leaves in the dark? In his pajamas? I watched the rhythmic motion of the rake—was he sleepwalking?

"William," I whispered.

He put a finger to his lips. "Listen."

Elmwood Cemetery's carillon tolled five times. Everyone had been complaining about the hour, which marked the first shift at the Gervais Street textile mill.

I walked down the back steps, pulling my bathrobe belt tighter. "Shouldn't you try to get some sleep? You'll be tired for your classes."

"In the European carillons—in the churches that didn't get bombed—the music would come from way out in the distance, you never knew from where or who was playing it. Just suddenly it was there. Most players use broken chords, impulsive arpeggios."

William began raking again. "The tolling for the dead was always six tailors—I've forgotten why they use that expression—for a woman, nine for a man, afterward quick strokes to tell the age of the deceased, then slow tolling of single strokes at half-minute intervals. You never forget it." He smiled suddenly. "Do you know what I was thinking about today? Our first anniversary, the canaries Bill and Coo."

I felt myself loosen, my limbs unfolding for the first time in months. *He thinks about Summerville too.*

"I loved Bill and Coo." The past becomes the present, my voice a caress. "There's never been a better gift. Except for Lyra."

"I was trying to remember their sounds." William is still raking, but haphazardly. "I was wondering if natural sound and man-made sound can be analogous. If the math of nature and the math of music are based on the same principles of melody and harmony. Take the concept of fifths.

Fifths are five parts, and an isosceles triangle has four sides, and then there are minor fifths, and integral numbers and—"

"Darling, do you feel all right?"

"I'm fine."

"Maybe you're working too hard, maybe we need a little more bill and coo ourselves."

"I'm fine. I just don't sleep well some nights."

A light breeze showers gold leaves onto the ground behind William. Fragrant wood smoke emanates from someone's chimney. *Why can't we just enjoy this beautiful time together?* "You seem worried a lot," I say. "How are things at the seminary?"

"Am I not taking good care of you?"

Don't mention his quitting the new job. "Of course you are. It's just—sometimes you don't seem very happy."

"Things are fine."

"Why don't you come back to bed? Maybe you could sleep for an hour."

Abruptly he shakes the rake at me. "You don't understand! I can't sleep, how many times do I have to say that, Louise? Tell me, how *many*?"

He hurls the rake onto the ground.

He almost hit me.

Nearly in tears, I head for the back door. At the steps I glance back: he's raking in the dark again.

The following Saturday, as was customary, I went to the farmer's market. Not much to be had this time of year, so I'm soon driving back down Assembly Street, left onto Elmwood, right on Lincoln. Nearing our house, I see two men coming through our front door—William and Bill Faherty, the heavyset neighbor who never did an honest day's work and let his children—teeth yellowed and decayed—suffer for it.

I park in the driveway. William and Bill Faherty are carrying our dining-room table onto the porch. Neither has noticed me as they maneuver through the screen door.

I call from the driveway, "William?"

I hear him telling Bill Faherty, "I told you this table was a beauty, didn't I? There's not a finer one in the whole state of South Carolina."

Bill Faherty notices me and says, "We best git it down the street, I got something I gotta do. Come on now."

I stride to the porch as they jostle the oak table down the sidewalk. You're sitting on the porch steps, staring. I'm yelling, my heart pounding— "William, I need to talk to you!"

They ignore me. I turn to you. "Where are your father and Mr. Faherty taking the table?"

You tell me your father has given our table to Mr. Faherty.

"That's impossible!" I run to the sidewalk. William has disappeared inside the Faherty house.

Across the street Rosa is sweeping her sidewalk. She saunters over. "Not my business, Louise, but that worm Faherty's been coming 'round your house in the daytime when you're not home but your husband is. Did he weasel that table outta your old man? He's gonna sell it."

"That can't be." William's home during the day?

I turn and run into the house, into the dining room. Only two chairs—the wobbly ones—remain. I'm so weak I have to sit down. This doesn't make sense.

When the porch door opens, I rush to William. "What have you done with our table? Why is it down there?"

He brushes past me. "I don't have time to talk about this right now. He needs a leveler and I've got some shims in the garage."

"Did you give that man my table?"

William stops. "I had to. That family needs a table, there are lots more of them than us. He admired it."

"You gave a man you barely know our best piece of furniture?"

"I had to give Mr. Faherty the table and that's all there is to it. I don't see what you're so upset about. It wasn't yours to begin with."

"Mrs. Moazen *gave* it to me. To *me*."

"Maybe you don't remember the wedding vows, Louise. Yours *is* mine."

He stomps past me into the dining room, stops, stomps back. "That man is dangerous. He has a large knife collection, pays to stay on his good side. We didn't use the table much, he liked the quality of it. That man was a soldier."

"What is *wrong* with you?"

"You have no right to act this way," he shouts. "You must be mad with somebody else and taking it out on me."

I notice you in the doorway, the frightened way you clutch your ragged teddy bear.

William marches through the house, goes out the back door.

I fall into a chair. How can he be so mean? I'm sobbing in front of my child. You walk over and kneel down and lay your head on my thigh. And suddenly I remember the lovely plastic women shredded on a bathroom floor.

Chapter Seven

I can't seem to stay in this hospital bed—I keep floating across time and now it's midday Saturday on Lincoln Street, dark circles around my eyes from sleeplessness as I sweep the front porch. Since the dining-room table disappeared, I've been profoundly dispirited—no, since William *gave* my table away. (He put a check for it in Uta's mailbox, but Uta marched over and threw it back at him, said she'd rather him owe her, which made William so angry he left the room.) Listlessly I push dirt toward the screen door. You're on the porch steps playing with the cat—*talking* to Fluffy, actually.

William appears, says he's going to the farm. You sing a chorus of "Oh please can I go, please please please?" William suggests we all go. I can tell he's trying to make up for the table—it'll have to be a whale of a trip for that to work. On the way, he drives by the new airport in West Columbia and parks beside a small hangar. You and he get out of the car—a weekly airport trip is his latest obsession. You sit on the taxicab fender and William leans against it, smoking his pipe, staring at small planes taking off or landing.

"That's a DC-3," he tells you, pointing. "It has a top speed of two hundred miles per hour, has a tail-dragger landing gear, two propeller engines."

You listen eagerly. I suspect, disturbingly, that you think if you act

interested in what interests your father, he may act interested in you. You
say you want to ride in a plane one day.

"Oh you can't," he says. "Planes are for businessmen and soldiers."

When you and William get back in the car, I tell you, "I bet you'll ride
in a plane someday. I bet you'll do a lot of important things."

William gives me a sharp look, drives on toward Orangeburg. We follow
the Bamberg Ehrhardt Road—my real mother grew up in Ehrhardt, you and I
went to that abandoned old house to retrieve several paintings when you were
a teenager. We turn onto the Barnwell Road and pass through Whetstone
Crossroads with its railroad station. You're impressed that we have our own
railroad, until William explains the concept of right-of-way. He shows you
the two ponds that are the far north and southwest boundaries of the farm.
Listening to him give you information for the future, I warm up a little. The
land was 683 acres, about six miles square, he says, when his grandmother
owned it. You ask how come the farm keeps getting "littler." I correct you
with "smaller" and he adds, "That's just the way it goes, I guess."

We stop at the cemetery and William gets out and inspects it before
we drive on to the house ruins. I begin to feel better. The country's loamy
aromas—this is the scent of small towns too, of when I'd walk down
Brantley streets in the summertime breathing the deep musk of ripening
tomatoes in a neighbor's garden. While you and William dig in the ruins,
I take a long walk in the woods, dragging my hand along the scaly trunks
of the loblolly pines that will one day be harvested to send you to college.
The shade and shadow of the forest become Gilead's balm. I pause on the
pine-straw path, listen to the trees creaking in the breeze. I have to forgive
William: holding a grudge is not going to make anything better. Pick your
battles, isn't that what people say?

You, in patched overalls, come running through the trees, screaming,
"The Yankees are coming!" You grab my arm and shake it. "Get the silver.
Get the muskrat."

"I think you mean *musket*, sweetheart. You know that war is not really
a good thing, don't you?"

"But they're after us! They want to knock us down dead. Daddy says
we gotta run from the Sherman flames."

"He's just playing a game."

When you and I emerge from the forest, William is mowing around the perimeter of the house. My lighter mood evaporates—the two toppled chimneys seem more jagged than ever today. I gaze anew at the great mass of broken bricks and blackened timber, a tomb of a house. William had recently discovered a picture of it in its prime, all the 1840s family, including two dogs, posed on a portico of Doric columns and fanlighted windows. Reduced now to rubble by man's inhumanity, by the most deadly war in American history. Abruptly I shiver as I stare at the sundered walls, two or three feet tall where once they had been thirty. I look out at the nearby fields: I can almost see bloodied bodies strewn in the grass.

William continues mowing, sprucing up the ruined house he loves more than he loves—I can't finish the thought.

What if he came home one day to find someone had given his farm away?

New York taxi, wandering in a cemetery, raking in the dark. Impulsively quitting one job after another. Giving away furniture I love. What does it all mean?

⌒⟲◯⟳⌒

While I was preparing supper the next night, someone knocked on the back door. I opened the door in surprise: Uta never came to the back door.

She cried, "I have terrible news. I went to the store this morning and Flo had heard it from some people on Park Street."

"What's wrong?"

"Max Wells was killed yesterday. He's dead."

"What?" I sat down in shock. "Oh my God."

"He was trimming trees—he fell off the ladder and broke his neck."

For no reason I got up and numbly walked over to the window. News of sudden, unexpected death is an emotional tornado; I looked outside as though checking for damage. "He was always smiling. I met him my first day at Laidlaw. The children love him." *He felt like an old friend. Someone who realized—*

"I never knew a finer man," Uta said.

Uta sat down at the table and I rejoined her. "Some mornings all the teachers would find flowers in our rooms," I said. "It seems so unfair. Did you know about him helping poor families during the Depression?"

"He told you about that?"

"Just recently. I truly admired him."

Uta studied the rings on her right hand. "I did too, but not for that. That story's not true. Max was never a collector for a furniture store."

"What do you mean? He made it up?"

"Oh no. It happened—there was a man who saved some poor people from losing their possessions in the thirties, but it wasn't Max Wells. Max appropriated the story. He read it in a book. He was a reading man, he was. He wanted a different past so he gave himself one."

"How do you know?"

"Because one day *I* read it in a book too. A book of WPA interviews. There it was, pretty much like Max told it. Think about it, Louise—Max's mother was a high-yellow Negro. What South Carolina store in the 1930s was going to let a half-colored man handle money?"

I sat back in my chair. "You're right. I never thought about that."

"That story doesn't matter—Max was as fine as they come," Uta said. "He aspired to what the world wouldn't let him do. I think that's pretty admirable. I'd be grateful if you'd go to the funeral, which is really a homecoming service, with me."

"Will we be welcome?"

"I don't give a flying fig. If I have to barge into a Holy Roller church to see Max off, I will." Uta got up. "And you can't wear black. It's disrespectful."

I wore a blue dress to the funeral. Uta, in purple, gave me a that'll-do-nicely look as I got in her huge white Cadillac, which she almost never took out of her garage. Although it had push-button gears on the dashboard, driving with one arm wasn't easy. It was a dampish, cloudy day. As Uta headed north toward Camp Fornance, she explained that she bought the car with her husband's insurance money. She said Max's death felt like such a bad omen that she'd uncorked "that green jar" and left it open all night. Perhaps it was all done now—all that bad soul gone.

"At last I'm truly rid of him."

I didn't know what she was talking about, but we're all made slightly irrational by loss.

I'd known lots of black people, but I'd never been in, as we put it then, a colored church. This one was red brick, set on a lot bordering the railroad tracks, with a white wooden steeple containing a single bell, now tolling. Some people told stories about the Mercy congregation "speaking in tongues," but whenever I'd driven past the church all I'd heard was singing. Uta turned her white whale of a car into the gravel parking lot, and we headed inside. The chancel was all gardenias, huge arrangements of roses everywhere else, vases filled to overflowing, upright funeral sprays, a carpet of white roses across the burnished mahogany casket. The women who cooked in the Laidlaw cafeteria had on their best dresses. And tropical headdresses: red hats, blue, pink, even one a flaming orange. People were taking their seats, big Negro men slapping one another on the back, little boys in short pants running up and down the aisles, a handful of teachers from Laidlaw, including Ed Hindeman.

Gathered in a semicircle below the simple wooden altar, a choir of thirty women rocked back and forth as one, heads back, eyes closed, humming in harmony, tears streaming down the faces of several. Various people walked up front and spoke about "Brother Max" and his smile and his gardens and his work in the church and his faith in Jesus. A handsome man in a pinstriped suit told us that Max had grown up on a farm and spent his early years picking cotton; that that was why he squinted sometimes, from those early years of staring into the sun to see if it was quitting time yet. Another man talked about Max's kindness to the children in the Bottom, how he put a collection box in the white junior high and got teachers and students to donate old clothes.

"Amen" cried two women in the choir. Another in the front pew called out, "Jesus is happy today. Jesus gets a good man today."

A woman in a red hat told the story of how Max saved the furniture of poor people during the Depression. When she finished, someone murmured, "That man was a good man," and someone else answered, "Don't you know the Lord be happy today. Saved them folks, he did."

Uta glanced at me and smiled.

I couldn't keep up with the eulogies for listening to the music. After each person spoke, the choir sang song after song that I'd not heard for years, since I was growing up and black women walking to the poor end of Brantley would stroll by the house singing in the twilight. I felt filled with those spirituals that always admitted to despair without losing hope.

> *Hush, Somebody's callin' my name,*
> *Hush, Hush, Somebody's callin' my name.*
> *I'm so glad that trouble don't last always.*
> *I'm so glad that trouble don't last all day.*
> *Oh my Lord, oh my Lord, what shall I do?*

This was the music I needed now. I wasn't sure why, at least not consciously, not yet anyway. Maybe the soul does tell us what the mind has yet to grasp. All I know is that, as though they belonged to a time now gone, the old hymns I loved, "A Mighty Fortress" and "Faith of Our Fathers," slipped through the open windows and floated out toward the railroad tracks.

A large Bible was placed on Max's coffin, the best coffin money could buy, I hoped. The Bible rested on a gold stand and people began going forward and placing money under the stand. Uta whispered that the collection was to pay for the funeral. I was mortified that I didn't have much in my purse, but I gave Uta what I had and she rose and walked forward and added two twenty-dollar bills. A burgundy-robed woman in the choir stepped forward and as people filed by the casket, some crying "Oh have mercy on our brother," her solo, a contralto "Amazing Grace," floated in and out among the mourners. In the middle of a bar she paused to murmur, "Thank you, Jesus," and then she sang the second verse with the choir coming in softly behind her. People stopped moving, just stood still to listen. When the final "Thank God I'm free" faded into the corners of the room, for five minutes not even a whisper was heard.

❧❧❧❧

A half hour later Uta and I are walking through Elmwood Cemetery. Max's funeral procession has wound down Park Street, turned onto Elmwood Avenue, and passed into the cemetery, a long line of cars heading slowly toward the back section. Max is being carried to his final rest in a gold Lincoln Continental. Uta suggests we wait until the private burial is over before we go pay our respects at his grave.

"I think I must show you something," she says quietly, almost to herself. "Yes, I think I must tell someone. You are the right one." In her purple silk dress and matching hat, her ringlets piled high on her head, she looked like something from another century. I found myself thinking that maybe you children were right, maybe she was part sorcerer.

She walks purposefully, points to a mimosa tree, a wide circle of low thick branches, each branch shooting off at waist level into two or three smaller branches. "Looks like a family tree. It's a sculpture, isn't it, mothers with their children all gathered in a circle."

We pass plots outlined with iron fences amid magnolia and cedar trees. In the distance the choir at Max's graveside is singing "He Will Carry You Through."

Uta smiles. "He got mileage out of that story."

"I still don't understand why he lied about himself. He didn't have to."

"I wish lying was the worse thing anyone did, Louise. Since that story was what Max wished he'd been, and he had such a good heart, to me, that story *is* the truth. Sometimes the truth is all that matters, sometimes it isn't what matters at all."

Uta points to a tomb adorned with broken tree branches. "I want that on my tombstone, the cut branch for the end of the life cycle. Maybe a cedar branch—it's bad luck for anyone to harm a cedar, maybe that'll keep the crows away."

We pass a small tombstone on which a carved gate opens backward to reveal a star. I wonder why we're walking so far away from Max's grave. On my right looms an eight-foot statue of a woman with a penitent face standing on a rock to embrace a huge cross. Uta stares at it. "You know that hymn 'Rock of Ages'?" She doesn't wait for a reply. "The Anglican priest who wrote the poem the hymn's based on—he calculated how many sins a person who lived to be eighty could commit in a lifetime. Two and a half billion sins. I do not sing that hymn."

She points to another tombstone bearing a woman's name and the inscription: *She was a good woman and full of the Holy Ghost.* "I imagine they'll say I was full of something else."

I almost laugh out loud. Uta stops and says, "We're here."

She leads the way inside a rusted wrought-iron enclosure. A family plot, ten tombstones, five very old table tombs with nearly illegible script, the others modern and upright, block letters, and a smaller gravestone adorned with leaves surrounding an iris.

"Meet the Moazens and the McClarys," she says. She walks over to a modern tombstone and intones quietly, "Henry, I'm sorry. Two wrongs do not make a right, it didn't fix anything, and I'm here to say I'm sorry for trying to interfere and I hope it didn't cause you any discomfort."

She turns around, whispers over her shoulder, "You did deserve it."

"My husband, Henry," she explains. She looks at the smallest tombstone, says very softly—"Now this." She reads the name out loud: "Elizabeth McClary Moazen. My daughter."

I stare at the dates. *Oh no.* A six-year-old. The same age as Lyra. "Oh Mrs. Moazen, I don't know what to say—I'm so sorry for your loss. I didn't know."

Max's choir is singing "Jesu" in the distance—*Oh receive my soul at last, this is my prayer.*

Uta leans down and brushes dirt off the tombstone decorated with carved flowers. "It took me a long time to decide to use the iris—Greek Iris was the messenger of the rainbow, a woman's soul couldn't be released from the body unless Iris cut a lock of her hair. Max Wells prepared this grave. I held the lantern that night, and he put the stone in the ground."

"The funeral was at night?"

Uta is slow to answer. "There was only a burial of a sort. There are so many rules for this cemetery. Max could have got himself in a heap of trouble. Not supposed to put anything in Elmwood without permission."

She turns to me. "There's no body in that grave. Despite what it looks like, it's only a memorial stone."

"I—I don't—"

"There's nothing to say, dear. There's no body because I don't know what happened to my baby. She may be alive—by now she'd be about your age. Maybe I even have grandchildren." Uta brushes dirt off of the gravestone. "After I lost my arm, Henry said I couldn't properly take care of our child—Mackie—he hated that I called her after my mother, God rest her soul—and he said we should let his sister in Baltimore keep her for a while. I cried and screamed but I was still recovering, was still doped up from the operation, in terrible pain. I tried to call the police but they thought I was just an hysterical woman, and who listens to a woman who contradicts her husband? Especially one with only one arm."

"How long did she stay there?"

"It isn't unusual in Ireland, you know, that a child goes to relatives when times are hard. Then the parents go get their little one. Mackie never came home."

The gray mist hovering over the cemetery turns into a soft sprinkling of rain as Uta traces the stone garland of leaves around the iris. "I used the acanthus leaves because of Greek legend too—about a little girl who died and her nurse gathered up all her toys and put them in a basket beside the grave. The basket was set on the roots of an acanthus plant and when the leaves came out, it curled around and over the basket to protect the toys and the child."

Her voice grows faint. "Henry didn't send Mackie to relatives. He gave our child away. He didn't like children—I ask you, what kind of man doesn't like, much less *love*, his own child? While I was sick he signed the surrender papers to an agency, and she was privately adopted. I think money changed hands. He said he never knew who took her."

Uta's words—worse than *anything* I can imagine—seem to knock the breath from me.

"I begged Henry to tell me the name of the agency, but he said it was done and couldn't be undone. I hired someone to look for her, to look for a trail to follow, but there was nothing. She just vanished. I almost went off my mind, I tell you, I almost ran away from Henry. I didn't go for hoping he might someday tell me something—even accidentally—that would help me find her. He never did.

Henry just died. Part of me had died when my little girl disappeared. I couldn't look at other people's children for years—that's why I quit teaching before retirement. After Henry died, I made a grave for Mackie; she died to me when she was six. I went to see Max—a friend sent me to him—and asked would he dig a grave secretly. I wanted to bury some of Mackie's things, a bird's egg she loved, her favorite dolls. I'd gone as batty as the Sweetes burying those old clothes, and no way was the cemetery going to agree to this, so I offered Max money and he said he'd do it but he wasn't taking money for helping a woman who'd lost her child."

I go over and lay a hand on Uta's good arm. "I've needed to tell someone," she says. "I won't live forever and I need Mackie's memory not to die with me. If I'd married a different man—who can predict what fate puts on us—we'd not be here right now. I'm asking you to share this story—you and that dear child have helped free something bottled up in me for a long time."

"I'm honored," I whisper.

"Louise, you need to know that you too can survive anything."

I stare at Uta's unbending profile, outlined against a grave for a missing child, and think, *I could never survive that. I could never survive losing my family.*

Part V: Lyra

2004

Chapter Eight

One evening I walk into the dining room of my parents' rancher and sit down at Uta Moazen's oak table, which is always covered with a tablecloth to hide its gouged surface. This is good furniture haunted by history. You come home from school one day and the dining-room table has flown the coop. It was November when my mother closed the door to the dining room on Lincoln Street and didn't speak for hours. Days passed and she barely looked at anyone. She never sang to me anymore, never danced me around in a circle.

Yet outside our house it's beautiful. The last of the leaves are falling, falling, falling, all over the lawns and sidewalks and in the street. The world is raining color.

I'm dawdling on the way home from Logan, shuffling through the leaves. Leaves are like palm-prints, I think as I pick up two maple specimens for the scrapbook I'm making for school, sticking one leaf behind my ear in case I grow up to be Hawaiian. The runway of color is a mystery, how leaves can turn yellow and red and orange but fall onto the ground later and get crackly brown and soon they're nothing but dust and brittle stems. Something so beautiful just goes away. I wish the leaves would stay. My mother says to remember that leaves are like old skin, that the trees stay alive and will make new leaves next year, so there's really no reason for me to be sad. Things always come back around, she adds. I still feel sad—I've noticed that the dining-room table hasn't turned up yet.

I sit down in a pile of the leaves in the driveway. It's like a cemetery. I begin picking up my favorite colors; I'm partial to the coral of the maples. When I've gathered my favorite twenty-five, having neatly piled them away from the others, I run into the house and come back with a kitchen fork and my mother's hymnal. With the fork I dig a grave and place the leaves in it, arrange them one by one like my mother does flowers, the prettiest in the most favorable position. I'll put them in this safe place to await that rebirth my Sunday school teacher is always talking about. I turn to "The Burial of the Dead" in my mother's book; I understand only a few words—something about "ashes," which I remember from when the stoves blew out. I skip the service, say a silent prayer, and sing "Shall We Gather at the River," a song my mother likes so I know all the words. I'm about to cover the grave with dirt when she comes walking down the sidewalk.

She stops and stares at the half-buried leaves, asks what I'm doing.

"It's a funeral. For the colored leaves."

She gazes at the hymnal open to the burial service and looks startled. She kneels down beside me, staring at the grave I've dug.

"It's the paintbrushes," she whispers. Then her voice rises. "Didn't I *swear* my child would never feel this way? Didn't I?"

She grabs me into her arms, murmurs against my hair, "Oh, sweetheart, don't—let's don't bury the beautiful colors."

Although no one talked about history, and I spent years running away from it, it has stalked me everywhere. In childhood I never got over reading—and rereading and rereading—*Jane Eyre*, especially about Bertha the "hyena" madwoman locked in the attic. When I was in junior high and just beginning to paint, I happened upon Goya's "black paintings." When I looked into the vaulted chambers of *The Madhouse*, at those dark and wounded creatures in their subterranean dungeon, I couldn't put the book down. Dark grays and lifeless browns and charcoal shadings, the shadows and shapes of misery and defeat. I lay on my bed and studied the library book for hours. One day the book disappeared. My mother had returned it.

These were not our best days together. In my teens I watched her continually subordinate herself to my father: he made all decisions, and she went along with little objection no matter how strange or paranoid his ideas were. And no matter how much his decisions hurt or inconvenienced us both. The king was *cracked*, if you asked me. She didn't talk to me about this anymore than she acknowledged our past, but occasionally I did remember my father's defacement of the lovely women on a bathtub decal. So we could spend time together, my mother repeatedly took me to her favorite movie, *Sunrise at Campobello*. Finally I realized that the film's claim on her wasn't her admiration for FDR so much as Eleanor Roosevelt's perfect self-sacrifice. Years later I wondered why my mother didn't notice that Mrs. Roosevelt eventually became much more than anyone's wife.

It was in art school that my nightmares—in daylight and in darkness—began hinting at my family's unspoken past. I was perpetually restless one spring, pacing endlessly. I couldn't paint—brushstrokes kept changing at will, they were long and sensate and brimming with color, then suddenly choppy, sharp, abrupt. Fragmented and dull gray-yellow. I felt out of control and frightened, so I began going to art shows and museums once a week, hoping that would help. Soon I'm in a small gallery in a white mansion near campus, a show from New York, people doing their milling, IVs attached to glasses of cheap Chardonnay. A painting begins following me. I walk by it, stare, start walking away. It grabs me back, demands a second look. French, Hugues Merle, nineteenth-century pre-Impressionist. *La Pauvre Folle*. The lunatic is the central figure, a desperate woman with stringy black hair; sitting beside a well, she holds a piece of firewood swaddled as a baby. The women and children nearby stare at her—they're light, airy, cherubic, and horrified. One young girl keeps a small boy from going too near the deranged woman whose wild unfocused eyes come straight from hell.

I've seen such eyes before.

I walk off. Get another glass of wine, intently swill alcohol into my bloodstream. I can't stay away—I go back to the painting, almost against my will. The eyes of the crazy woman scratch marks on my arm and suddenly—for the first time—I *know*. The past really did happen.

Another glass of wine and I go to a pay phone and call my parents. When no one answers, I buy a postcard, address it to them, and write drunkenly: "Plato was right about art—memory *is* the mother of the Muses. Pentimento everywhere. *Now* is always reciting the story of *Then*."

I mailed the card that afternoon. I was told it never arrived.

I sit in the waiting room and wait. Hospital time has no end or beginning, no day or night, no mealtime or meaning. It's standing in a still pond—movement occurs in the distance, nurses go up and down the hall, the muted intercom requests a doctor, the woman whose husband is dying cries softly. Life is happening but you're only vaguely part of it. I've painted that many times—aren't most of my pictures metaphors of estrangement? The whole point of my abstracts. What did those first reviews say? A "cool silvery tonality." Except when I painted Lincoln Street.

Later I part the drape into my mother's ICU room and find the nurse Darlene. She has pulled the sheet up and is massaging my mother's swollen, blue-veined feet, tender hands kneading the misshapen bulge on her right foot, a car-accident injury that never healed properly. I remember only vague details about the accident, something weird about our car in the Lincoln Street driveway, but I have the feeling—for no reason I can name—that it was important.

"Do you think she might get better?" I ask Darlene as we walk out into the hall.

"Honey, no. She's tired, she's gonna die."

My lip trembles. "How do you know?"

"She told me she's ready to go. You get yourself ready for her to pass."

"She *spoke* to you?"

"Not with words, but I could feel it. Working with the sick you get so you can sense things. She can't let you know she's ready 'cause it's terrible to you, her going, and she don't want to disappoint you, make you feel bad. Kinfolk naturally want the loved one to keep fighting. That's why most people die in the middle of the night. After the relatives go home, they feel free to do what *they* want."

We head toward the elevators. "Your mama's got a big soul," Darleen adds. "Maybe she didn't give herself credit for how special she is, that's part why she is. I'd go to see her about Annette's work and Miz Copeland would smile at me like I was the exact person she'd been hoping to see."

I watch as Darlene waves and gets in the elevator. I feel like I should thank someone for her soul.

When I go back into the ICU room, my father is standing beside the bed, studying the computer monitors. He tells me if a number goes up or down. Eventually he leaves and I watch the spring sky out the window.

❧❧❧❧❧

Dr. Dumaine comes to the waiting room every morning at seven. He says Louise is a little stronger today. He returns later and says she is still improving.

The next day he says Louise has fallen back a bit.

The day after that—raining today, is it still spring or has summer come?—he says she's even weaker.

He comes early the next day. Head bowed, he says that Louise is failing. Too much fluid in her lungs, her heart is so weak. We may be nearing the end.

The unimaginable happens. My father's lips begin to tremble, his shoulders shake, tears flood his eyes. The extraordinary sight of his emotion overrides my own. I've never seen him show affection toward anyone. Does he really love his wife?

I go sit in the first-floor atrium and stare at the cloudy skies in the ceiling. Did he really cry?

❧❧❧❧❧

Mother grows weaker and weaker. I bring her a pot of African violets in bloom—her favorite indoor plant. A crisis comes, her heart almost stops but then corrects itself, as though she wants a little more time. Or maybe—just maybe—she'll live another year or two. If it means being helpless, I know her well enough to hope she does not.

My father stands in her room all afternoon, dozes in the chair by the bed as her breath rasps in and out. Friends and relatives come and go. I stare out the window at the Columbia skyline; maybe what I've never liked about my hometown is its claim to fame as the defeated victim. Elmwood Park was built after the famous fire, but defeat drifted like poison gas through our rooms anyway. I turn around and gaze at my mother. Isn't death the defeat to end all defeats?

Maybe not.

One day I say to my father, "I'm surprised Betty Tyler hasn't come by."

"She died. She was in the hospital for a while and Louise wanted to visit her but couldn't drive of course. I knew the Tylers wouldn't want anyone bothering them."

"You wouldn't take her to see an old friend who was dying?"

He gets up and stomps out, calling, "You don't understand these things."

When my father isn't in the room, I whisper to my mother or sing her favorite hymns. My early training comes back and I'm standing beside her in the Earlewood church, I'm twelve or thirteen, and five hundred singing voices rise around me like swelling seas, a leviathan of sound, extraordinary and grand in this town that prizes the reasonable, the practical. The wild thoughts that flood me like a berserk river have their counterpart in such sound, and suddenly I'm aware that my mother's voice is exceptional, is beautiful, that she is magnificently strong when she sings. She stands out, can be heard above the rest, her alto resonant, powerful. She's suddenly new to me: someone special, *more* than just my mother. She knows *abandon*, what I feel when I paint. Here her breathing, timing, the balance of light and dark, are perfect. Here she is utterly herself.

I think about that day as I drive through the misty early evening. That day she was remarkable, strong in the artistic way I valued. Yet for years I implied that I saw her as anything but strong, patient endurance not being my idea of courage. Was it hers? Many women turn sour when they stay in an unfulfilling marriage. My mother never complained; a sweet spirit was never totally crushed.

As I pull into my parents' driveway, I gaze at a twelve-foot dogwood tree—something's odd. I didn't notice before but—*Jesus*—the dogwood's lower branches have been removed and the top foliage shaped into a giant sphere. It looks like a water tower. A tree ten feet away is the same. Two globes hanging in the sky. I stare at the other shrubbery. Most boxwoods have been pruned into perfect round balls, except for the two that are rectangles. My father has made the front yard into Versailles. Round fat balls and cones everywhere, palatial gardening for a carport rancher in a declining neighborhood. The azalea bushes look like a tall row of children's wooden blocks. It's a wonder we're not on a tourist map.

I see again a 1950s Checker cab, part yellow and part burgundy, colors clashing like two yard cats fighting over a food bowl. I laugh out loud. You can say this for him—he's never been boring.

He once brought home a large velvet painting he'd bought at a yard sale, a bare-breasted chain-mailed woman astride a rearing white horse. My mother took one look, forbade it a room in the house, and headed for the aspirin. On the carport my father repaired the broken frame and touched up the paint; I can still picture my mother covering the perky bare breasts with a blanket afterward in hopes no neighbor would notice them. My father uncovered the painting every morning so "she could get some sun." I wanted to kill him when the school bus stopped at my house and boys I knew leaned out the windows to whistle at her. One day a stranger offered my father a hundred dollars for the velvet beauty. Which he *never* let us forget. When I was a teenager, I prayed he would spot Jesus in the backyard—that would make sense, crazy-wise, be easier to explain. Eudora Welty said that if a man thinks he's a streetcar and runs up and down the street at regular hours but isn't hurting anyone, who cares? Miss Eudora was clearly not related to that charming fellow.

Abruptly I remember a gallery director who said my paintings were "iconoclastic, occasionally incomprehensible, *never boring*." There's a scary idea.

Inside the house I settle on a ham sandwich for dinner. Women have been bringing food at least once a day, it's been ages since I've seen fried chicken and butter beans cooked with bacon. Not to mention the "sweet tea" that tastes like sugar water. I didn't realize this world still existed. Each woman says how much she loves my mother; earlier today, a neighbor, eyes red and puffy, insisted on vacuuming and doing the laundry. Another woman told me how much my mother helped her when she got breast cancer. I gaze at the old brass lamps that have been rewired and rewired, at an old vase collaged with china shards sitting atop the oak bookcase. I pick up the vase and study the patterns—so many chaotic colors. Everything in the room is history. I always wanted my mother to have nicer things, but these objects seem right now, more her, more both of them really.

I lie down in my mother's room, and the room gently rocks the child in me as I study another of my grandmother's paintings—a lone young woman with bowed head floats in a wooden boat under a ghostly white moon. A melancholy picture, the only time my grandmother painted a human figure. Maybe it's my new favorite. Most of her pictures are melancholic: did she intuit that her life would be brief? A life cut short by bad luck, an inheritance that fits us. In our case art *is* family. I get up and open the closet door and look inside. My mother's shoes—lined up in a tidy row—break my heart. I run a hand up and down the sleeve of the blue suit she wore to my wedding, notice a cardboard box on the shelf bearing my name. After I pull it out, I plunge through tissue paper and unwrap a small wooden ladder: it comes with the memory of Uta as I watch the tiny boy and girl—it still works—*plop plop plop* to the bottom. Nice metaphor for aging. A small box underneath the toy contains three white satin Christmas balls. I pick one up but drop it suddenly—it's made of human hair. Then I remember. Uta's hair, *that* Christmas. A note in the box in a strange hand reads, "I finally found her and she didn't care."

In a flat clothes box lies a white linen baby dress encased in plastic; a tag pinned to it reads: "My mother was making this for her unborn fifth child when she died of the flu. I finished the dress and Lyra wore it on her

Christening Day." I slip the eighty-year-old garment out of its bag—white eyelet embroidery around the tiny neck—and hold it against my cheek to feel the texture of my family's women. I've never seen it before. Why is it separate from the other old linens? For the future—a christening gown for my mother's second child? And for the grandchildren she dreamed of?

I also find a picture of my young parents in front of a huge bell tower. Photos of each of them under live oak trees dangling Spanish moss. He's in a suit, she's in a flowered dress. This must have been their honeymoon in Florida—they got married on Christmas Eve because that was the day my grandfather married my grandmother the painter. My God—did they have sex for the first time on Christmas Day? Romantic. I look up for a moment—those years they were barely speaking, when money was so short my handmade clothes embarrassed me, yet Christmas was always made into an occasion. To relive the good one, or to make up for the desperate weight that holiday carried later? In one old picture my father is holding out his arms as though to invite her to dance—flirty, boyish energy in his eyes. Did they really go dancing once upon a time? The back of the photo reads: "Christmas Day at the Singing Tower in Lake Wales." He's so lithe and handsome, she's so dark-eyed beautiful—people, given the choice, I'd have requested as parents. A folder under the pictures is crammed with old sheet music. Hymns, gospel songs, African American spirituals—I stare at a tattered copy of "Somebody's Callin' My Name." Also many sentimental 1940s ballads. The most yellowed, embellished with pink roses, is "I Love You Truly." An ecstatic star decorates the right corner and written below the star, in my mother's fluid, youthful hand: "For the Big Day! My dream come true!"

After I repack the box, I sit and stare at my name scrawled on its side in my mother's elderly hand. She made sure I'd look at these things. I open the box again and take the photo of my parents beside the bell tower and prop it up on a dresser.

∾⊙∾

As my mother worsens, for reasons I cannot name, I begin riding over to Elmwood Park nearly every day. I park and sit and stare at the Lincoln

Street house. Sometimes I walk up and down the street. The lawn-service guys now recognize me and wave.

One afternoon, long-buried fragments come back—

... the endless hours of screaming, my mother kneeling beside their bed crying, she sounds hurt bad. He yelled at her over and over again. Finally it's quiet, night has gone out the window and sunlight creeps up the sides of the old house, dances on the windowsill where someone forgot to pull the shade, seeps under the front door that no one locked, crawls through a kitchen window where an unopened can of salmon sits on the counter and a terrified cat hides behind a refrigerator. Outside that kitchen window, a lone mockingbird sings a two-note song in a dogwood tree. Wooden houses creak, a stone house rumbles awake. A milkman, in a navy jacket with "Ray" stitched on the pocket, leaves long-necked bottles on every stoop.

A child, bathed in a pool of light, wakes up on a cold wooden floor. She's me. I lay on the floor all night so I could see into their room. Grayish winter shadows stripe the scratchy wool blankets as I climb onto my bed. I hear a sound and get down again to look into my parents' bedroom. My father is sprawled atop the covers, he's wearing pajama bottoms streaked with red and his arms are flung out from his sides like a cross. My mother is still on her knees beside the bed, slumped over, holding on to the bedspread, and she's crying like when my baby cousin died. I want to disobey her and run in there but I'm scared. After a while she slumps lower, I think she's asleep.

I tiptoe into their room. Then I turn around and gallop back to my bed, I don't want my daddy to grab me and make my arm hurt again.

But I want my mother to wake up, so in a minute I pad back into their room. I touch her but she doesn't move. Red goo oozes from a bandage on my father's arm. I reach out to touch it, jerk my hand back because he moved. He's asleep though, I can tell because of how he's breathing. I rub my finger in the goo, the color of red Kool-Aid. Then I lick my finger—the red stuff tastes sour. Like when I cut myself with that knife I wasn't supposed to use.

My father stirs again, and I turn and run back to my bed and pull the covers up over my head, curl into a ball and slide way down where no one can find me. I think about my father's photographs of dead Civil War soldiers lying in a field. The soldiers had blood on them too. I didn't know that some soldiers are mothers. Maybe my mama and my daddy are dead.

Part VI: Louise

1957

Chapter Nine

I think I've been dreaming—I was back on Lincoln Street. Seems like Max was there.

I feel you across the room, Lyra. Did I ever tell you I buried the afterbirth when you were born? Supposed to bring a newborn good luck— it's at the foot of a dogwood tree in Summerville, maybe I did tell you, I've forgotten. I loved it that you were born in the spring, that time of promise, but I often thought of you as a Christmas gift too. That 1957 December, it's ironic that it began in such a lovely way. Despite the sadness of Max's death, despite your father's erratic behavior, I still believed—I guess naively—that life was a journey of amazing promise. Christmas was coming, midwinter unfurling its crimson streamers. Time of color, joy. Season of miracle. And before the world fell apart, we did have one.

It's dark, late, you're snuggled under your wool blankets and the patchwork quilt your grandmother made, when I tiptoe into the room and lean across your bed and part the curtains. Fluffy issues a yawn and nestles closer to you. He's mellowed since you stopped dressing him in doll clothes.

"Look outside, honey."

You brush sleep out of your eyes and sit up. I gently push you toward a window. You gaze outside, turn to me with wide bedazzled eyes. "Snow! It's *snow!*"

Together we behold magic. The world is *white*. It's nighttime but it looks like a million lights outside, you say, like light is coming from under the ground so it looks like daytime except fuzzy like fog. I raise the window and we hear twinkling noises and you say it's like two stars bumping together, and it's so still outside, as though the world has stopped, quiet and tinselly at the same time. Snow *is* a miracle in a subtropical land, as mysterious as a virgin birth. White down falls and falls as I lift the screen latch so you can stick your hand out, and you catch a huge wet snowflake but it disappears and you try to catch another and we laugh out loud and I whisper, "Shush, we'll wake your father."

With my arm around you, we watch white crystals mount higher and higher on the garage roof, the snow gets deeper and deeper, like maybe it'll keep falling forever, and you say that soon we'll be Eskimo people and live in a house made of ice and cut holes in the ground where our food of fish will come from.

I think about the first time I saw snow. "Let's go outside."

Hand in hand, coats over my nightgown and over your bluebird pajamas with plastic-spotted feet, we scurry past your sleeping father in entirely inappropriate shoes—who in South Carolina has snow boots? You say that now we have Up North trees because they're covered with lacy icicles, and you run to see one up close and fall smack-dab into a big white drift. I giggle like no mother ever does and pick you up and whirl you around and maybe we'll both catch cold, but how often does a child see such winter beauty? I pull you toward the tall evergreen near your swing set; we walk underneath the low-hanging branches and as it snows around us, we're dry and safe. We hold hands, looking up through the green limbs as white crystals float down from heaven.

I reach up and come back with a palm filled with snow. "Make a wish, sweetheart."

You say you'd like more snow for Christmas Day and a sled like Up North kids have.

"Now kiss the snowflakes."

You giggle because of course you're kissing white sloppy goo in your mother's hand.

"Now kiss the best mother in the history of motherland."

You do, and I shake snow from a tree branch down onto you, combing the white crystals through your hair. "I christen you a Southern child of snow. Here's to Lyra the Queen of Winter."

I sing—very softly—"In the lane the snow is glistening" and feel as happy as you'll probably ever remember me. I'll carry that snowy night in my pocket for a very long time, as you travel down road after road in another direction, until I can't bear it anymore and one day I take it out and leave it on the sidewalk to melt.

❧☙❧

That snowstorm came a few days before the demon arrived—the demon with prayers and screaming and blood and being thrown to the floor. It's still that first night and William remains slumped by the bed mumbling. I've got to stop the bleeding. I run to the bathroom; you're crouched on the floor hiding by the tub. I tell you to stay quiet as I rifle through the medicine cabinet. I run through your bedroom and rush over to William and grab his left forearm. The sight of the blood makes me queasy again, but I wrap the wounds with gauze and apply all the pressure I can—

He jumps up suddenly and the gauze falls away as he shouts, "That child has to confess. Where is she?"

I grab William's wrist, hold onto it for dear life, he doesn't seem to feel any pain. "God likes prayers to be quiet," I whisper. "Come kneel with me and we'll say our prayers together."

I can't think what else to do but this works, and William becomes docile and kneels down and lays his head on the blood-spattered sheets, crying. I wrap his wrist, this stems the bleeding, and I tell him that God is listening, and I'm going to get some water to wash the wound, everything will be all right—

"*No*," he screams. "You cannot leave."

He forces me back to my knees and abruptly I see the razor blade on the bed, dried blood on its edge, and reality dawns. It wasn't an accident.

"Oh my God," I cry, gaping at my husband in shock as I say over and over—"What has happened, what's wrong? You cut yourself on purpose? Oh my God—you tried to—"

He begins walking in a circle, he's off-balance, leaning over and holding that bandaged arm—the bandage is coming loose—close to his chest. When he runs into the kitchen, I pitch the razor blade under the bed and run after him, follow him back to the bedroom. He and I go back and forth in front of Lyra's door, and I'm crying in some voice I've never heard, "Come and sit down, William. Come and sit down and talk to me, please."

But he sprints through the house as though chased. Lyra must be terrified, I think, must wonder what to do, she's cold and hungry by now and I hear her crying but softly because she doesn't want him to hear her. William reappears and throws me down beside the bed again, his red hands on my shoulders, and he says that we must pray all night for forgiveness, for those we have killed, and I tell him I will pray, though my voice quakes with terror as I begin the Lord's Prayer and William says, "That's right, we will ask him to spare us."

I think I must do something about my baby and I stop praying. "William, please let me check on Lyra—"

He screams, "*No No No.*" Then he turns and talks to someone who isn't here. When I look at my husband, he's not William anymore, he's someone else. He screams at me to pray, and I begin praying again, rotely, as though my exhausted mind has separated from my body, and as I pray my faith in life drains away, my blood feels spilled onto these sheets too, and there's William walking down the aisle with his college degree, how spiffy he is in his uniform, I can just imagine what young French girls thought when he marched in to save the day, and there he is again, William, so shy on our wedding night, and we're splashing in the Fountain of Youth in St. Augustine, and I steer myself into that past. I am no longer beside this bed and my husband is no longer bleeding and screaming at me and—

—from her doorway Lyra watches us, I see her watching her mother and father in a room turned red, a room of screams to God. While I'm still on my knees mumbling prayers, she lies down at the end of her bed so she can see me, but she doesn't look at her father. It's dark night now, dark long past supper, the dark of bedtime. I know she wants to come to me but is afraid of her father, and I pray under my breath, *Please God, don't let her come in here.*

William jumps up for the thousandth time and runs to the living room and then back, and I slump against the bed as he yells at me so loudly I clap my hands over my ears.

"You tried to kill me! My own wife—you despicable woman."

I'm crying insensibly though my mind can't yet form the fact I know—that Lyra and I are alone now. I'm a child once more myself, something has gone wrong, someone is not right and I don't understand what has happened, and my own father is crying for the love he can't bring back, we know now that the person we count on can't be counted on anymore, and this is my husband William to love and to cherish who throws me to the floor, and till death do I pledge thee my troth, this stranger, this person of sin and blood and razor blade—

William moans and talks to spirits. He tells me I'm going to hell.

Lyra jumps down from her bed and runs to our door and stands there shaking, and I'm desperate to go to her but William might follow. I gaze helplessly at my child as more belief in life drains out of me. William falls down beside me, he's still mumbling to God, and it's getting darker and darker, and then it's a little lighter. For hours William babbles and cries—I never look up. I sense morning after a while but I don't want morning anymore. When I do look up, Lyra is standing in the doorway—she'll paint doorways and windows forever—and I know she wants her mother to come to her right now—*please God, let me go to her*—and she cries out but I barely hear her as William begins screaming again—

And on the night goes.

While William shouts and moans, the stark white moon slips into the room. The solstice is coming early for us, this moment when time changes from one direction to another, this moment which marks both the beginning and the end.

❧❧❧❧

It's the next day, Saturday, and there's still blood on his pajamas, still blood on my dress, but it's afternoon and he's back in the house after hitting the dogwood tree with the car. Blood is seeping out from beneath the bandage on his wrist but he won't let me look at it. He's been rummaging through household objects, or he'll begin a project—"I think I'll fix that leaky faucet"—only to abandon it twenty minutes later and take up another. He's painted a kitchen cabinet on the inside only. Often he just disappears. I'll find him on the porch steps—still in his pajamas, crying. Talking to himself. I drag him inside—

It's night now, it's always nicer in a hospital at night. With no eyes to see, my reality is what I hear. It's reassuring when the night nurse comes by to check on me, she has a soothing voice and always whispers, *Hope you feel better soon, dear.*

I doubt I will.

During those terrifying days, I realize now, there wasn't as much blood as I thought there was. But while it was happening it felt like a gory spectacle.

I think it was around noon that Saturday when I tried to phone a doctor and William jerked the phone away, said if I tried to use it again he'd cut the line. He took all the pots out of the kitchen cabinets, said the stove wasn't safe to use and unplugged it, said he did not trust Mrs. Moazen and that I was forbidden to talk to her again. He walked through the house several times as though giving a tour to someone, and then dashed out the front door and flailed down the street. I tore out of the house and chased him, crying, "William, William, please come back."

I'm sure Rosa watched from her front window, even the Fahertys on the corner undoubtedly saw William run by in his pajamas. Mrs. Flo, who delivered flour and milk to an invalid on Lincoln Street every Saturday, saw me running after him. Finally he went back in the house. Before I followed him, I noticed you and Johnny in his front yard, where I'd sent you earlier, both of you staring at our house.

❧❧❧

That afternoon William raised his right hand into the air and held it there for four hours, staring at the ceiling, not uttering a word no matter how much I tried to get him to talk. A fixed stare, vacancy, as though in a waking coma. When he finally lowers his arm, he still doesn't move from the bed. I smell urine. He hasn't spoken in seven hours. I leave a bowl of soup by his bed but he never touches it. Often he seems to be asleep, but his eyes are eerily open.

Eventually I go to Rosa's and get you and put you to bed; you stare at your father as we walk past him into your room. I tell you that things will be better tomorrow and pull the covers up around your neck and kiss you.

"I love you, sweetheart. I know things feel—*funny*—right now, but it's all going to be okay." As I leave, I wonder how.

I close your door tightly and drag a kitchen chair into the master bedroom and sit down; I'm between William and your door. I watch your father until I finally slump over and fall asleep. My dreams are terrible: a body on a bed, and I'm wandering in the backyard in Brantley—

I awake with a start. Morning light. William slept through the night; his eyes are closed but his arm is back in the air. How can he hold it there? There's a soft knock at the front door. I stare at the clock—seven-thirty. I stand up stiffly and smooth my dress. I look like I've been in an automobile wreck. At the front door I peer through the lace curtain and come eye to eye with Rosa.

Her face is less made up than usual; she's wearing pedal pushers, a white shirt, a cardigan. Her subdued outfit takes me by surprise. If she'd wear that to PTA meetings instead of low-cut dresses, people would be friendlier to her.

When I crack the door open, she says, "Louise, I wondered if I could do anything for ya. I've had a few men problems in my time."

Of course they all know.

"That's very kind, thank you. My husband isn't well, he's sleeping, maybe a cold coming on."

I wait for Rosa to tell me that any fool knows William has a lot more than a cold.

"Well, maybe Lyra would like to have some dinner with me and Johnny. I been wanting to test my goulash recipe, the man who gave it to me was a count or something—or maybe a no-count. I know him from back when I was a secretary. They fired me when I got divorced, I couldn't even get a charge card in my name after that. I was secretary for this toy company that made pogo sticks. Don't that just beat all?"

Pogo sticks? I start laughing, too loudly, hysterically.

She's still smiling. "So I'll give the kids some dinner?"

I hear William stirring. "Thank you, but it's Sunday, we should get to church this morning."

"Are you sure? Lyra'll be fine at my house, I give you my word."

Was William getting up? "I'm sorry but I have to see if my husband's doing all right. Excuse me."

I step backward, am about to close the door when Rosa steps forward. "Louise, I know when a man's gone off his head. You should call the cops. Uta and me can take turns watching Lyra—we already talked about it, and you know it ain't no small thing when she and I agree. You gotta look out for yourself and your little girl. Ain't no tellin' what he'll do."

There's a crash in the bedroom. "Rosa, I have to go."

Our back door is open when I reach the kitchen. I run down the back steps and scan the yard. Noise in the garage. Inside, William is perched on a wooden bench—he's put on a shirt and work pants, and he's looking down at his hands mumbling to himself. He looks so fragile—he's misbuttoned his shirt—but when he looks up, he doesn't seem to recognize me.

"This is your fault," he growls. He stares at his hands again and I think he means the bandaged wrist.

"I'll do anything for you, William. Please let me change the dressing on your wrist. I think you should see a doctor."

His eyes are inky dark. "I know what you've been doing behind my back."

Then I hear you calling me from our back steps. I step out of the garage and yell, "Lyra, go to Johnny's house."

You look hurt but scamper down the driveway. William is pacing in a circle in the garage, counting aloud; he reaches a hundred and stops.

I plead, "*Please* come in the house."

Miraculously, he goes inside and gets in bed and closes his eyes. Soon he seems asleep. I stand in the bedroom doorway—I've no idea if he really is asleep. I walk to the front door. Is it safe to get Lyra? I hesitate on our porch; I don't see you or Johnny but Rosa is walking toward me. She waves me to the sidewalk, her face determined.

"Louise, Lyra told me a little of what's going on. You got a gun in your house?"

"I don't know where his army pistol is, I've looked."

"Well you gotta find it."

"William wouldn't hurt us."

"Listen, this ain't just about you and yourn. He could take that gun and come raving into the streets. Shoot anybody. Has he got someplace he keeps stuff from the war?" When I say no, she asks, "What does he care the most about? What's his favorite stuff?"

I go back inside and peek into the bedroom—William is still sleeping. I tiptoe into the hallway. He had recently lined up all his books about the Civil War on the second bookcase shelf and ordered me not to touch them. Even when he attacked the bookshelves yesterday, he left that shelf alone. I pull the books off, careful not to drop them on the floor, and find a paper bag containing his service revolver.

When I go across the street and give it to Rosa to keep, she says, "You need to call somebody."

We both hear the back door of our house slam open. William sprints down the steps. I rush back to our house. When he sees me, he runs up the stairs to the empty apartment and knocks, then runs back down, taking the stairs three at a time. I'm certain he'll fall but he doesn't. I call to him but he doesn't respond. He notices the downed dogwood and stops to stare at it. Next he runs to the car and looks at the dented fender and says, "I knew that man would do that," and crawls under the car.

Uta stands on her porch, watching; I pray that William does not see her.

He peers out from under the car as though looking for something or someone; suddenly he screams so loudly everyone on the block can probably hear him. He rolls out from under the car, his head tucked, opens the back car door and takes the bench seat out and throws it on the ground. I start toward him just as he climbs into the driver's side and starts the engine—

Everything that happens fast happens slowly.

The roar of William starting the car, the crunch of tires on driveway gravel, William spinning the car around toward the street, it nearly hits the back stoop, comes within a hair of the outside staircase, it's weaving wildly, going way too fast.

The scream isn't coming from me, it's from Uta, who's running toward me, who seems an unlikely screamer. Then I realize that my husband—I can see his intent eyes behind the windshield—is aiming the car directly at me.

"Run, Louise, get out of the way."

Uta keeps yelling, but no, William wouldn't hurt me, William loves me, he's just tired and confused—

The front of the car bears down, everything feels unreal, time is slow and objects out of focus. I hear yelling, it sounds like a child's voice, I notice the grating sound of the taxicab engine, feel the vibrations of the ground nearby. I gaze trancelike at the front of the car, and suddenly see William's face clearly, that's our car, that's William driving it—that's my husband—*he's going to run over me.*

If I keep still, this will stop, I won't have to live through any more, I won't have to figure out what to do, where it all went wrong, I'll just stay right here and it'll be easy, he's going so fast, there's no question, the only awful thing will be my—

The world goes to slower motion. Another sound. A child's voice. You're running down the driveway. Rosa is chasing you, shouting at you. You're screaming in a high-pitched voice—

You're running toward me.

"Lyra, no. *No.*"

I dive for you and we hit the ground and I shove you away just as a wheel runs over my right foot. I shriek in pain as the car roars by. William whips the car around in a circle and heads into the garage. You're screaming and crying as I grab you and try to get up, but I fall back down, pain shooting up my leg. I try to rise again, I hear people running into the driveway. I have to get away before he comes out of the garage. I throw myself onto the injured foot and pull myself up with you in my arms and limp-run down the driveway as fast as I can.

Chapter Ten

For years, I tried to decide on the right word for the first days of your father's breakdown. Much more than *chaos* or *pandemonium*. *Bedlam*? The word I favored was *maelstrom*: a violent whirlpool of strange sights and sounds and events. A tornado whipped through our house and sent everything flying—lightning hitting us a second time. I was in shock through much of it; for the first time I understood, at least partially, what shell shock had done to William. What it feels like to go frozen and numb internally, even as you must outwardly, and relentlessly, confront and deal with what is terrifying you. It's a nightmare you do not wake up from.

You cannot realize how unprepared I was for what happened during those days. The 1950s exalted being ordinary, *normal*, coloring within the lines; it was a cruel, unforgiving time for those of the "wrong" color, income, or chemistry. Imagine for a moment this prehistoric era: only primitive psychiatric drugs and no one admitting to taking those, no books on mental disorders in every bookstore, no talk about depression on television. My college curriculum included a class in "Moral Ethics" but nothing vaguely resembling the "Abnormal Psych" of yours. As was typical, I thought most patients in mental hospitals had schizophrenia, the diagnosis given virtually every patient then, which meant you were deranged beyond repair. I had no idea that in places like New York and Boston—remember, there was no real "media" then—poets and artists with mental illness were well-respected. Most people I knew believed that a "nervous breakdown" resulted from over-exertion, that the sufferer simply needed rest. Isn't that what doctors told Virginia Woolf and Charlotte Gilmore Perkins? I didn't know that the euphemism "nervous breakdown" was created when psychiatrists realized madness was, as they put it, a genetic *defect*. Exactly who was going to admit to a family of defectives? Instead, we had a benign word for what isn't benign at all.

Mental illness has always been tricky business in the South—some would say because we have a lot of it. The South has always specialized in eccentrics, harmless oddballs on street corners waving Bibles. Flannery O'Connor made being "turned funny" into legend: oddballs, then and now, provide regional character. Can't this heat make anyone a little strange? Remember the woman in Brantley who gave away all the trash cans in her house and removed the doorknobs? But local color wasn't always amusing. An eccentric who truly *misbehaved*—that was something else. No one could say what separated harmless idiosyncrasy from the madman's evil, but everyone knew when they saw it. Those who vaulted, usually not at their choosing, over that barrier were hidden in back bedrooms, sometimes tied to a four-poster, or remanded to jails and asylums when relatives couldn't cope. You've no idea the extent to which I and everyone around me had been taught that the mentally ill were *other* people, another race—primitive, violent, dirty, and dangerous.

And now—my husband, your father.

I'm on the sofa in Uta's house, shaking all over. You're sitting on my lap, leaning against me sucking your thumb. I rock back and forth, trying to breathe normally. When I close my eyes, the car's coming straight at us. *He almost killed us.* Uta has my foot soaking in a dishpan, it hurts terribly, it's swollen but I don't think any bones are broken. I drink the brandy Uta has provided and ease you off my lap, tell you to stretch out. I lean over, my hands to my temples. *He could have killed Lyra. He could have killed our child.*

"I going to call a doctor," I say when Uta walks into the room with a tray of food. "If I can't get a doctor, I guess it's the police. Oh dear Lord."

I gaze at Uta, say the words I fear: "He's lost his mind."

Eventually I phoned the general practitioner I'd chosen for your vaccinations because his middle name was the same as my mother's maiden name. Dr. Dumaine—for years he's asked me to call him Ernie but it's never felt natural—arrived an hour later. He was heavyset even then; at thirty-five he looked middle-aged, as doctors were supposed to in 1957. He had a lazy left eye, that laconic manner and gruff affability that still endears him to women and children. When he arrived, he couldn't park in our driveway because of the downed tree, so he left his car at the curb and headed to the front door.

I called to him from Uta's sidewalk. "I'm over here, doctor." I limped forward, shook his hand, thanked him for coming.

"What's wrong with your foot, Mrs. Copeland?"

I pointed at our house. "My husband's—he's been—not himself—since—I guess it was—yes, it was—Friday afternoon. He—injured himself—he's very upset." My voice broke—"I don't know what to do—"

We looked up. William was yelling from inside the garage.

The doctor said, "You go in your house." He guided me to our back steps. "I'm going to look at your foot in a few minutes. Go inside and make coffee. Has your husband been drinking?"

I said no and climbed the steps slowly. At the back door I hesitated, looked down the driveway—I wanted to walk down Lincoln Street until I could take a right onto Elmwood Avenue and get on that new freeway and disappear.

Inside the kitchen I put the coffeepot on the stove and cleaned up a bit—your untouched cornflakes were still on the table. I heard yelling outside and hobbled to the window. William darted by, followed by the doctor. William stopped and Dr. Dumaine said something, and then the doctor put his arm around William and led him to the back door. When they came in the kitchen, William saw me and turned and ran back to the door, but the doctor grabbed him. He dragged William into the bedroom. William tried to punch him, but Dr. Dumaine was larger; he threw William onto the bed, whipped open his black bag and withdrew a hypodermic needle, and plunged it into William's thigh. William looked stunned, lay down quietly, and in a moment closed his eyes.

Dr. Dumaine came in the kitchen. "Let's look at your foot." He examined it, fashioned a small splint with gauze and a tongue depressor. I poured us burned coffee and described William's behavior. We went into the bedroom, and Dr. Dumaine inspected William's wrist. There were five cuts, three close together, of different sizes, and two others at uneven distances.

"Two hit veins," he said, "but—fortunately—only nicked them. You did a good job stopping the blood loss." He asked about weapons in the house, applied a sterile solution, and sewed across William's wounds.

In the kitchen I poured him a second cup of coffee. He asked, "Did something happen Friday, something out of the ordinary? Has he been feeling bad lately? Worried about something?"

I said I hadn't noticed anything unusual. "But when this began he talked about God and sin, and he wanted to pray. He prayed most of the night. He's studying to be a minister, but I never heard him talk like that before."

The doctor took off his glasses, polished them with the tail of his tie. "During mental breakdowns people often become very religious. I don't know why."

"Could it have been some kind of accident?"

"No. I'm sorry, but he meant to do this. A suicide attempt always has a reason, even if we never know what the reason was."

He gazed out the window at the encroaching darkness, then looked at the wall clock. "Your husband should sleep through the night." He gave me a long look, said now he remembered my coming to his office. Where was my daughter? After I told him, he said, "She should stay at your neighbor's house for now. Has he tried to harm anyone else—you or your daughter?"

It took me a moment to answer: "William wouldn't hurt us."

"Well then, you try to get some rest, and I'll be around bright and early tomorrow morning."

When I asked about his bill, Dr. Dumaine patted me on the shoulder. "Don't worry about that right now. You need some rest and to get off that foot. That's an order."

When I walked him to the front door, I could barely keep from crying out: *Please don't leave me here alone.*

He hesitated at the porch door, glanced into the dark driveway, stared at the downed dogwood. "Your husband hasn't tried to harm anyone else, you're sure about that?"

"He did drive the car dangerously. You have to understand—this isn't like him, this isn't who he is." I hesitated. "He could have hit someone."

The doctor turned around. "Let me call my wife. I think I should stay here a bit longer."

∽ᴏ･☉◯℮ᴐ

While William slept, I fried a hamburger for the doctor and we talked and drank repeated cups of coffee. I wasn't hungry, I couldn't remember eating anytime in the last forty-eight hours—at least I didn't have to worry about my new diet. Dr. Dumaine and I discovered we were distantly related: his great aunt had been married to my mother's brother, who died in World War I. As the night wore on, he told me about going to medical school in Charleston; he'd been there about the same time we were living in Summerville. We talked about the differences between Charleston and Columbia; he said he still missed the Low Country, said I spoke with the "beautiful Charleston brogue," which made me blush. For a moment the world seemed normal, like it was before my husband tried to kill himself.

Finally I said, "I need to get my daughter from next door."

"I don't think you should. We don't know what will happen when William wakes up. Can't she stay with your neighbor?"

"She's never spent the night away from me. She'll be scared, she's already scared. It's awful what she's had to see. She needs her mother."

"How about this—I stay here with your husband and you stay over there with her? You need to stay off that foot too."

I said he was very kind but I didn't feel Lyra could stay at Uta's. Wouldn't it scare her even more if neither of us could come home?

The doctor settled onto the living-room sofa with a book, and I limped over to Uta's house. You were asleep on the hard Victorian sofa; Uta had covered you with an afghan and was dozing in an armchair beside you. I whispered that the doctor was staying the night and knelt down and woke you gently and walked you home. You said it felt "funny" to be out on the street so late, that the world had gone still like it did when it snowed. I told you that in our house there was a doctor, maybe you'd remember him, he gave you your school vaccinations. The doctor was staying with us late because your father was sick. At our house I told Dr. Dumaine I'd sleep in your bed tonight and he said that was a good idea, and you and I tiptoed past your sleeping father. In your room I whispered about Christmas and how your cousins would be coming to visit. I could feel the fear in your clammy skin as I pulled your pajama top down over your head. I almost broke down but forced myself into what I hoped was a reassuring smile.

I made you sleep by the windows. During the night I awoke over and over again and twice I got up and went into the other room to lean down and look at William. I wondered whether to call my brothers. I couldn't call my stepmother; she had no patience for people who didn't behave correctly. My brother in DC or the one in Florida? So far away, what could either do? If William was having a "breakdown," he'd hate anyone knowing it. Wasn't it bad enough that the neighbors knew?

Was it possible William would wake up okay tomorrow? Maybe tomorrow everything would be better.

∽◦⊖◦∾

First I felt it. Moving air, breeze—no, breath. Someone's breath. I opened my eyes. William's bored into them. I almost smiled. Then I remembered.

He leered at me, his eyes dilated. Instinctively I pulled back, one hand reaching for you.

"Are you feeling better," I whispered.

He kept breathing on me, studying me. My heart beat a chaotic rhythm. He leaned back and without a word strode into the bathroom.

I stared at the clock on your orange-crate nightstand. Six-thirty.

I held my breath as William walked back through the room—he didn't look at us. I heard him get back in bed, heard him tossing and turning. Heard his breathing even out.

I should have left Lyra at Uta's, I must get her out of the house.

It is Monday, isn't it? Has to be. I rocked you playfully, whispered that I was going to walk you to school early, you could play in the schoolyard until the doors opened. Hurriedly I got you dressed, threw on a dress myself, and we sped past your sleeping father, though not quickly enough that I didn't see how you stared at him. I made your lunch and we scrambled out the door—Dr. Dumaine was still asleep on the sofa—and we both ate an apple as we walked, me still limping, through the early morning chill. Several houses now had green wreaths on their front doors. We headed through the Logan gates and over to the swing set, and I said you were to stay in the schoolyard until the doors opened, you were not to go anywhere else. There'd never been any trouble here, but when I looked at you I almost burst into tears—you were so small in your green jumper and plaid jacket, a small child alone in the schoolyard before school opened. You got out a coloring book from your book bag and attacked the outline of a house with a dog and a cat lolling in its front yard. What your home ought to be. I started walking away, calling that I'd see you that afternoon. When I turned around, you'd stopped coloring and were watching me leave.

I shuffled back down Lincoln Street berating myself, stopped when I was halfway home and turned around and limped back to the schoolyard, pain shooting up my leg. I could see you, you were all right, you'd be fine. When I stumbled into our yard, William was on the porch holding the iron, looking at it oddly. The doctor, tieless now and minus his glasses, was saying he'd like William to come inside. William threw the iron down and ran into the house. As I hobbled onto the porch, I could hear him in the hallway babbling about the farm, how he had to get down there to fix the leak in the roof. He ran into the living room, the doctor following.

Dr. Dumaine gave me a troubled look and crossed to his black bag. He caught William and jabbed the needle into his arm. In a few seconds we got William back into bed. I retreated to the kitchen while the doctor talked to William for a while.

When Dr. Dumaine walked into the kitchen, I cried, "I don't know what to do, I just don't know what to *do*."

He sat down. Unshaven and rumpled, he looked as exhausted as I felt. "He needs to go to a hospital, Mrs. Copeland. I've tried to talk to him about that but he refuses to consider it—some people fight the idea even when they know they need it. While I was talking to him he suddenly froze, went rigid, stared at the ceiling with one arm in the air. Has he done that before?"

When I said yes, he looked worried. "How long was he like that? When he came out of it, what happened?"

"Four hours. He acted wild afterward. That's when he drove the car dangerously."

"He was probably catatonic. A catatonic patient is very dangerous—this isn't safe for you and your daughter. I don't have much experience with nervous breakdowns, but I know he needs to be in a hospital."

"No one can force William to do something he doesn't want to do."

"Then we get an involuntary commitment. In an emergency, only one relative and one doctor have to sign. Are there mental problems in his family, in his past?"

"He had shell shock during the war, that's all I know about." I put the coffeepot on the stove again. "I can't send my husband to a hospital against his will. He'll never forgive me." I turned around. "If I have to, I'll send Lyra to her grandmother and take care of William myself."

"He needs treatment he can only get in a hospital. This will protect him too. The law says anyone who's a danger to himself or to others, or who clearly needs treatment he's not competent enough to agree to, should be committed."

"I can't lock him up. I know what people think about anyone with mental problems. There's a poor woman in this neighborhood nobody will even speak to. William's a good man, a sensitive man. I can't treat him like he has no say in what happens to him."

"I know this is hard. But there's more dignity to commitment now. A public hearing is no longer required, he won't have to wait in jail for a judge to sign the papers. We'll get him in a private hospital, and it'll be very orderly and quiet."

Lyra in the schoolyard. Alone in the schoolyard before school opens. Because she can't be in her own house. Because her own house isn't safe.

I got up and stared through the kitchen doorway at William's rigid body, the arm in the air. "*Why* is his arm that way?"

"I don't know, I wish I did. Come sit down."

Dr. Dumaine led me back to the table. "Your husband's not the only one who needs help. You do too."

"What do I have to do?" My voice had no inflection, no tone. My singer's voice was gone.

"First we decide on a hospital. A private sanitarium is going to be expensive."

A good wife would never do this. A good woman supports and protects her husband and her child.

"My husband is a student, he's not been working lately. I'm only a schoolteacher." I paused. "We have one thing that's valuable, but it's not in my name—a farm. William loves that farm to death. I can't imagine selling it, it's our daughter's inheritance."

"Anyone involuntarily committed loses certain rights, I'm afraid—I doubt William would be allowed to sign legal papers." The doctor thought for a moment. "Did you say shell shock? If he's a veteran, he can go to the VA hospital. It has fine facilities, they learned a lot about treating mental problems in army hospitals. You sit and rest. I'll call and get things started."

He peeked in at William and went to the hallway phone. It sounded like he was arguing with someone. I looked around the room. Cleaning up the dishes from last night seemed pointless. Abruptly I realized—I forgot to call school. I didn't call and I didn't show up.

Dr. Dumaine walked into the kitchen. "The VA hospital doesn't have a bed available on their psych ward." He lit a cigarette and smoked in silence.

"The only thing we can do," he said slowly, "is call the state hospital."

"The state hospital on Bull Street? No. *No.*"

I paced across the room, hands shaking, voice taut. "I won't do that. Everyone knows how people are treated there. I've heard that most patients never come home."

"There've been many improvements in recent years. I've seen the progress myself."

"But the shame—what will people think about William if he's sent there? The place looks like a prison. Awful things could happen to him there."

Dr. Dumaine ran a hand through his hair. "It's not ideal, I admit. But he could just stay there until a bed opens up in the VA hospital."

I stared into the bedroom at William. "I can't do that to him. He's not crazy like those people."

"You know this is serious, Mrs. Copeland. I'm not trying to *make* you commit him. But if you don't get him into a hospital, you and Lyra must stay somewhere else until he becomes less agitated. We can try to find someone to look after him, but I don't think that's the wisest choice. There's a new medicine now—chlorpromazine—I'm told it works wonders at calming a patient down. But he can only get it in a hospital. He may not get better without going to one."

I stared at Ernest Dumaine but his features were blurred, as though my eyes could no longer focus. I went in and looked at William; he was tossing back and forth, even with his arm in the air. He no longer seemed quite real. I felt his hand on my back, his long tender fingers, as I walked forward at the cemetery to lay roses on my father's casket. I saw you in the schoolyard alone, saw you running down the driveway as William aimed the car at us—

I went back to the kitchen and nodded. *Why do I feel like I'm deciding whether the man I love will live or die?*

Suddenly time stops and I watch the past, which had been so simple, waltz out of the room. I know that nothing will ever be simple again. Terrible things may happen to William. Terrible things will be said about him. Terrible things will be said about the woman who threw her husband into the lunatic asylum. I go back and gaze at William while his life is compromised in the hallway where Dr. Dumaine talks on the telephone. We're on the porch that first night. I'm singing to William. It was a week later that he kissed my hand. Soft feathery waves against his forehead, smooth skin like a child's, long lanky body, my husband, my love, my child's father. Who does not know us now.

As I stand there stroking your father's arm, I recall his story about ring shake, how a hurricane can cause the internal layers of a tree to separate. Even though the tree survives and looks all right on the outside, internally it is forever changed.

❧⚬◯⚬☙

So many decades later and you're leaning over my hospital bed weeping. You must have been equally anguished when—amid screaming and confusion—someone important to your life disappeared. But no one asks how you feel, or tells you it's all right to be frightened and sad. Rather like the silence of a brokenhearted father staring at his wife's paintings night after night after night.

William was resting quietly when the police car arrived, followed by the white van from the state hospital. I stand on the sidewalk while Dr. Dumaine speaks to the hospital attendants—I know I'm cold in the December air but I can't feel such things anymore, I've lost any sense of being in the world. I keep picturing you as I left you in that schoolyard. How can this be what my life has become—I am forcing my husband to go to a place where it's said that people inside, locked up like animals, pray to die. I wish I could go instead. I wish I could die today.

The attendants and Dr. Dumaine head into the house. I'm trailing like I'm not sure where I am—I hear myself talking to the doctor but it's not my voice anymore. He's telling me what will happen after William gets to Bull Street, about some place called "intake." I should not come there today, I should wait for his call.

He holds out a document. "You do have to sign it."

I stare at the form, sign it. *But that can't be my signature.*

Then we're in the bedroom. William sees the men in white and screams, *"No, no, no—I won't I know I'm not going—"*

He tries to get up. "You bastards—she can't do this—she's stupid—"

The attendants head toward him with the stretcher. I scream, "Please don't hurt him—"

William is still yelling. The doctor is holding him, saying, "We're just going to get you a little help, you won't be there long, do you understand me?"

William puts up a hand to shield himself.

"He's a veteran," the doctor says to the policeman. "Maybe the uniform is scaring him. Can you wait outside?"

"I'll stay in the other room," the officer says. "But I have to make sure no one gets hurt."

Oh, Lyra—I know you came home early, how much did you see?

William breaks free of the doctor's grasp, rears up and scrambles out of bed, heading for your bedroom. Dr. Dumaine jerks him back by his shirt and it rips; the two men in white grab William and while he wriggles and screams, hurling profanity at me, the men trap him in a straightjacket and tie it in the back.

William begins to cry, I'm leaning over him crying too, murmuring, "Darling, I love you, this is only for a little while so you can get better, and I'll be there as soon as I can and it'll be all right, you'll see, you'll get some rest and the doctors will make you well, and I'll be there to see you every morning and every evening and—"

William begs, "Please, please, please."

I turn to the doctor and scream—*"I can't do this!"*

William cries harder as they carry him toward the living-room door. I'm following the doctor and imploring the orderlies to be careful. When we get outside, William is suddenly quiet. He stares at the sky as though frozen. Across the street neighbors have gathered to stare; I see Rosa drag Johnny inside their house. Dr. Dumaine and I stand on either side as the stretcher goes into the rear of the van. The van driver speaks to the policeman, the officer gets in his gray car, and the white station wagon pulls away.

The people across the street begin to go home. I stagger to our front steps. Uta, watching from her porch, rushes to our house.

Chapter Eleven

Our lives are over, I think as Uta walks me onto our screen porch.

I make Uta go home and stumble through our hallway and back to the bedroom. I collapse in tears onto sheets stained with dried blood, lay my cheek on the pillow still indented by William's head. I try to breathe back into being the husband I loved those warm nights in Summerville. But I can't make him reappear. He's gone.

I want a mother to tell me what to do. To tell me I did the right thing. To say it will be all right.

Suddenly I hear you—you're on the back steps, crying. *Please let her not have seen much.*

I pull myself up, brush my tears away, rush through the back door and take you in my arms. You feel unnaturally small and fragile, a child with a bluebird's bones. I rock you and pray that neither of us will break.

The South Carolina State Hospital ambulances did not pass through the wrought-iron gates of the front entrance, did not meander down the magnolia-studded main drive. They didn't pass the stately redbrick Mills Building, home of the original South Carolina Lunatic Asylum. Your father didn't see its lovely curved staircases and white columns that day, although later he did tell me the building's semicircular design was to allow the sun to move across patient rooms from east to west—even in the early 1800s, William explained, light was considered restorative to the mentally ill. The Mills Building was innovative: fireproof ceilings, central heating, one of America's first roof gardens. Its Doric temple portico and Palladian windows still exude graciousness.

Ambulances entered the hospital through the twelve-foot-high back gate topped with barbed wire, which sat beside the dilapidated brick morgue.

The state hospital's past was as turbulent as Elmwood Park's—disturbing history shadowed us at every turn. When its doors opened in 1828, few patients turned up: people associated a "home" for the mad with poorhouses and prisons. Insanity was dishonorable, so sending a relative to a public madhouse was an admission of family shame. During the Moral Treatment era, the asylum's image improved. Tourists were encouraged to visit, to admire the elegant building, to see that the mad were not "beasts." But visitors often taunted the patients or threw tobacco to provoke them into fighting each other for it. The hospital did not fill up until the Civil War, just as the Confederacy commandeered its grounds to imprison Union officers. During the burning of Columbia, when locals thronged through its gates, the asylum really was a refuge. Most old Columbia families have one or two ancestors who spent a night in the madhouse, although you rarely hear anyone bragging about it.

The asylum survived the Civil War, deteriorating severely during Reconstruction, when South Carolina became one of the poorest states in America. It took thirty years—hospital administrators called in Dorothy Dix to appeal to a stingy legislature—to improve overcrowding by completing the Babcock Building. But hundreds of freed slaves and newly impoverished whites, with nowhere else to go, inundated the new building, whose bricks were made by convicts to save money. Every year thirty percent of the patients died, usually from tuberculosis or poor sanitation. Local authorities sent their epileptics, alcoholics, mentally handicapped, and indigent to the asylum, and overcrowding led to more mechanical restraints. Sometimes the treatment itself killed: draining someone of forty ounces of blood to "calm" him, for example. There was barely enough food. A troublesome patient might be left in pitch-black solitary confinement for months.

This background I got—many months later—from your father.

New buildings in the early twentieth century helped alleviate the hospital's problems. But not for long. When William arrived there, its 6,000 patients lived in facilities intended for 4,500. Faith in curing the insane had been replaced by custodial warehousing. The wards were filled with old people no one wanted, with "hysterical" women committed by husbands seeking control of joint property, with criminals the jails didn't have room for. The hospital complex was a small town made into an island by locked gates and brick walls and barbed wire, a city-state of two hundred acres and fifty buildings constructed over a hundred years.

Many patients regularly tried to scale the ten-foot-high walls. Getting caught got you stripped and locked in solitary, herded to the bathroom— branded by your nakedness—past the jeering of other patients. It got no lower than this, being ridiculed by those ridiculed by the world.

❧◉❧

When the stoplight turned green, instead of going left or right as everyone did at Bull and Elmwood streets, I drove across the intersection. A uniformed man stepped out of the guardhouse and asked my business.

"I'm to see a social worker—at the Williams Building—let me see, I have her name somewhere. I can't seem to find anything today—" I flipped through papers on the seat beside me. "I know I have her name—"

"Ma'am, are you a relative of a patient?"

I stared at him as though I wasn't sure. But of course, I *was*. I had a loved one in the *mental* hospital, didn't I?

I gave him William's name. William's *good* name. Was that pity in the guard's eyes? He stepped away to check a big book—were there that many names? *The Book of the Damned*?

Stop that.

He gave me directions, and as I drove down the tree-lined boulevard

I thought of Max Wells—dear Max, he knew something was wrong with William. I passed the Babcock Building, a massive brick Renaissance structure with long four-story arms extending from a center section. I braked. Hundreds upon hundreds of large windows with small glass panes, many broken or chipped, each covered by rusted iron bars. Bars over dirty windows, more bars, peeling paint, an unkempt building reeking of despair.

I've put my husband in prison.

It took me a few moments to start off again. In the modern admissions building, a social worker introduced herself as Mrs. Ravenel. She was thin and angular, black hair in a French twist, green eyes—maybe in her late forties. She led me into a small office.

"Please sit down, Mrs. Copeland. I'll be your primary contact at the hospital during your husband's stay. It's best not to contact the doctors—we have a huge number of patients and if relatives try to speak with the doctors, it keeps them from their work of caring for the sick."

"How will I know how my husband is doing?"

"You call me. Anytime." She leaned across the metal desk, her voice gentle. "I'm sorry, but you can't see your husband yet. It's hospital policy that the patient not see any relatives for the first ten days. During that time we're trying to determine the best course of treatment. It takes thirty days to completely evaluate a patient's illness."

"He has to stay for thirty days?" I sat back, felt around for the wooden spindles of my chair. Lately I couldn't feel anything well—chairs, steering wheels, children.

She handed me a pamphlet. "This will explain everything. What he can have in his room. And you'll want to deposit money on account for him. He's not allowed to have cash but he can draw on whatever you provide to buy things at the canteen, cigarettes or soda pop or a magazine. You can also bring him writing paper, a few books—no knives, matches, or any sharp objects. No razor. No ties or belts." She pointed at the pamphlet. "This also lists visiting hours. We discourage phone calls to a patient, it's not practical."

"What's happening to William now? I feel terrible that I can't see him." *Won't he think I've abandoned him?*

"He's on the top floor of Babcock—the ventilation from the dome is best there. That's a—serious ward. As he improves, he'll be moved to a lower floor. He's closely observed every day, given a shot if he's agitated. Or water immersion."

William in that terrible building. What did he think when he looked out his window and saw iron bars? "Is he still tied down?"

"Restraints are usually not needed on a regular basis. There are new drugs called phenothiazines—I can barely spell it. Miracle drugs, really, at calming patients down. I wanted to ask you about William's background. Has he been under a strain lately? Do you know anything that might have precipitated his psychosis?"

Undoubtedly I looked confused; *psychosis* wasn't a word often bandied about in those days, at least not in my world.

"I'm speaking of when a patient loses touch with reality. Some hear voices, imagine they see things that aren't there. It's common in schizophrenia."

"William doesn't have schizophrenia," I said. "He's a very smart man."

Alicia Ravenel nodded. "I'm sure he is. But I have to be honest—without drugs, he's very agitated. That's often initially true in an involuntarily committed patient. If you can think of anything that's been disturbing him lately, it could help us help him."

"He has seemed a little—well, not himself for the past few months. He's been doing eccentric things, sometimes it's like he's become a different person."

"That's not uncommon. Often a mentally ill person can be completely different when the illness worsens. And that confuses those around him— there's nothing you can *see* as in most physical illnesses. Don't blame yourself for not realizing what was happening."

She stood up. "If there's anything I can do for you, please call me."

I thanked her. But she'd be no help with what I feared most—*after this, will my husband still love me?*

❧❧❧

I always prided myself on my knowledge of language. I marked agreement errors in newspapers, corrected television news anchors out loud. Words made sense of life: literature converted the universe into pictures that made it mean something. Language helped us master our fears, celebrate our joys. But suddenly I was assaulted by enemy words: *Psychosis. Catatonia. Schizophrenia. Phenothiazines. Mental illness.* I hated them—they meant nothing I wanted to picture.

I drive out of the hospital grounds and park in front of Laidlaw. This last school day before Christmas break had ended at noon. I stare at the empty schoolyard, remaining fall leaves scattered here and there, everything still and silent. In my room I find the chaos left behind by a substitute. I put the dictionaries in the bookcase, pick up the scraps of paper the new janitor never sees. Midday light filters through the blinds, leaves thin stripes across the dusty blackboard. How happy I've been in this room. On the blackboard I write, in a stiff forced hand: "Welcome to a New Year." It will be the first thing students see in January.

I grab a dirty eraser and obliterate the words, chalk dust flying. After a moment I print the same words again and stand back and stare at them.

He will get well. Just have faith.

I climb the stone stairs to the second floor, walk past silent lockers and the closed library door. Footsteps in a vacant school building echo like gunshots. Swatting at the chalk dust on my dress, I let myself into the main office and walk over to the closed door labeled "Principal" and knock.

Ed Hindeman greets me warmly. "Do sit down, Louise. I'm so sorry to hear your husband is ill."

I remain standing. "Mr. Hindeman—Ed—I want to apologize for missing these last days before Christmas. I wouldn't have done it if there'd been any other way."

"I know you wouldn't. How's your husband?"

I tell Ed that William is in "the hospital," and he says, "I'm sorry to hear that. Where is he? Baptist is a very good hospital, but so is Presbyterian."

What do I say? What will he think of William? I take a deep breath. "He's in—the state hospital."

Did he flinch?

He comes over to me. "Tell me what I can do."

"I'd appreciate it if you'd say something to the other teachers—so they won't ask me. I just can't talk about it."

He walks me to the door. "They do some very good things over there—don't listen to what people say. I know who should be told and who shouldn't. I'll take care of it."

I gaze at Ed. How stupid of me—of course it wouldn't be wise to tell everyone. I wish him a good holiday, say that I'm lucky to be working for such a fine principal. He looks embarrassed. He accompanies me to the outside door and stands watching as I head for the staircase.

∾∾◎∽∽

I made sure to get home before you. When I heard the porch door open, I walked through the dining room to find you hesitating in the front doorway. I picked you up, spilling your Christmas drawings onto the floor, and planted a ferocious kiss on your right cheek.

"How's my perfect little girl?"

You gazed over my shoulder. "Is my daddy here?"

I asked about the school Christmas program, said I was sorry I couldn't come but I went to see about Daddy, he was doing just fine, he would have to stay in the hospital a little while to get well and then he'd be home and we'd all be together again. You said I'd forgotten to put on my lipstick. I ignored this and blathered on, fooling no one, certainly not you, about getting a Christmas tree and how we'd decorate it and make some nice things to take to Daddy.

"Does my daddy still have on the shirt with no arms?"

"Your daddy's fine, Lyra. I need to run an errand and you'll have to stay in the car, but afterward we'll go to Krispy Kreme, how about that?"

Soon we're driving toward the east side of Columbia. We pass Doug's Drive-In, where women in white boots bring hamburgers to the cars, and I ask if you remember going there one Saturday. You say you don't.

The Columbia Seminary, a branch of a Virginia divinity school, sits on a slight rise at the edge of the city. As I get out of the car, I recall the day William first registered, when he walked me around the campus of stone buildings and old trees—magnolias here too—and I took his arm and imagined sitting in some nice church listening to my husband at the pulpit.

That seems like a hundred years ago.

I head toward the administration office located in a Gothic stone palace with an arched carriage ramp, white cupola, and notched roofline. It feels like pictures of ancient European fortresses. In the registrar's office I ask to see William's advisor. A sixtyish silver-headed man in a dark gray suit appears and ushers me into his office. Professor Charles Estes, a specialist in the Old Testament, is so tall he seems awkward—he must have to duck through most doorways. He invites me to sit down as he settles into a black leather armchair behind a mahogany desk; on the wall facing me are oil portraits of somber seminary presidents in church vestments.

"This is an unexpected pleasure, Mrs. Copeland. I was looking forward to meeting you at William's second service."

Second service? When was the first? "Well, of course I'll be there."

"I told him we need to schedule it soon. Even if he's to pursue another option, he needs pulpit experience for graduation."

"Professor, I'm here because William has been taken ill. He may not be able to come back until next semester."

"Not a serious illness, I hope. We can give him an extension on papers and exams. We'll need a letter from his doctor. What has him down?"

I take a deep breath. If a letter is required, I have no choice. "He's in the state hospital. He's been working too hard. He just needs a rest."

Charles Estes regards me silently. "I'm sorry to hear that," he says finally. "We've been concerned about William for quite a while. Ever since he dropped out of his ethics class. I'm sure you know that when William led his first service it was—well, not very successful. We called him in for counseling."

I know nothing, apparently. "He's a very private man."

"You don't know what happened? Frankly, he botched his first service. Mumbled all through it, we couldn't hear a word. I called him in and told him he needed a good strong voice to preach God's word. I told him what

I tell a lot of the men—preaching is salesmanship: you sell 'em something they don't even know they want to buy."

Charles Estes looks pleased with himself. "Everyone understands that that's just a little joke. But William had a conniption—said that wasn't how he thought of Christian service. He lectured *me* about Jesus throwing the buyers and sellers out of the temple."

He rolls his eyes as though we're sharing a private joke. "We finally recommended that he switch from the Master of Divinity program to the Master of Arts in Religion. He can teach theology. Or become a Christian education director. He can still be very active in a congregation, but he'd be relieved of the ministerial duties that might be difficult for him. The salary is a bit less of course, but we pointed out that he's lucky to have a wife who works and can help him out."

William not become a minister? Be supported by his wife? He must have felt humiliated. "I'm sorry, I don't understand this."

The professor pushes his fingertips together in front of his chest. "William does not—how shall I put this—well, he doesn't have the necessary social skills. Social duties are an important part of a pastor's job. Your husband is—well, a little too—unusual."

"He's worked so hard to get here. He's just been tired lately, worn down, when he gets some rest I'm sure he'll—"

"I'm sorry if this is upsetting, Mrs. Copeland. Perhaps we sensed whatever trouble has necessitated the state hospital. It's odd how he talks about the Civil War as though it happened yesterday."

"He's just in the hospital for a short time." *This can't be happening.* "He wants to be a minister so badly. It has to do with his wartime service—he's a decorated veteran. I think he needs to—well, make up for what he had to do in the war."

The administrator's phone rings; he tells me he has a meeting to attend and stands up. "Do give William our regards. When he's up to it, perhaps his classmates can visit. The seminary maintains a certain ministry over there."

I shake his hand, ask, "When was William told he couldn't be ordained?"

"Very recently, actually. I believe it was last Friday."

Friday. The day the world blew up.

On the way home, you ask me to sing a Christmas song. I say I can't right now, that I'm not sure I know any songs anymore.

I do, however, have an insistent racket in my head—

> *If a man believed he'd sinned terribly,*
> *God said do not kill and he did,*
> *upon orders of his government wouldn't change it*
> *and he needed to atone, needed to make—restitution.*
> *He'll preach Thou Shalt Not Kill*
> *And then he's told he can't,*
> *What then?*

You're looking out at Christmas decorations, humming "Rudolph."

"Stop singing, Lyra. This isn't the time for Christmas songs."

Your severed voice hangs in the air as you regard me with a shocked look on your face. Your bright eyes grow dull, as though receding into their sockets. I feel like I've slapped you and narrowly miss hitting a curb. I slow down but can't look at you.

"I'm sorry, sweetie. Come on, sing some more."

You gaze out the window and say you wish it would snow.

Chapter Twelve

Christmas was awful. How dare the world be joyous? Even before your father was committed, Rosa had hung strings of red lights (what else?) along her roofline and balcony and porch railings, plastic swizzle sticks hanging from them like icicles. Some evenings Uta stood outside and frowned at the scarlet spectacle—she said she'd given some thought to arson. As cooler air invaded, Rosa paraded around in a black coat with a fox-fur head. One Saturday before your father's breakdown, we ran into her in Mrs. Flo's store and she called, "Hey Louise. Hey Miss Lyrey, how are you, babe?" After you said you were pretty all right, Rosa added, "You come over sometime and I'll show you my Christmas statues—got Santas and Marys to beat the band, I've been collecting 'em for years. It's a wonderful time, Christmas." She unhooked her fox's mouth from its tail, wagged it at you and growled.

In the days after William's commitment, though, Rosa and Uta both brought us food or some toy for you or a piece of fabric that might make a nice dress for me. Uta urged me to come play the piano, but I always said no. She asked what I had planned for Christmas but I had no plans, I'd have to call my brothers and cancel soon. Uta said, well then, she'd be expecting the two of us for Christmas dinner and we'd be having Yorkshire pudding, which you were positive was custard. I told Uta I'd "have to see." Truth was, I couldn't even imagine Christmas.

174

Another day Uta came over brandishing a pair of scissors. She headed for the kitchen, took a dishtowel and wrapped it around her shoulders, and sat down.

"I'm ready. Louise, I want you to cut off these foolish ringlets."

"What?"

"You heard me."

"Are you sure you want to do that? You need a beautician."

"I want *you* to cut my hair. This is special, letting go of this old fashion. One's hair is magical—think about it, when you cut a lock from the dead it'll last your lifetime, you can keep a live part of the person you love. How I wish I had a lock of Mackie's hair. Now come on, let's get to it."

"I don't know how to cut hair."

"My dear, aren't you doing a lot of things you don't know how to do?" She looked at you, said why didn't you go in the living room and color in the Christmas book she'd brought you. After you left, she asked, "How are you managing?"

"I can't talk about this, Mrs. Moazen. I'll just break down."

She regarded me soberly—her black eyes bright. "So cut my hair, dear. I might have a ball to go to."

While I haltingly snipped here and there, she said, "You know that tour they give of the capitol building? I'm fond of our state seal—that part where the woman is walking over swords and daggers." Uta got up to look in the mirror, turned back. "Let's have a little more off." She sat down again. "At the bottom it says *Dum Spiro Spero*."

"'While I breathe, I hope.' I took my honors class on the tour."

"Far superior to 'May the Wind Be Always at Your Back,'" Uta said. "Seeing as how an Irish wind can blow you on your behind no matter where it's coming from."

I laughed. It felt like many years since I had, and I went on trimming the old woman's wispy white hair, and you came in to watch the long strands fall onto the floor and asked Uta could you tie it up into balls and use it as snowballs on the Christmas tree we didn't have yet, and Uta said that was an excellent idea, hair was magical all right, she'd known hers would come in handy some day, and I wondered if maybe that was inappropriate and

Uta said it was her hair and she was making you a present of it. You began rolling her hair into snowballs, adding scotch tape to hold the hair in place, and the three of us found ourselves laughing, though I grew silent once and listened to the sounds of laughter, thought of the carousel that used to be where Uta's house was—or so she claimed—how lovely laughing women and handsome men must have ridden on it, this would have been the same years that my mother was a young painter, and did my mother ever ride a carousel, if so maybe she'd have painted one, and then I remembered the painting that always puzzled me, the one canvas that was not dark and heavy—though the animal portraits weren't either—but this seascape had incredible yellow light against a cliff over water, and suddenly I could see that yellow light, it hung in the air over you and Uta *dum spiro spero*-ing for all it was worth, and I reached over your head to put my hand into that light and for a fleeting moment the world was itself again.

∾∾∾

On the sixth day after William was admitted to the hospital, I was called in for a conference with the social worker and Dr. Dumaine.

"I wanted to see you," Alicia Ravenel said to me, "because the staff psychiatrist has recommended electric shock for William."

I slumped down in my chair.

Dr. Dumaine asked how I was "holding up" and then said, "I saw William this morning. The thorazine calms him down but only with very large doses. Too much can cause involuntary muscle movements. Which can be permanent. We need to try something else."

My voice quavered. "But isn't electric shock dangerous?"

"It's quite safe these days," Dr. Dumaine said. "And often it does correct whatever's awry. He's to have unilateral shock—only on one side of the brain, that produces less memory loss. I wouldn't advise this if I thought it would harm William."

Alicia Ravenel added, "He'll be sedated. Right afterward he'll be a little confused, a few patients cry, he'll have a headache. He might have trouble sleeping."

"But what's *wrong* with him?" I was nearly shrieking. I lowered my voice. "The day of the breakdown he got bad news about his career. Did that cause this? Was it the war?"

"Either might be a factor," Dr. Dumaine said. "For a lot of men, their youth, and the idealism that often protects the young, ended abruptly on the battlefields. Mental illness can lie dormant for years until something unleashes it, and wartime horrors could certainly do that. Some soldiers have more severe reactions to combat than others. Those men might have had severe reactions to other things that no one noticed. A mental problem might be made worse by war, or some other stressful experience, but might not be caused by it."

"I thought of something," I said. "William won a medal at the Battle of the Bulge. That battle was in December. He's never told me exactly what he did to win the medal."

Dr. Dumaine thought for a minute. "How long have you been married?"

"Seven years. We got married while William was in college on the GI Bill."

"The euphoria of courtship might have kept William's illness at bay—everyone's at their best when falling in love. After that brutal war, when he saw so much death and destruction, he found a woman he loved and probably thought—things will be all right. But a marriage settles down and you have children and a bit of the luster wears off. That leaves you open to more influences. Wartime trauma sometimes has delayed reactions."

I hate that awful war, I thought. Wasn't it enough that it killed two cousins and turned my oldest brother into an angry stranger too fond of the bottle? It killed William's brother and a decade later it's trying to kill him too? Haven't we paid our fair share?

"Does it ever end?" I asked. "Does what war does to people ever end?" *What might we have been without it?*

Dr. Dumaine put a hand on my shoulder. I wanted to lean against him and cry my heart out. "There's no way of knowing for certain what's caused William's breakdown," he said gently. "And there's no reason to think he won't recover. But we need to stabilize him."

❧⊙❧

Because of the shock treatment, I couldn't see William until Christmas Day. Until then, I distracted us by making fabric animal Christmas ornaments to give to neighbors and friends. As I sewed I reminisced about "the old Christmases" in Brantley, the twenty people around two tables. Giving only vague reasons, I had cancelled this year's holiday reunion. As Christmas got closer, Lincoln Street looked as though it'd drifted Up North, what with everyone trying to make the subtropics look like fir trees and frozen ponds. Uta installed what she called "a solstice altar" on her porch, a pine tree sprayed with artificial snow, with various trinkets and photographs of Uta's ancestors underneath, including a silver-framed portrait of a five-year-old girl. Mattie Sweete made cookies every day and set them on her steps for anyone who happened by. In Rosa's front yard stood a six-foot Santa that a "client" who ran a garage had made by fusing melted tires into a figure and then painting it. The tread was still noticeable—Santa looked like he'd been run over. Eventually I got out our decorations and unwrapped the metal bells and tinkled one in your ear, reminded you that when you were a baby you'd lie under the tree and swat at the bells. You giggled—at the wise age of six—over the idea. How sweet that sound was, my child laughing. I took out the wooden crèche and set it up on the mahogany inlay table under the front window—I was proud of that table, I got it by saving Green Stamps for four years. But often I'd find myself in the bathroom crying. Later I'd reappear and say we should play a game, or maybe I'd read to you. I read you *A Child's Christmas in Wales,* going to great lengths to explain where Wales was, and read "The Night Before Christmas" twice, rather desperately.

Our Christmas had one saving grace, which wasn't our Christmas morning in Uta's stone house or her Yorkshire pudding, which you pointed out was definitely not custard. The saving grace started with Rosa, who had a Christmas Day drop-in. To your surprise, I—who never visited Rosa—marched you across the street. Rosa came to the door, music and laughter wafting behind her, a tall glass in her hand, and said, "Louise, I am so glad to see you. Merry Christmas. You and that gorgeous child come right in here." I didn't even flinch at Rosa's tight red pants and low-cut white blouse—"I'm a red velvet cake," she explained cheerily, herding us into her living room. From her record player issued Elvis Presley's "Blue Christmas." Maybe it was Elvis' lonesome lament, maybe it was the bathtub-bourbon eggnog, maybe it was the mix of neighbors and "clients," and definitely it was the absence of your father that made me put my coat on in fifteen minutes. As we were leaving, Rosa pulled me into her kitchen (painted purple) to ask me for a recipe; she shuffled around in an index box containing as many phone numbers as recipes.

Abruptly she turned around. "You did the right thing. Nobody may say so, but you did. It ain't easy being the one what's gotta go it alone. Ain't easy doing what everybody's got a big fat opinion about, even when they don't know the half of what's up. I should know."

It took me a moment to respond. "Thank you, Rosa."

I collected you, and Rosa walked us to her front porch and for some reason came across the street with us. She—bright-eyed and coatless—said she'd love to come in—I hadn't asked because I was tired and wanted to be alone. I heard a noise in the dining room and for a moment I thought *William is home,* but of course he wasn't, William was locked up in the state mental hospital, that's where William was. Rosa said she needed a glass of water and she and I walked into the dining room. There, to my surprise, stood Uta, and behind her—*there was our dining-room table.*

"It came back," you whispered.

Uta smiled. "Merry Christmas, Louise. Faherty is no match for two women."

My hand flew to my mouth and I said, "Oh my, oh my," and then burst into tears.

Rosa marched over and ran her hand across the smooth oak surface. "It was right much fun to explain to sneaky Faherty about my friend the chief of *po*-lice, and my fellas were good sports to move it during the party."

I said over and over again that it was the nicest gift in the world, I'd missed the table so much and it was just the most wonderful thing, especially this Christmas, and soon I was going to fix a huge meal and they were all going to come to supper—

When they left, while you played with your new toys—you loved the little desk that opened and had a drawer underneath for your colored pencils—I polished the table over and over and over again. I called you and grabbed you up and danced you around it. *No matter what, there's still this wonderful child and a beautiful table for the future.*

❧⊙❧

Later on Christmas Day, you and I visited your father. I packed a picnic basket for William—a roasted hen with stuffing, green beans cooked in bacon drippings, and a jar of tea. I was nervous and yelled at Fluffy, who got in the way as we were leaving the house. I kept saying things like "Won't it be nice to see Daddy?" As we drove down Lincoln Street and the old houses flew by, I tried to calm down. We passed several children trying out shiny new bikes.

At the hospital gatehouse, I told the scowling guard, clearly disgruntled to be working on Christmas Day, "We're going to Babcock." I gave him William's name.

He checked the book, nodded. "You know that little kid can't go in, don't you?"

You glared at the man with the crew cut and called across me, "Hey mister, your head got run over by a lawnmower."

The guard said you had a mean mouth on you and I apologized profusely, explained to you what "impertinence" was. How could you be so rude on Christmas Day? Then my voice softened. "I know it hasn't been easy, sweetie. We'll have a tea party at our new table tonight."

I pointed out the Mills Building as we drove along. You stared at the patients in bathrobes, some with coats thrown over their pajamas, walking back and forth across the lawn or sitting on park benches. You said they looked asleep, or real tired. That they all looked sorta lazy, like they didn't have anywhere to go.

"Johnny says some people locked up on Bull Street who're walking around are really dead."

"That's an unkind thing to say. Johnny shouldn't make up such stories.

These are people who've been sick. Lots of people have had—nervous breakdowns." Though I knew no one who had besides William.

I braked at Babcock and you stared at the massive brick building. Endless barred windows. "Johnny says my daddy's in jail."

Isn't it bad enough without the meanness of children?

"This is a hospital," I snapped. "Come on, honey, let's go see your daddy. He's going to stand at the window and wave to you."

I gave you the everything-will-be-fine smile—by now I could patent it. I looked at my watch, took your hand, and we walked closer to the building. "Look up, Daddy's in that window on the fourth floor. Count eight windows from the end of the building. He's waving at you."

"That's a little midget like at the State Fair. My daddy's big."

"That's because he's so far away. See him? Wave to your daddy."

You really didn't see your father in that barred window, did you? Didn't realize it was him. But you waved. Probably to make me happy. I looked at you hopefully, put you back in the car, and went in the building.

Babcock had two rows of rooms divided by a corridor on each ward, a nineteenth-century asylum design that allowed too little ventilation in our humid climate. I was shocked to see empty beds running like a train down one side of the hall: did some patients have to sleep here? I passed dozens of aimlessly wandering men in dirty bathrobes. I tried not to notice the cockroaches and filthy floors, tried not to notice the smell of dirty clothes, bedpans, mildew. Tried not to notice the man, unshaven and unkempt, who yelled that he'd give me fifty dollars if I'd take him home. Tried not to notice a white-uniformed attendant—thankfully they weren't called "keepers" anymore—shoving a red-faced, screaming patient down the hall. As I passed tiny rooms left and right, someone was shouting inside one, someone else was crying. Another man, pacing the hall terribly fast, stopped when he saw me and hissed, "Get out of here while you can." I shrank back, clutched the picnic basket, and hurried on.

I turned, with relief, into William's room. He was stretched out on his bed, wearing his standard white shirt, khaki pants, leather bedroom slippers.

"Merry Christmas, darling," I called, my voice unnaturally high, straining too hard for cheerfulness. William stared at me as I set the basket down. I embraced him and kissed him on the cheek. "I'm so happy to finally see you. We miss you so much."

He did not respond to my touch but said hello, regarding me warily as I set out his dinner. "I didn't make a turkey this year," I said, "just a roast chicken. I'll make a big turkey next year when we're all together."

I gazed around the room—just enough space for a single bed and a wooden desk and chair. Gone were the Dorothy Dix days when someone would have put pictures on the walls. A metal portable closet, paint peeling, held William's clothes. On his desk, some books and writing paper. The walls were a dirty green, the ceiling light bulb swinging naked, and his window—he was lucky he had a large window—had two cracked panes and one missing. Beyond the glass was a network of rusted iron bars placed so close together not even a hand could get through them.

William sat at the desk to eat. He murmured something about the dinner being good but other than that he was quiet and didn't look at me as I told him about our day, omitting the table. He stared out of the window often—it was a warmish December day and the room was stuffy. I said maybe I could bring him a fan but he said they weren't allowed, some patients might try to cut themselves with the blades. I fell silent, then I asked if he'd been going to the dayroom to listen to the radio. They had a television there, didn't they? I'd seen one in a store downtown and they were amazing, people said that sooner or later everyone in the country would have one. I couldn't imagine how, they cost $1,300, who could afford that? I asked if he'd gone to the Christmas Eve church service—I'd heard the chapel here was lovely—and he said no, he didn't feel like it. I asked if he'd seen the doctor this week and he said he thought so. I asked if he needed anything and he said some cigarettes. I said surely there was something else, but he said no, he didn't need a thing.

He hadn't looked at me at all. "Remember our first Christmas in Summerville?" I said. "That wonderful silk dress you gave me, I still love it. I let it out and wore it to Christmas dinner at Mrs. Moazen's house."

"What silk dress?"

"You know, the year we had Christmas dinner with those people from the academy."

He looked blank. I thought, *He doesn't remember. The shock treatments?*

Outside the window the chapel bells began ringing. I waited for him to say something about them, but he didn't. I asked how the hospital food was; he said it wasn't very good. No word differed from any other in tone, none carried inflection, the signature of personality. The speech of someone who was very far away. He was calm, all right. So calm maybe I should check his pulse.

I talked about how much Lyra missed her daddy, assured William that everything at home was fine, that I'd paid the bills on time. I'd get the car oil changed after New Year's. Did he want me to go check on the farm? "I could clean the cemetery down there if you like."

"What cemetery are you talking about?"

"On the farm. Your family's farm."

He looked perplexed, turned and gazed out the barred window. Did he not remember it? How can he not remember a place he loves so much?

I didn't know what to do so I began cleaning up. I'd leave the iced tea in case he wanted some later. I'd brought a pound cake to leave too. He nodded a vague thanks. I said I'd better go because Lyra was in the car—it'd been a long day for a six-year-old. I went over and laid a hand on William's arm. "We missed you so much today, darling. It wasn't the same. But you're getting better. I can see that. It'll be just a little while. I'll talk to the social worker this week and see when you can come home. You're going to be fine. We love you very very much."

I kissed him. He thanked me for coming and watched as I picked up the basket and opened the door into the hall. I made it to the first floor before I collapsed on a hallway bench near the administrative office and covered my face with my hands. A nurse passed by and asked if I needed help; I smiled wearily and said no. After she left, I leaned back against the cold wall.

How long will he be this way? As though he does not exist?

I closed my eyes and wished I didn't exist anymore. Then the strangest thing happened—in my head I heard the music of my youth, music I didn't want to hear anymore—"I was building a dream," which was banned from the radio when 18 million were jobless, songs of struggle and hopelessness that spoke to what everyone felt then. Songs about being together and surviving. I remembered singing Gershwin's "One of these mornings, you gonna rise up singing," and after a while I felt like maybe I could get up again and go out to that car this Christmas Day and sing to my child. A country had survived. In time we would be all right too. We had to be.

Then I heard the guttural, labored voice of Ethel Waters—when I first heard "Suppertime" on the radio I'd had to sit down—and the pain of that grieving song settled over me, that woman with a broken heart, whose husband has been murdered and won't be coming home that evening or any other. That woman will be eating alone forever. *Will I as well? A table but no family?*

It took me a half hour to drag myself up from that bench.

⟋⟋⟋◯⟍⟍⟍

When I come out of Babcock and rejoin you, I don't say much—I've run out of energy to try to fool us both. After the drive home, you play with your new toys. I turn on the radio's Christmas carols and then turn them off, finally settle down in the living room with a novel. After a while we both go to bed—I've been having you sleep with me since William was committed.

I lie awake a long time. *How could this happen to us?*

A few hours later I wake to you screaming. You're under the blankets shaking, crying, "Go away, go away."

I pull you out and take you into my arms. "Sweetheart, you're dreaming."

Half-crying, clearly terrified, you babble—"There's somebody in the corner, a man, but he's little, he's not right, not like he's supposed to be. He's littler than Mr. Max who died, he's staring at me, he's mad cause he's all little. It's *Daddy*."

"Lyra, it was just a dream."

"Why is he so *little*? He looks all hurt and mad 'cause he's locked up, and he's coming to get me."

"Sweetie, no. Your daddy's not there."

"Yes he is!" You pull away from me and scramble under the covers again. "The little man, my daddy's got blood on him."

❦❦❦

I didn't realize that taking you to see William locked up behind bars was a terrible decision. I didn't realize it until you began having that nightmare, which you had for years. Perhaps I didn't realize it because I was still in shock myself.

Sometimes a shock—lightning hitting a chimney, or war, or the loss of a dream—damages the foundation of a house forever. Despite the decades of change, I've never been able to enter the present world where mental illness shows up in everyday parlance. During these years that I've not talked about what happened to us, I've sometimes given money to people on street corners who're obviously ill. Other times I've hurried away from them as fast as I could.

I've had a nightmare from those days all my life too. In it, I've gone somewhere and when I come back, our house has disappeared. I'm homeless.

I can still see him on the front porch. Definitely not a dream. The Lincoln Street landlord who wouldn't let you have a dog. I don't remember when he came. Big leering man, cheap shiny suit—I never liked him—puffing his cigar smoke in my face.

"Mrs. Copeland, see here—this is a fact—decent people can't live where there's a deranged man. Lots of folks saw your husband running up and down the street half naked. People are afraid he'll come back and do even worse."

I was too exhausted to point out that anyone locked up in the state hospital wasn't likely to go anywhere anytime soon.

"Y'all been good tenants but people are scared of you now. Neighbors want you to move and I have to keep in good with them. I don't know as I can afford to let you stay."

"Please," I begged. "We can't move right now, we just can't."

"I'm sorry, but you got kin in that place it makes folks nervous and they cain't sleep at night." More smoke in my face. "Having tenants like y'all are now, well, that means I'm taking a big risk. Could cost me."

Finally I comprehended the opportunistic gleam in his narrow eyes. I wanted to scream that he was a coarse, unprincipled oaf. Instead, I asked him to wait, and as though sleepwalking, I went back to the dining room and crossed to the oak sideboard. I leaned over it for a moment, steeling myself. I didn't have anything else. I took out the rectangular box of my mother's silver.

Chapter Thirteen

Sometimes in this hospital I imagine I hear bells ringing. I suppose that's a holdover from your father's obsession with them. Or from my childhood when each farm in the country had its own bell with a distinctive tone, so that if one rang in the middle of the night neighbors would know which family needed help. I even read once that in an American foundry in 1953, a large bell was cast from the metal restraints used in US mental hospitals. Craftsmen threw iron handcuffs, steel leg irons, heavy lead chains with neck rings into a large square oven. *Chink-chink* of steel and iron hitting the oven's sides, then the gurgle of metal bubbling at nine hundred degrees. This bell, when rung, would symbolize hope for the mentally ill. The music of survival, as it were.

I've often wondered what happened to that bell, but I've never tried to find out. The fact is, given its limited diatonic scale and the difficulty of accurate tuning, a bell is not really a musical instrument at all.

I still think about it sometimes—what happened to William in the state hospital, how bad was it? I was terrified for him of course, partially because the lobotomy had just come into vogue—thousands were performed in the 1950s, proponents calling it a "merciful euthanasia of the mind." It didn't seem "merciful" in Tennessee Williams' play about it. Electric-shock treatment was also fairly new and at that time equally primitive; I'm glad I didn't know then that it was discovered when butchers applied electrically wired pincers to a pig's head, convulsions and subsequent coma enabling them to cut the animal's throat more easily. Not a reassuring genesis for a medical treatment administered to someone you love. Not too long after your father's breakdown, a famous writer would shoot himself because he believed shocks given him for depression had destroyed his memory, thus his creative source.

No bells tolled for Mr. Hemingway.

Along with new drugs that caused a condition similar to Parkinson's, fever therapy and histamine treatment were common when William was in the state hospital, as were injections of ether and malaria. It's hard to imagine that a doctor would deliberately raise a patient's body temperature to 106 degrees or try to infect him with a dangerous illness. Patients were regularly forced into tubs of freezing water, but there was no talk therapy. Did anyone ever say a kind word to William? I've no idea. But after being shocked, after he stopped trying to tear off his leather restraints with his teeth—Dr. Dumaine told me this much later—pretty much all your father did was lie there and stare. No doctor came to his room now because he was quiet. The bells of the hospital church—the Chapel of Hope—told him when one day ended and the next began. Sundays were when his wife came. An attendant shaved him every other day. Every two or three days, a nurse came by and asked how he was. He always said he was fine.

The New Year arrived with an unusually cold winter stuck to its heels. No more snow fell on Columbia, nor even in the Up Country foothills, yet the air crackled, the ground crunched, chapped lips blistered, the reddened hands of those who didn't have proper gloves burned. Car batteries died and children stayed indoors even at school recess. A severe ice storm blew in and left us without electricity for five days. The city closed down. Everything simply *stopped*. A state I already knew well. A pecan tree in the backyard lost two large branches, and the blue hydrangeas seemed unlikely to survive. Rosa gave up her low-cut blouses for bulky warm sweaters, and Uta said she wasn't coming out of her house until April. Eight people died in car accidents caused by black ice. Snow is gentle, but ice is sharp edges; its lacy beauty is cold and deadly.

The oil stoves huffed and puffed and during the days without electricity I was thankful for them. But their ugliness depressed me, so when the ice storm ended I asked Melvin Sweete to move the living-room stove into the garage. That fireplace was reopened and soon there was a wood fire. You clapped your hands and I smiled for the first time in weeks. Every night we lazed in firelight, you drawing the fire, me grading papers. Often I'd simply watch you—you were my reason to get up every morning. One evening I put my papers aside and sat beside you on the floor. You leaned against me and I put my arm around you. I closed my eyes and imagined your father and me sitting on the couch watching our children play together on this warm hearth.

A local man delivered a supply of firewood, and many mornings before school I carried in aromatic cedar logs and laid them on the hearth so they'd be there when I got home. Creating something that made our lives warmer and brighter helped me. Isn't this what women always do? In bad times we get up and fix *something*. I pictured my father and grandfather and brothers carrying logs into the house in Brantley. Marooned now from that family—for I'd still not told them the truth about William's illness—it was strangely comforting to carry wood and stir embers.

I know I acted as though your father had simply gone on a trip. Others didn't ignore the truth. One afternoon I heard Johnny Truesdale taunting you: "Your old man is down in the loony bin chained to a pole drooling and pissing on himself."

You hit Johnny upside the head and got to stay in your room for an entire Saturday afternoon as a result, even though Rosa said, "Kids will be kids," and Johnny wasn't really hurt and he shouldn't have been so mean. You said two girls at school asked you, giggling, if you were gonna go live in the nuthouse too. There were whispers at my school as well. Fellow teachers who were suddenly nicer to me or looked away when I came down the hall. Although no one mentioned William, I avoided the teacher's lounge: who knew and who didn't? The neighborhood was no better. As I was leaving Mrs. Flo's store one afternoon, I heard a woman say to another, "I think that's the lady who stuck her husband down on Bull Street. Not that I wouldn't like to get rid of mine from time to time, but no decent woman does that." Children still pointed at the house and sniggered. The milkman wouldn't meet my eyes. One morning I found a note on the front door: "WHY DON'T ALL OF YOU GO TO THE CRAZY HOUSE? This is a decent neighborhood. GET OUT."

I appreciated anew what black people had endured for generations.

Often I felt as though my husband had died. But there was no way to grieve—I'd become a widow in secret. I visited your father every weekend and often on Wednesdays during my free period. I'd put on an optimistic face—which used to be so natural—as I walked to Bull Street, wondering if anyone I knew would see me entering the grounds. My shame covered a continent. At least William wasn't blaming me. He never said much during my visits except to ask about the car or bills; he did remember the farm now. But the flatness in his voice remained, and my optimistic mask always fell off as I walked home. I'd look down at the sidewalk and there would be the face I used to have.

Uta made us go to the movies once a month, which suited you just fine though I protested that I should stay home and do my housework. One afternoon Uta kept you and sent me out to "breathe without care for a few hours." I went downtown but couldn't get interested in store windows, so I went to a see a new picture—Joan Crawford's *Autumn Leaves*, having no idea it was about a woman who commits her deranged husband to a mental hospital. I almost got up and walked out. Joan is also married to a younger man who has electric shock; I averted my eyes when the doctor put electrodes to Cliff Robertson's head. But what relief at the movie's end—after he's released, he's well and the couple lives happily ever after.

Once in a while I went to Uta's house to play the piano, hoping music would soothe me. Occasionally it did. I let you visit at Johnny's house now, and Rosa volunteered two "men friends" to clean up the debris in our yard after the ice storm. I watched from a window as they sawed up what was left of the dogwood tree. Once a month I met with William's social worker; once a month I asked when he could come home. Once a month the social worker said the staff doctor felt William was too listless and depressed. Perhaps he'd be allowed a trial visit later. He'd started going to the library, which was a good sign. Now he also walked over to the canteen every afternoon. He was improving, was more alert. It was just a matter of time.

During Laidlaw's second semester, I prepared my classes for the following year's integration. I played the *South Pacific* soundtrack, had them dissect the song "You've Got to be Carefully Taught." I waxed at length on *Porgy and Bess*, explaining that a white South Carolinian was the first novelist to portray blacks positively, but half the room never got beyond Porgy's plan to travel from Charleston to New York in a goat cart. I found myself faltering as I spoke of believing in a dream, however impossible. On my way home that day I stopped by my fellow teacher Clarice's house, which I did frequently now. She invariably asked, "How are you *really?*" But I never talked about William. "I'll just break down," I always said. I was truly afraid I would.

It got worse.

One Saturday morning someone knocks on the door. I don a sweater and find a man in his early twenties on the porch. Tousled black hair, somber brown eyes. He's holding a paper bag and introduces himself as Jack McHenry, William's seminary classmate.

I shake his hand, invite him in out of the cold.

"Thank you, but I can't. I've got a heap of studying to do today." He nods at the bag. "These are William's books. We had a lot of the same classes. I cleaned out his locker. I hope he's going to be all right."

"Oh, he'll be fine. He'll be back at those books in no time."

"He plans to reapply?"

I pull my sweater around me. "He'll be back by next semester."

"He's reapplied and they've accepted him?" When I look confused, Jack McHenry hesitates. "Oh no—you haven't got the letter, have you?"

"What letter?"

"I thought surely—I hate to be the one. I'm really sorry. I thought you knew." He looks away. "You should call Dr. Estes."

"Why? I don't understand."

"I'm sorry, Mrs. Copeland, but William's been expelled."

I gape at him. "I went over there before Christmas and explained, and Dr. Estes said he could come back."

Jack McHenry shifts from one foot to the other. "I'm so sorry. The scuttlebutt, nobody's saying this directly or course, is that it's because of the state hospital."

I shrink back against the front door, hands shaking. "But he'll be fine in no time," I insist loudly. "Dr. Estes said William could come back next semester."

"Either he didn't tell you the truth, or he changed his mind. William's a smart man but unusual—he hardly ever says anything in class but when he does it can be so original it confounds the professors. Made it easier that he hadn't been coming to class lately. Rumor is that when the administration made him change programs, they discouraged him from continuing at all."

I drop into a webbed lawn chair on the porch, gaze at Jack McHenry. "They wanted him to withdraw *before* he got sick?"

"I think everything went wrong after that first chapel service, when he was so nervous. He made Estes mad about something too, I don't know what. William got a raw deal—a lot of us think so. Please tell him hello. Maybe I could stop by and see him sometime."

I gaze at the bag of books, a rectangular monument on the gray painted floorboards. Mechanically I stand up and thank Jack McHenry for coming by. Voice trembling, I ask if he wants some coffee before he goes, and he says no, asks me again to remember him to William. He turns and walks toward the bus stop.

∾∾۞∾

When I come back in the house, I ask you to go outside and play, and you say you don't know anything to play, and I yell—"Go out and play, Lyra.

Now." You look frightened as you scurry out the back door. Your coat is still on a kitchen chair, and I carry it outside, hand it to you and say that I'm very tired and need to rest. You pull on your coat but don't button it and I don't care. I feel you watching me as I plod back up the steps. Even when it gets dark, I don't come look for you, don't call you in.

Cold, no doubt frightened, you finally come back into the house. I haven't turned on any lights. I'm sitting on the side of the bed, staring. I see myself walking across the room, the person I used to be is over there, the room is different too, as though someone has sneaked in and taken everything we own. If I could feel anything, I'd know that our dreams truly are over. The secure life, the house of our own, the garden I'd dreamed of.

You run to my door, stand there shaking. I look up at you but I can't get up, I've run out of courage. Drowning in the river of my own despair, I do not reach for the small figure left on shore. Unforgivably—though I love you more than breath—I leave you there alone.

This river of despair—this year I lost my husband and our dream, this year you lost a father *and* a mother—this river will snake between us for life.

❧⬥❧

The letter came.

I stand at the kitchen table staring at the imprinted return address. At William's name. I've never opened a letter addressed to him: I take all the mail to the hospital and he opens the bills and gives them back to me to pay. I sit down at the table, push the envelope back and forth. It's wrong to open another person's mail. Don't I already know what the letter contains? I leave it on the kitchen table for days, untouched. I go to school, you go to school, I push it aside while we eat supper. It watches me every time I walk into the kitchen. Some days I come in the house and imagine it will have disappeared. But it's always there, mocking me with white rectangular silence.

Sunday comes and I drop you off at the church for Sunday school and drive to the hospital in a slow rain. I check in at the nurses' station and walk down the hall, my Sunday heels clicking against the tile floor. William is lying on his bed wearing his pajamas, a half-opened book beside him. I smile brightly, kiss him, say I'm happy to see him, and put down the basket of food—fried chicken, lima beans, a corn casserole. He sits up straighter, thanks me, asks what the weather's like outside.

"Still chilly, raining a little."

He asks if the oil bill has come. I say no. The seminary letter is in my purse. I take a deep breath. *Go on, give it to him. Get it over with.*

I go to his closet for his dirty clothes, ask what he's been doing. The hospital library is a pretty good one, he says, though very disorganized. I say it's wonderful he's been reading so much and launch into a story about a student who's having trouble reading. How lucky we are to have had good educations.

William looks toward the window while I talk, as though studying the bars. I fall silent, don't finish my story. "Darling, something's come up." I sit down in the one chair. "It may be—well, it's—"

There's a scream in the hallway, the sound of rushing feet.

William says, "There's a fella who starts screaming the same time every day. They probably don't give him his medication on time. One day they beat him up to keep him quiet."

The bells from the chapel toll in the distance, one two three four, and on until eleven. William says, "I went over there the other day to see what the chapel looked like, and as I was coming out the door a car stopped along the sidewalk and this big woman leaned out her window and asked me, 'Where do they keep the patients?'"

William laughs: harsh, shrill, mirthless. "I asked her did she want the really crazy ones or the ones only half crazy?" He laughs again. "I told her she'd better be careful because we're all over the place."

I walk over to the window. Stare down at the magnolias slicked with rain. "I wonder what we'd be doing if we hadn't moved to Columbia."

"For starters, nobody would have put me in this place."

It's the first time he's mentioned the commitment. I've been waiting for his anger. I bite my lip, taste blood as I say, "Darling, I'd have given anything if it'd been me. You were ill, all the doctors said you needed to be where you could get better. If only there'd been room at the VA hospital. We thought a room would be available by now."

I wait for him to blow up. He looks away, asks if I'm going to church today.

We might as well face the whole thing. I reach down and click open my purse. "You're going to be released soon and we're going to get our lives back like they were." *Or as close as we can.*

"I imagine the seminary is wondering when I'll be back."

My heart jumps. "If anyone should understand a—a crisis like this, it should be a Christian seminary." *Why did I say that?*

I snap my purse closed and kiss William on the cheek. "I need to pick up Lyra. I love you, darling. We miss you terribly. But you'll be home soon."

Speeding out of the room, I stop and lean against the wall to catch my breath and calm down. I start back down the hallway, pass awkwardly shuffling men (too much thorazine); another man is sitting on the floor rocking back and forth and cursing the blank wall. Ahead are two attendants in white uniforms. Sometimes I notice a contemptuous look in their eyes. I stop the unkempt attendant with greasy brown hair and ask if he cares for the patient in room 3219. When he nods, I cry desperately, "That man is a decorated war hero, he's studying to be a minister."

"Is that a fact, lady? I bet he's met the Queen of England too."

He laughs and heads down the hall.

I will my legs to move. I pass the nurses' station, walk through Babcock's front door; from the portico, I stare down the main drive toward rain-slicked Elmwood Avenue. I can see the square outline of Laidlaw, the turnoff to Lincoln Street, even the shadow of Logan Grammar and Elmwood Cemetery, and beyond them that open and inviting ramp to the interstate highway. Then my eyes narrow and all I can see is the hospital's ten-foot brick wall.

The winter dragged on. Many alone hours of firelight for your mother during those days, after you'd gone to bed. Flames leaping as though to escape the slow blue burn beneath them. Strong oak logs gone to ash in a half hour.

Firelight. Warms or destroys. A painting of a forest fire—what made my mother paint such a thing? Made her want to portray desolation? Firelight. Flames. Gives light, erases gloom, kills. Fire in the brain, mania. Possessed by fire. Fire in the brain. Fired up. Set on fire. Lightning bolt hit the house, could have caused fire. Should I have realized then? Lightning bolt, electric volt. Fight the fire in the brain with electric fire. Lightning bolt, doomed house. Electric volt, doomed memory.

Firelight. Fire painting. Fire in the brain.

Firelight making soft shadows and shapes, the room softer, warmer. The light made me feel better and sometimes I could barely stand to look at it.

Spring came slowly, dragged its warm and soggy body onto Lincoln Street in late March. When the rains ceased, the red camellias—always the first-comers—bloomed in Max's garden and along our front sidewalk, soon the jonquils too. Heartbreaking colors stole into the neighborhood overnight. The grass turned new green, was so light-filled the yard looked happy. Birds woke everyone at six a.m. Children played outside again. Rosa put all her rugs on her front banister and beat them with a broom. Uta, in her new short hairdo, began volunteering at a children's hospital. Unlike them, I was not made lighter by the new season; despite the warmer temperatures, I kept having fires in the living room, sitting beside the hearth to read. It was too warm, and damp air often forced smoke back into the room. Finally, fearful of black furnishings again, I cleaned out the fireplace and read in your father's chair by the living-room window. Outside, the world turned a shade brighter every day and eventually I smiled a little more, or suggested we go downtown and look in store windows and get a hamburger and a Coke.

Over the past months I'd learned how to take care of us—I knew the men at the auto garage, knew how much the light bill should be, knew how to mend a screen door. But somehow that didn't translate into more confidence. Either I didn't have the self-confidence gene or I'd used it up chasing your father before we were married. Or it was destroyed by that mental hospital. I wished I were as bold as Rosa or as no-nonsense as Uta. If so, and I thought of doing this many times, I'd march over to that seminary, that *Christian* seminary, and give them a piece of my mind. I'd make a scene, embarrass the people who threw William out on the street like old furniture. But it wasn't in my character to do that. Instead, from that year on, I focused myself on turning you into someone who could be bold. It was shortsighted of a teacher not to realize that example is also instruction, though I think you've managed fine—you haven't shied away from giving me a piece of your mind from time to time.

You now knew, from overhearing me mumbling in my sleep, that your father had been, as you put it, "electrifried." I endeavored to put this into a better context but there was simply no way to. I told you that difficult things can happen in life, it was best not to discuss Daddy's illness with anyone. That if anyone mentioned it, or said anything unkind, you should hold your ground and say that your father was simply ill and that it wasn't nice to talk about sick people behind their back. Sometimes when I felt sad, I hugged you so hard you said it hurt. "You're everything in the world to me," I'd say. When I looked more lost than usual, you'd draw something to show me or ask me to sing, though often my songs were sad—I favored a hymn that ended with "There's no sorrow on earth that heaven cannot heal." Other times I'd sing "Songs My Mother Taught Me" or "Only God Can Make a Tree," or belt out happy tunes from my college days, but they always sounded hollow. One day, after you'd read the novel in a classic comic book, you said, disturbingly, that we were now "Robinson Crusoe people."

One day when I couldn't stand the crushing weight of helplessness another minute, I stopped by Ed Hindeman's office and said, "Ed, give me something you need done. Anything. Something I can help out with."

He looked at me soberly and I thought—*Maybe he doesn't want anyone with mental illness in the family to be too visible at school.*

Then he smiled. "Louise, do sit down. I've got tons for you to do."

Spring passed and early summer arrived and the school year ended on an upbeat note. I'd arranged to have the Laidlaw art teacher give you private lessons; I paid for them by giving her daughter voice lessons. For six weeks, while the music teacher was on maternity leave, I directed the school choir. I organized faculty and student discussion groups about desegregation; the school board asked me to organize them at other city schools. But no matter what I tried, what good came about, I felt remote and removed. As if I didn't quite exist.

Your father remained in the hospital, though he could pretty much do as he pleased. Sometimes he seemed his old self, though quieter.

"Your husband is prone to depression," the staff doctor treating William explained in a three-minute conference in June, the only time I ever met with him. "He may still be subject to paranoid delusions. He says rather odd things."

I explained that William had always had an unusual way of expressing himself. The doctor said, "Well, let's wait a month and see where he is then."

⸙⸙◯⸙⸙

A day at the farm helped. With my hair tied up in a scarf, I push the lawnmower around the cemetery's gravestones and feel lighter—maybe because it's summer vacation, having so much time to relax, to play with my precious daughter, who's getting taller and smarter. Yet how sad your seventh birthday seemed without your father. I lean back and wipe perspiration from my face; I never realized mowing was such hard work. When the grass is cut, I plant azalea cuttings along the wrought-iron fence. It's a lovely day, not as hot as usual, a slight breeze wafting through the loblolly pines as they lean against each other and clack like old friends talking. You're down at the ruins, where you go to make up stories. There are always dogs in your stories, never any adults. I think of the bullying, dog-hating landlord and my mother's sterling and swear under my breath.

I walk to the ruins, sit on the broken brick wall to watch you. You look so much like your father, same fair hair and coloring, those startling blue eyes. I think about the day we brought you home from the hospital. William had run off that afternoon to an insurance office but when he returned we bundled you up and drove you home in the Chevy we'd just bought. William was nervous handling you, left most of that to me. You'd been a bit of a surprise for us—which is irrelevant since I had been simply *dying* for you to show up. A surprise also lay in the Summerville living room. A handmade cradle, burnished oak, beautiful. William was beaming with pride.

"My father was right good with a hammer and saw and taught me a thing or two. Seemed like she should sleep in a good strong tree."

Tears filled my eyes that day. Nothing makes a man more appealing than his love for his child.

That *was* love, wasn't it?

As I watch you dig around the ruins with a toy spade, I wish you could remember *that* father. Is William different since the hospital? He's more alert now, more interested in the world. He asks about you occasionally, always asks about the house. Sometimes asks about my weight—have I "fallen off" any? I have, I've been dieting again. However, when I recently told him how much help Uta and Rosa had been, he said I shouldn't "bother" the neighbors; I assured him I never spoke of his illness to anyone.

He never seems upset or worried. He seems—polite.

What happens when I finally tell him about the seminary? When he's stronger, when he comes home—that's when I'll show him the letter. When we can sit down and make new plans.

You're digging with sudden intensity, dirt flying over your shoulder. I call to you, "What are you trying to find?"

"Treasure."

"What kind of treasure?"

"Gold dublins."

"I think you mean *doubloons*."

You stop digging; I watch you skip from one end of the ruins to the other. It's going to be all right. It won't be the *same*. We'll have to turn in a new direction. There are many things William can do. He'd love teaching history, he certainly knows enough about the Civil War. He could run a small business. He could go back to working with forests. I gaze up at the sunlight, feel its warmth on my face.

You run into the pine forest, arms flailing, hands reaching out to touch each tree you pass. William and I are truly blessed—such a sweet child. Independent, fearless. So—*normal.*

No one knows what causes mental problems. Not even the doctors.

What if it does run in families?

Stop thinking that.

"Don't go far," I call out. *Don't go too far away from me.*

Carrying a flowerpot, I trail you into the woods where sunlight sprinkles light-stars between the tall pines. The trees were planted at uniform distances, row after symmetrical row. I love the cozy interior, the maze created by the rows, gossamer filaments of light raining down. But the symmetrical spacing is disorienting—hope I'll be able to find the way out. I scan the ground, find a foot-tall loblolly sapling and dig it up. I'll be able to tell William that the farm is fine, the graveyard clean, and I'll have a young tree from his family's soil to put in his room. Maybe someday we'll plant it in the yard where the dogwood once stood.

I look around for you. "Lyra, it's time to go home."

No answer. I head deeper into the woods. "Lyra—honey—come on."

The forest is still—silent sunlight, silent trees.

"Come on, Lyra. Now."

When there's still no answer, I drop the pot, begin running, call your name over and over again. *Where is she? What if I lost her too?*

"I'm over here."

Relieved, I walk in the direction of your voice, passing through rows of trees into a sudden clearing. You're standing atop a four-foot-high mound of wood chips and sawdust; golden sunlight cascades across it like a mystical, ethereal waterfall. Hacked-off pine branches are scattered below, a striking reality. Someone has chopped down a dozen tall pines, must have dragged in a mulching machine. Poachers. You run down the hill, wood chips flying. I'm still staring at the downed trees, the inert hill of wood pellets, the pall of sawdust. Another kind of ruins. You ask can you take some sticks home and I say you have enough sticks in your own yard. Perhaps you intuit the future—you slip a wood chip into your pocket anyway.

Retrieving the sapling, we return to the car, where I water the tree from a Mason jar. You hold the tree as we ride along, and I say that maybe soon you'll have a brother or sister to play with at the farm. You clap your hands—you want a sibling so much—and upend the sapling, but catch it in time. All three of us make it back to Columbia safely.

Chapter Fourteen

William is coming home!
Some days that was all I could think about.

I stared out the living-room window at the oak trees just hinting of color. *We'll be a family again.* He had improved so much since he'd begun working in the hospital library, cataloging books, annotating the card catalog, spending long hours reading. He wasn't as silent now. The library was more restful than Babcock. What he was reading was a little unnerving—everything he could find about the hospital. When I visited him now, we met in Babcock's visiting area, a long reception hall of ceiling fans, huge arched windows covered with wire grilles, folding chairs set in small groups. William usually leaned against a window— milk glass, which blocked any view outside. The air was always filmy from cigarette smoke: sometimes he seemed ghostly as he stood smoking and talking. One day he told me that Babcock was named for the hospital superintendent who ignored horrible conditions there, when clogged toilets, bedbugs, lice, and dirty bathwater were common. The Columbia hospital had always used more mechanical restraints than other mental institutions, he added.

I suggested we walk over to the canteen.

The sidewalks were crowded—nurses in white, orderlies in blue or white, patients in twos or threes but more often alone. Some with the vacant stare William had had right after shock treatment. Others shuffled along awkwardly, clearly drug-induced woozy.

"Being dazed is better than getting knocked unconscious or strapped to your bed," William said.

Over the past few months he'd "seen a lot." He recited the list of drugs used in the hospital over the years: iron, quinine, alcohol, potassium bromide, chloral hydrate, strychnine, sulphonal, potassium iodide, calomel, opium, morphine, digitalis. Increasingly uncomfortable, I asked how he knew all this. He said the library's disorganization made the hospital records easy prey. Did I know that John C. Calhoun's family incarcerated the famous man's brother here? Around 1838. The man got out okay. Soon afterward, though, one-fourth of the patients had pellagra because the food was so bad. In 1891, one patient murdered another.

Was he telling me this to make me feel guilty? Sometimes, mercifully, he talked of other things. Of going fishing with his father. How his brother, on his first day of running a gas station, accidentally left the pump running all night, dumping the entire week's gas onto the ground. I learned that in her early life his mother had been a milliner, and this tickled me, given that you were always putting something on your head, especially kitchen pots.

When I met with William's social worker about his release, she said he might not recall much about the first days of his breakdown.

"And unless he asks you, I wouldn't bring it up—it's best to let him lead any discussion of his illness. He's had a counseling session about dealing with the outside again; we advise that he never reveal his hospital stay on a job application unless directly asked. Unfortunately, that's the state of the world."

"What can I do to help him?"

"Be patient, don't expect too much at the beginning. Be optimistic, don't bring up problematic subjects, anything likely to elicit internal conflict."

How long, I wondered, can I wait before showing him the seminary letter?

Alicia Ravenel added, "If things don't work out, William can be recalled with just your signature or Dr. Dumaine's."

I begged her not to tell William the hospital could recall him that easily. No matter what happened, I would never send him back.

When you were in your thirties, I realized you believed your father had been "away" for four years. You were certain he'd missed your entire childhood—in a way, that was true. A father who never shows his child affection is pretty much an absent parent. You were shocked to learn he was hospitalized for less than a year.

How long didn't matter. I knew from my own experience what I couldn't say out loud: Childhood loss is a giant, and giants have their own large truth.

William's coming home! Soon!

I'd been scrubbing the floors for days. I'd made new bedroom curtains and bought a television set—I found a cheap one in a store going out of business and, despite your protests, was waiting until William came home to try it out. I talked excitedly about going to the mountains to see the fall leaves. Did you remember the trip to the Smoky Mountains when you were four? You said you didn't, though I believe you did. You were sitting on the living-room floor drawing; your drawings were beginning to look quite professional. I went to my closet and came out with a shoebox of old photos and showed you a picture of yourself and your father in a mountain stream. William was smiling, kneeling beside a younger you wearing a ruffled bathing suit. You stared at the photo impassively.

You left off drawing to help me clean and polish—Uta said our house looked like it had been run through a washing machine. Entertaining you many afternoons while I sewed a new dress for your father's arrival, she regaled you with Irish stories. Your favorite was the legend about the handsome young man who fell in love with a beautiful girl and went with her to her country but got homesick for his own. The girl gave him a white horse for the trip home but told him he had to stay on it, he must not get off. He did anyway, to pick up a stone, and he turned into an ugly old man. He was one thing, then he was another, you explained to me, giving me pause.

Rosa interrupted us, bringing a vase of flowers. She also proffered a small bottle of "love elixir." I blushed and stammered out a thank-you, ignoring your question about what it was for.

After Rosa left, you asked, "When my daddy gets home, will he be old now? Will he be crying again?"

I picked you up. "No, sweetheart. Everything's going to be wonderful now."

A slant of soft titanium light. A long night sighing its contentment, phantom lovers' whispers in the breeze outside the window, old houses and old memories of young women on a carousel, laughing. Midnight. Moonlight. I get up and go to the kitchen for a glass of water, water on the tongue feels cold and sweet. I was dreaming of making love. I walk back into the bedroom in my filmy cotton nightgown with white eyelet embroidery, and stop and gaze at our bed, moonlight filtering through the new dotted swiss curtains, blue like his eyes, aquamarine melted to cobalt by fire. We've not been together in so long, what will it be like? I yearn for the touch that is like dancing, or swimming, the body moving without intent, like singing, running through a field of flowers, that's what love can be. I touch my breast timidly, so full of longing, for William, for another baby, for life to fill me with new history, new hope. Whispers and wind, soft cotton and songs of a new baby, a husband who loves me again, all that blond hair falling into his eyes, slender limbs, the way he would smile in Summerville coming up the sidewalk when I least expected it.

That man will walk in the front door in just a few days. Not the same man, exactly. I'm not the same woman. But we'll get to start over.

I laugh and whirl myself around the bed.

⊸∽⊙⊶⊶

A beautiful Saturday afternoon in October, colored leaves falling outside
the window. I'm wearing my new dress—lustrous emerald green silk,
with a lower neckline than usual. I stare in the mirror on the bedroom
door. Lord, it looks like something Rosa would wear. Well, not really,
Rosa would want it tighter. I have on my favorite piece of jewelry—my
mother's Victorian cameo. I finger it absently as I walk through the house.
I've bought real cream for our coffee and a tin of the special pipe tobacco
William likes. I linger beside the dining-room table, run my hand along
the polished surface. What he'll say about it, I don't know, but we'll have
our first family dinner in here tonight. The whole house smells warm and
inviting from the simmering pot roast. I cross into the living room, regard
the fireplace—I'll show him how I can build a fire and not burn the house
down. If he insists, the oil stove is in the garage. No. By wintertime I'll
make him understand how important a real fire is to me.

What if it happens again?

It won't. He won't ever go back there. It's over.

I walk to Uta's to say good-bye to you. When she opens the door, she
says, "My, my, Louise, aren't you the picture today."

"You're beau-ti-ful," you whisper. I pick you up and kiss you. You say,
"Mama, you have perfume on."

"That's the Chanel your daddy gave me one Christmas before you were
born. It's a special day."

I skip down Uta's front steps and get in the car, you and Uta waving
from her porch. I drive to Bull Street; at the gate, I tell the guard, "I won't
be back. My William is coming home today!"

I park in front of Babcock, glance at my watch. I'm too early so I walk
around the building, through the passageway to the inner courtyard, an
exercise space enclosed by barbed wire. The courtyard is empty, eerily
quiet. Across from me loom four stories of barred windows. At one window
a face appears—a silent staring face. What if it isn't okay? What if I'm the
world's most foolish woman? I turn and stride to the front of the building,
climb the stairs and sit, heart pounding, on a hallway bench.

When I enter William's room, he's sitting on the bed dressed in a suit, his suitcase beside him. I kiss him on the cheek, breathe in his aftershave.

"Oh darling, this is wonderful day for us."

We walk down the stairs and stop at the admissions office, where we both sign his release form. I feel him watching as I scrawl my signature—in a trembling hand—beneath "Released to the Custody Of." I hate that it reads like that. The admissions officer hands William his driver's license and the money left on his hospital account. William looks off as though embarrassed.

After he stows his suitcase in the trunk, he walks around the car looking at the tires, says they need air. He slides behind the steering wheel and rests his hands on it, and for a terrible second I wonder if one can forget how to drive. Of course not, how ridiculous. He starts the car and backs up, but passes up the main drive for a service road circling the hospital complex. He pauses at the white-steepled church, then drives on and turns right at the Williams Building, goes down a hill that ends up behind Babcock. From here the massive building—its two wings of barred windows—looks even more the prison. The concrete sidewalk is cracked, weeds sprouting through it. The gracious cupola, seen up close, has broken windows.

He stops the car and stares at the building for a long time.

Eventually he takes the main drive, past the Mills Building, through the wrought-iron gate. What is he thinking?

"I cooked a roast, darling, I thought you might like that."

He remains silent.

"How about we go to the mountains soon, remember how much fun we had there?"

William nods. This is the adjustment period, I remind myself.

As we drive down Lincoln Street, he says he's hardly been aware it's autumn, since most trees around the hospital are magnolias.

"It's nice to see the oaks. Nice to be free again."

∼◦◦⊖◦∼

How tired I feel. I can't speak about the rest, Lyra, I just can't—I thought I could but I can't. I'm sorry. I'm too tired to go on. There are things you're better off not hearing. You know how our lives were later.

Just remember—you were always my dream.

Part VII: Lyra and Louise

2004

Chapter Fifteen: Lyra

One morning my father takes me aside at the hospital and says that perhaps we should make the necessary "plans." On the way to the funeral home, he says it's highway robbery that funerals now cost eight thousand dollars, and we argue about where my mother should be buried. Then we spend a surreal hour in a world of walnut furniture and subdued lighting and gold brocade drapes, including a tour of the "showroom" of top-of-the-line caskets. In the lobby, as we're preparing to leave, my father and the funeral director talk about World War II.

"When we landed at Normandy," my father tells the director, who's deceased father was in the Invasion, "we had this life preserver, terribly heavy with all our gear tied to it, supposed to keep us from drowning but didn't always. I didn't take that life preserver off for four days. I was hoping it worked on land too."

The funeral director laughs. My father tells him he almost lost his legs during the 1944–45 winter. "They were frozen solid from crawling around in the snow, and one morning I woke up in a medic tent and heard a doctor talking about whether to amputate or not."

These are stories I've never heard before.

Genuine respect shows in the other man's eyes as he teases my father, "Bet you didn't have that mustache in the army."

"You can say that again. Patton would have given me to the Germans."

The funeral director claps my father on the shoulder as we leave. As we're walking toward the car, I wonder who the pleasant man beside me *is* when he says, "He's probably trying to cheat us."

In the hospital cafeteria later, I notice that my father has become thin but has almost no wrinkles. He looks up from his pork chop and says, "That woman in the waiting room, the older one whose son has that blood disease, she used to work at the seminary. She was a secretary there right many years. I told her I had known a few people over there. She knew exactly who I was talking about."

I don't say anything. He never mentions the seminary.

"They kept me from using my education," he adds.

My God, he's talking about the past. Long ago when I asked questions about his childhood, he told me to mind my own business, so I try to sound nonchalant. "Who did? The seminary?" I poke at the wilted lettuce of my salad, keep my voice flat. "What did they do?"

"They put me in the state hospital, that's what they did."

My fork clatters against my plate. *Jesus H Christ.* It's taken him forty-seven years to mention it—do I dare ask anything?

The *seminary* put him in the state hospital?

Risk it. "How did that happen." No inflection.

"They ruined my chance to use my academy education," he says. He stares into space, seems to have forgotten I'm there. "They were training me to work with mental patients. They knew I wanted to be a missionary, but they had an outreach program at the state hospital, we used to pick up some of those people and take them to events, some were awful people from the back wards. Animals really. The seminary wanted me to understand what it was like for those patients, so they put me in there with them."

I'm on a new planet. Green men must be everywhere.

"They made me go there," he says. "That's why I'm the only person to ever have only one electric shock." He gazes at me dead-on. "I am the only person to ever have just one shock. They forced me to go there."

I nod as though I understand. All around us others continue eating bad cafeteria food, unaware that the world is flying off its axis.

"Several people in charge—they had something to do with what happened to me, they had it in for me. I kept journals to prove it, I wrote about the war and everything that happened on Lincoln Street, maybe I'll give you those notebooks someday."

He wrote it all down? I want to beg for the journals, for what I might learn about my family, and about myself. "I'd love to see them."

"I started writing a book about what they did," he goes on, "but I'm gonna give them a chance to apologize to me first. I'm still the only person in the state hospital to have only one shock. I wasn't supposed to be there. I got immersion therapy later."

He stands up. "They kept me from doing what I wanted to do. Psychiatrists are dangerous. They can get inside your mind and control your behavior."

Not always.

I stumble after him toward the door and ambush a meal cart, apologizing to the nurse behind it, muttering that I finally have proof that mental health care in South Carolina needs a little work.

◈◈◈

My father heads for the elevator. Watching him disappear inside it, I sit down on a bench in the hallway. *Is he completely delusional now?*

The "truth" depends on the teller. "No razor," she says. "Not sick," he says.

I close my eyes, remembering a day I was taken to school too early, before the doors opened—

What happened that day?

I felt abandoned, didn't I? Suddenly I'm like Little Annie who's an orphan. My mother doesn't even know she put my shirt on backward. I take my coat off and struggle to turn it around. Two birds are sitting on top of the tetherball pole, singing. No one comes to school this early—the other kids will call me weird. Nothing's right now. I look at a book for a while. Then voices. Some third-graders head into the yard; they start hitting the tetherball and it goes around and around the pole. More people and cars, the cars are the teachers, they park behind the building, near the cafeteria. Teachers eat a lot. Noisy, lots of kids. I sit in the swing and listen, cries and whoops and yelling, only three days until school ends for Christmas. Johnny's late, he's always late. The bell rings. I go in the bathroom and make sure my shirt is right so the teacher won't notice. Arithmetic and reading and learning songs. I want everything to go back like it was before. The teacher frowns at me—I missed four words on my spelling test, I don't have a perfect average now.

Then what? What did I do?

Recess. I remember recess. Johnny comes over, he's got on that shirt with Mickey Mouse on it, he wears it all the time.

"Hey Lyra, how come you came to school so early-like?"

"I wanted to." I walk off in a huff. I stare at the schoolyard gate, start toward it.

Johnny calls, "Whar ya goin'?"

"Home."

"You can't go home, school ain't over yet."

I don't look back at him. "I can to."

"You're gonna get it for playing hooky."

"It's not hooky, I been here lots longer than you."

Johnny catches up as I go through the gate. I turn to him. "Where are you going?"

"I can cut school good as any girl in this whole damn town."

I don't bother to tell him that my mother says *damn* is a bad word.

We walk in silence for the next two blocks.

Down the street, near my house, there's a gray car with a yellow bubble on top and a long white station wagon with writing on the door. Looks like the car dead people go to the cemetery in. A group of neighbors is standing across the street.

Johnny says, "Damn—there's a policeman at your house."

I stare at the white station wagon. On the door is a picture of the Bull Street hospital.

Johnny sees it too and stops dead in his tracks.

"Damn fire and hell. Somebody's going to the loony bin."

⚜⚜⚜

I run away from Johnny and creep in our back door, hesitating in the kitchen. In my parents' bedroom my father is screaming, "*No, no, no—I won't—I know you're—you're not going to—I won't go—I won't—*"

The doctor who gave me shots is leaning over him. A policeman is on the other side. My daddy is trying to get up, yelling, calling the men names I'm not supposed to say.

The doctor tells him, "We're just going to get you a little help, you won't be there long, do you understand me, William?"

Two men in white uniforms are in the living-room doorway. When my daddy sees them, he rears up and scrambles out of bed. The doctor catches him, jerks him back by his shirt and it rips; one man in white grabs him, the other man in white grabs him on the other side, and while he yells and cusses real loud, the men slip a white jacket onto him and tie it in the back—he doesn't have any arms now. Like Mrs. Moazen, only worse.

My mama is there too, she's wringing her hands like she does, and crying. My daddy's crying too, he cries louder than anyone I've ever heard and it seems like that first night again, when the praying went on, and my mama is saying over and over again that she loves him, that "this is only for a little while so you can get better—"

My daddy cries—"Please please please."

My mama's face looks as strange as my daddy's, they're both sick, they both must be going somewhere, to that scary hospital maybe. Who will be left at home with me? I hope Fluffy will stay.

My daddy is crying harder, tears roll all down his face, I didn't know a daddy could cry all the time, he still doesn't have any arms, and the white-clothes men are pushing him down on a carry-bed and tying cords to it, he looks like pictures in my history book, how they carried soldiers off the battlefields. He's yelling again—really loud—as they carry him into the living room, and my mother and the doctor follow and the doctor is telling the men in white that he'll be at the hospital within the hour but I know that Bull Street isn't really a hospital, it has a high brick wall to lock people up—

They don't see me, no one knows I'm here, I'm a secret person, like a ghost.

Soon they're in the living room, and I hear all this commotion as they go out onto the porch. Maybe I'll be in trouble because I cut out of school, but I don't think anyone will care today. I walk into the living room and watch from a window as the others go down the front steps. People across the street watch—Johnny's there but not Rosa. Mr. Faherty. No Sweetes. The man from Aiken Street who sells hubcaps. Two or three others I don't know. A teenage boy is pointing and laughing.

The men carry my daddy down the sidewalk. He's quiet now, he's stopped crying, maybe he's gone to sleep. Or maybe he died—they're putting him in that car that goes to funerals. Across the street Rosa is dragging Johnny inside their house, you can tell she's fussing at him and I don't mind this at all. My mama and the doctor stand on either side as my daddy goes into the car. He tries to get up but the armless coat stops him, and he screams bad words over and over, and my mama is crying again as the men close the door, and suddenly my daddy's cries sound like when you try to talk underwater, a stretched-out sound, and the doctor pulls my mama back from the white station wagon and he talks to the policeman, and the policeman gets in his gray car and starts the engine and the bubble on top begins to go around and around with yellow light, and slowly the white station wagon and the police car pull away.

The people across the street begin to go home, though some keep staring at our house as they walk away.

The doctor has his arm around my mama. Mrs. Moazen is there too. My mama is crying like she wanted to go to the hospital. She says over and over, "Nothing will ever be the same again."

I go out to the back porch and sit down on the steps. I don't know what to do—my mama is crying real loud and my daddy is *gone*.

With my father's version of his state hospital stay still in my head, I wander the rancher like a distracted burglar, staring at household objects I don't really see. I stop pacing—has he invented this bizarre explanation because even now the truth is too painful? Does he really believe this? I feel unfamiliar empathy for him—his life has not been easy. Or is this simply what he wants me to believe? I wish I could remember more. I do recall that after he came home from the hospital my parents seemed faded, like wet laundry blanched of color by the sun. Later that year my mother went in the hospital too, the regular kind, and when she returned she didn't smile for a long time and she didn't whirl me around anymore. What had I done wrong? Soon an imaginary friend—*Dandelion Rose*—came to live with me and that helped. She looked like an eight-year-old Rosa Truesdale, only with lime-green Raggedy Ann hair.

I go in my mother's room and decide to look through her business files, to see if she's left requests for her funeral. Anything to keep busy. In the scratched metal file box I find her teaching certificate, old savings-account books, my grandfather's will deeding her the Brantley house. I take several folders out and notice a white envelope taped to the bottom. The letter inside, on yellowed flimsy paper, is handwritten and wrinkled, as though it was once crumpled up. I gaze at it idly. One section catches my eye:

I don't get this. I was driving, you were just riding along, and no one got hurt. I got insurance for the car. I won't ever sue you like you think--you didn't do nothing wrong. I've never laid eyes on this kind of money and taking it would be stealing. I may end up sorry, but if you don't take it back I'm gonna give the fifty-thousand to my church.

I gaze across the room. *He gave away fifty thousand dollars?* While they took one vacation in forty years? Where did he get that much money?

Of course. The farm.

I've lost his letter to me about the sale. Maybe I threw it away. I was living in that roach-infested East Village studio with the bathtub in the kitchen, when he wrote that he was getting too old to take care of the place and there was no one else who could. I knew what he meant: no son. Swallowing my anger, realizing the money would give them a more secure old age, I asked him to save me ten acres that included the house ruins. He agreed, and I imagined building a small winter studio where I'd once played.

Place in the South has often stood in for human contact. The truth was—I wanted something that seemed like normal family tradition.

Six months later he wrote to say that the buyer hadn't wanted to divide the property. That since I didn't live in South Carolina, why did I need property there?

I called him and screamed, "You *promised* me." I'd believed that on this one thing—the *farm* for Christsake—he wouldn't let me down.

"I don't know what you're so upset about," he fired back. "You don't understand these things. That place is from my family and I'm the last of my line. I'll give you several thousand dollars, provided you send me a detailed statement about how you will use it. That ought to make us even."

I threw the phone across the room.

That Christmas when I went home, which I did only to see my mother, I wanted to visit the farm one last time, but I'd forgotten the directions and my father refused to tell me how to get there. I looked it up on a plat map at the county courthouse, disregarded the new "No Trespassing" sign, and walked around the ruins anyway. On that Christmas Day, my beaming father presented me with a clear plastic box bearing a metal nameplate extolling the history of his family and the land once called China Grove. Imprisoned inside was my handful of sandy South Carolina soil.

The worse my mother gets, the more haunted I feel, like I'm clawing at the door of some house I'll never enter. Avoiding my father the next day—I'm furious about the farm all over again—I tell the hospital I'll be away for a while and, without thinking, I start driving south as it begins to rain. In a half hour I leave the interstate and meander down soggy back roads. I spend an hour on dead-end two-lanes, pass through nearly abandoned small towns whose Main Street stores are boarded up. Several times I get lost and slow down, watch water beat against the open fields. I pause beside an old house that's falling down: the roof is caved in and a magnolia tree and eight-foot-tall weeds rear skyward from the interior. Nature always recovers, always reasserts itself. Always survives. I try another road. Kudzu everywhere, that vicious voracious vine turning trees into formless leafy humps. This road leads to one that feels vaguely familiar. Finally I spot the expanse I think was China Grove. I park and walk along a barbed-wire fence, camera over my shoulder. The horizon is green and brown, flat, still, damp, fecund. And minus its historic drama. The ruins were plowed under years ago. Human history doesn't exist here anymore.

I stare at the fields of soybeans where loblolly pines once held up the sky. No burnt shards left to gather and no vase to glue them onto. I take no pictures.

It's against the law to destroy a family cemetery, so I get back in the car and try to find it. Have they built new roads? I ride down one where several mobile homes nest together. Down another. Nothing but more farm fields. I'm near where the ruins were, so the cemetery should be a half mile away. *Where the hell is it?* I admit defeat—even if I could find it, I'd have to trespass to pay my respects to my ancestors. I stop the car and walk through the warm mist anyway, staring across the terrain I remember. My mother and I skipping through the woods, my father digging up his talismans. I'm back on that dangerously jagged wall—all the blackened boards, fallen chimneys, the spooky mist perpetually hovering. Our landscape of loss and defeat shooting through my veins. This place *was* our story.

But I'm not the first descendent who didn't inherit it—it's odd that the only family stories my father's ever told me have to do with this place. My great-grandfather's will inexplicably denied one son any land, and later the furious disinherited son smashed his parents' gravestones with a crowbar. I still remember the tombstones that looked vandalized. His sister, whose first child had died while a toddler, feared her deranged brother would desecrate her child's grave too, so she exhumed the child's body and moved it to a town cemetery. After that, the cemetery at China Grove ceased to be the family burial ground.

A legacy that fits far too well.

I look out across the fields. It's just acreage in the middle of nowhere. Not worth anything. A place where a man went crazy and a mother protected her child. Where another man and his child looked for things that can never be found, exchanging dirt that came to naught. After a while I acted like I didn't care that he didn't save me those acres. Didn't care that he never had a kind word for me. But staring at the damp fields, leaning against barbed wire, the soft fabric of my heart rips open all over again.

⌁◦◦◯◦◦⌁

When I get back in my car, my cell phone is blinking. The message from a nurse says my mother's condition has become "grave." Frantically I head back to the interstate, my pulse racing, and speed toward Columbia. When I arrive at the hospital an hour later, I run up the stairs and push through the ICU doors into my mother's cubicle. Her breathing is shallow.

My father, poised beside the machines, cries out, "She's going." He puts a hand on her pillow, six inches from her face.

My favorite cousin and another cousin from Brantley stand on either side of the bed. We watch my mother's breathing; the ventilator pumps like mad but no air seems to reach her. I take her hand, keep my eyes on her face; I want to witness her departure from the world. I whisper about the good times—the Thanksgivings in Brantley, all her brothers and their families, the table laden with ten vegetables, ham and roast and turkey, more food than any family could eat, and everyone brought a pie and there was laughter around the table and old stories were flying about.

My father takes something out of his pocket. "She left this." He hands me an opened envelope. "You should read it now. I already did."

Robotically I unfold the single typed sheet and begin to read aloud. The words don't penetrate. I stop reading because I want to focus on my mother's labored breathing. I tell her that I love her and look at the piece of paper again and read her requests for her funeral—the tone is disturbing. I stop in mid-sentence, look at the envelope: "To Be Opened After My Death."

She's not dead, I scream at my father silently. She wanted this read *after* she's gone. And if she can hear us, she knows we didn't do as she asked.

The cousins stare at the paper in my hand. I know they're shocked too.

Mother gasps. Machines whir. My father moves his hand closer.

I'm bent over her hand when I hear a muted, muffled voice: "I love you. I've always loved you."

The voice isn't mine. Not one of the cousins. A voice I've never heard say this. A hand that touches only a pillow.

I have always loved you.

❦

Mother does not die. Classy of her not to reward a deathbed scene she'd have hated.

How awkward now—the loved ones hovering, waiting for the beloved to die, and she doesn't cooperate? She breathes more easily, the machines are normal again. An ICU nurse comes in, says, "Y'all brought Mrs. Louise back. All that talk about Thanksgiving dinner—I'd stay around for that myself."

My ears are ringing—*I love you, I've always loved you*—did he really say that? I don't believe it.

The nurse adds softly, "Mrs. Louise isn't ready yet. Y'all go back to the waiting room while I check her over. Come back in ten minutes."

I walk to the waiting area, sit down, take out my mother's typed letter.

Dear William,

    You made a big point of telling me, more than once, that the dying shouldn't make requests for their funeral because it wasn't fair to the ones left behind. So if you don't feel like doing the following, don't trouble yourself. I'd like a closed casket and two hymns: "Faith of Our Fathers" and Leslye said she'd sing the solo "Come, Ye Disconsolate." I'd like my mother's prayer book buried with me. But if my funeral's too much trouble for you, just forget it. I wouldn't want to put you out.

I stare at the letter—dated four years ago, after Mother could no longer write by hand. He told her that even for her *funeral* she shouldn't ask for what she wants? So she gets back at him, from death, with sarcastic martyrdom? This is how my family ends?

I tell the ICU desk to call me if there's any change and go for a walk around the hospital grounds. It's raining hard. After I've circled the grounds five times, I drive to my parents' house. I don't even dry off but go straight to my mother's green hymnal on the piano. A book she sang from for forty years, her name in gold on the leather cover. I pick it up and fit my hand into the imprint left by hers, pebbled leather worn soft and smooth, caressed. The oil from her fingers seeps into mine—I can feel her holding on to this book. To her own voice.

As I thumb through the pages, looking for the second hymn she wants, a black and white photograph falls out, its rippled edges creased. My parents in 1940s clothes—their engagement photo maybe. They're smiling like nothing exists except each other. Staring at the picture, I feel completely crazy. I put it down and find the hymn:

> *Come, you disconsolate, wher-e'er ye languish;*
> *Come to the mercy seat, fervently kneel;*
> *Here bring your wounded hearts, here tell your anguish;*
> *Earth has no sorrow that heaven cannot heal.*

I curl up on the piano bench and beg whoever is out there to let my mother die.

Chapter Sixteen: Louise

Darling Lyra, you're here early this morning. Oh how I will miss you—

I feel stronger today. My mind's been stuck in 1957—so much of my life comes down to that year, but not all. Why, just a minute ago I dreamed about when my daddy and my uncle took us children down to Hilton Head. This was before there was anything there, the men were going hunting, though my father never shot anything, didn't have the heart for it. We were staying with family friends, I was probably nine, and Daddy and Uncle Billy were out one night scouting for game, but they came back to get us and took us to the ocean to see a herd of wild deer, must have been twenty-five, in the water. The deer swam across the inlet and went up on Daufuskie Island and stayed a while, and got in the water again and swam out so far we couldn't see them anymore. Daddy was smoking his pipe and kept saying, in a hushed voice, that he'd thought it was an old tale, the myth of the sea-deer. He whispered, "Louise honey, to see this means we've been chosen tonight."

I never forgot those swimming deer. Wild creatures driven to bathe in moonlight simply for the beauty of it, their luminous gold-nugget eyes twin beacons through light and shadow and the sighing of inland rivers and pine forests. Eyes of the miraculous, of ancient faith. I wanted to have eyes like that. I'm swimming myself and I was never a good swimmer, but

I seem better at it right now. Fortunately I'm not fat anymore, I did hate it when your father called me that. No one knows—save you—the terrible things he sometimes said to me; for decades, I haven't known from day to day what strange or hurtful thing might happen. I know you think I should have stood up to him more. I'd like to think I just didn't know *how* to stand up for myself. I felt so guilty that the state hospital ruined his career, our lives really. It was heartbreaking how no one would hire him afterward, him with an honors degree from the military academy. When he did get work, one job after another failed. But he kept going out to forage and I admired him for that. I'm sure he didn't *want* to end up as a night security guard, a shell-shock victim ironically carrying a gun for years.

After William returned from the hospital people shunned us—people at the church, neighbors; a department store got wind of it and cancelled our credit card. And don't think I don't know what happened to you—children who wouldn't play with you anymore, the Logan Girls Club all your friends were invited to join but you weren't. What came after William's breakdown was often worse than the breakdown itself. I so wanted another child, a large family—

Misfortune makes some of us punish ourselves, others punish someone else.

One year William was berating me—I forget for what but telling me, like I was a dimwitted child, that I didn't *understand* anything—and I was about to say I'd had it, but somehow I couldn't. I remembered how happy we were on our honeymoon. I remembered the shy way he held you when we came home from the hospital and how the Spanish moss draped across the crepe myrtle trees in Charleston when we went to Hampton Park to feed the swans. I remembered that he was sent a Dear John letter in the muddy trenches of war-torn Europe, remembered that he'd lost all his family when so young. I asked my sister-in-law why she put up with my brother's drinking, and that sweet woman looked at me and said, "If I don't take care of him, who will?"

I know that sounds ridiculously self-sacrificing to you, but I really believed in *for better or worse.* Even after William revealed his hideous revenge, I thought that to run away would be to think only of myself. I wanted you to have a whole family. So I made up my mind to stay and see what I could do to make things better, to play out the hand I'd been dealt. I was an optimist—things *might* change. Not much, as it turns out. But as Mr. Faulkner put it, we survived. Even after we left Lincoln Street—you were a handful in high school and your father tormented you—I was often depressed, though I'd never have called it that. I know I let you down sometimes. When Laidlaw closed because of white flight—I was principal then—and I was sent to teach in that massive, violent high school across town, I was miserable. An energy I'd always had went missing—

Sometimes it feels like I'm levitating—I can't explain it—floating— but I want to say something else—

I could never admit the failure of our family life, couldn't face that I hadn't been able to give you a happy childhood. Maybe I was afraid you'd blame me. Do you? Eventually it was too late to change anything, too late—partially my own doing—to recoup what I'd most wanted. I settled for company, did without comfort. Now William has ended up taking care of me: caring for someone may not be love, but it is loyalty. Such things matter at the end of life, even if the inspiration is obligation. He kept watch over me after my surgeries and he's checked my blood sugar every day and doled out my medicines, though he rarely lets me have the prescribed sleeping pills and painkillers, says I'll "get hooked on them." He brags that he hasn't had a day to himself in four years, which is accurate I suppose but wouldn't be if he hadn't refused Medicare home nurses. He told neighbors I likely had infections that could be spread and they should stay away. Thankfully they paid no attention to him.

But he has been here every day. Because he has, I haven't had to burden you with my old age, and I'm grateful for that. I haven't had to go to a nursing home. I've gotten to stay in my favorite chair and look out the window at the camellias I planted so long ago. And once or twice—just for a moment—there'd be a glimmer of the past, as though William's lack of warmth was a gray mist that sunlight suddenly broke through. Every autumn, even after I couldn't walk well, he took me to the North Carolina mountains to buy the winesap apples I love. One day while we were sitting on a motel balcony, he said, "Time is slowing down, Louise. Sometimes I remember your singing, it was something."

Shared history can be a powerful ligament. Like those twenty years I lunched every month with retired Laidlaw teachers. With them I was young and playful again. I've had wonderful times with friends. I've lost many of them in recent years, one year two died in the same month, but Clarice, who finally left Elmwood Park and moved to the suburbs, has been a godsend. For two decades we've talked on the phone at least once a day. Several times a day lately. In our seventies we went to every store opening in Columbia where something free was handed out. At one time I had a sizeable collection of neon Radio Shack Frisbees. Don't tell me I don't know a good thing when I see it.

If you don't laugh now and again, you really will go crazy.

Clarice and I have kept ourselves going in our eighties by telling each other the same stories time and time again and never letting on we've heard them before. But when Clarice broke her hip and was rushed to intensive care, I was too feeble to visit her. Suddenly I could no longer talk to the friend who'd become the sister I'd always wanted. I could barely look at the telephone. As it did when you left home decades before, loneliness invaded every cell inside me. Six days later—maybe it was seven—I had this stroke that has stolen my eyes and my voice.

Everyone says the mind and the body are connected. I think it's the body and the heart.

Lyra dear.

You're whispering something—did I hear right—oh please let my hearing not go yet—did you say something about the farm?

Lights, sound, shifting shapes, and night and day. I scarcely know where I am and then I hear you. I hope I see my parents again—I wonder if my mother will still be thirty. What did you say about the farm? I never told you that your father deposited the farm proceeds into a bank account only he could use. My teaching pension paid our living expenses. He had extra cash, I didn't. He also gave away a huge chunk of the farm proceeds out of paranoia. Wasted money. I didn't mind living with old things; I do mind that he was far more generous to strangers than he was to us. I never forgave him for those ten acres he denied you. That's been the story of our lives: your father has made countless decisions that affect you and me without ever considering how we feel. No matter who's been hurt, he's never apologized, never admitted to being wrong. I don't know what's wrong with him, I never have.

I should have said these things to you long ago. I did go to see the farm one last time—I guess it was several months after he sold it. I drove down while he was at work, passed the wooden shacks with vines growing out of their chimneys, turned onto the dirt road that cut through the piney woods, breathed in the cedars and pine sap, and found the old cemetery again, snug behind its wrought-iron gates. There was no sign of the new owner as I got out and walked through the grass. Oh how I longed for you, for the times you ran through that grass holding my hand.

Was that a nurse? I like that woman whose daughter I taught.

What was I saying—oh, my last day at the farm. For an hour that day I walked through the monochromatic stands of conifers, those unchanging green trees of sharp-pointed needles. At the house ruins I sat on the low brick wall, looked at the broken bricks, blackened beams, determined saplings struggling through the debris. I stared into the woods. This—family land—I'd wanted it to make up for the siblings that never came to make you less lonely, for what you had to endure. Is that too much to ask? But I was too tired to cry anymore, too defeated— how many times can one mourn the same loss? Then I found myself humming. I was surprised—by then I'd left the church choir and I rarely sang anymore, except when I visited Uta's and Max's graves. I was almost shocked—how lovely to hear my voice again, like finding an old friend in a strange city. I belted out the refrain—"I once was lost but now am found." I sang and sang, I sang as I had at Uta's funeral, I sang the old spirituals and the songs from my college days. Against the ruins of century-old destruction, I sang to feel the love I didn't have. I sang to keep from losing my heart for good.

~∽◯∾~

But you know what I just remembered? That last reunion in Brantley. Before it began, you and I went to my parents' house—the new owners let us stop by for a visit and the wooden swing was still right there on the porch, the swing I'd swung my childhood away in, and we sat in it and I remembered the times I'd brought you there as a child. And I thought, I've done some good in my life—some good teaching. And look at this beautiful young woman beside me. Like a silly goose, I turned and whispered to the house—*Look, Mother, look what we have made.*

The reunion—you must remember it—was at my uncle's farm in the country. I loved that rambling white farmhouse; my aunt who lived there married at sixteen and had ten children! Just imagine. I smiled all that day, spent that afternoon—your father never went to the reunions, of course—surrounded by my brothers and their families. Even now I can see myself standing beside the white board fence with my arms around the two gray-haired men who still called me "Sister." That day we laughed and told old stories one more time. I got something you didn't, Lyra—an easy childhood after my mother's death, siblings and cousins to play with and to love, a father who never stopped holding my hand until the day he died. That reunion day I looked out across fields I'd roamed as a child, and I gathered in the tender moments of my life—the lovely bits and pieces—for safekeeping.

Loss is the inevitable coda of a long life. But at that reunion I felt our wonderful days at China Grove again as I watched the strong, graceful sunlight in the distant trees. Almost coral in color and moving in waves as all light does, I don't have to tell a painter this, it spilled liquidly, like a wistful melody, across the tree limbs and pine-needled ground. I hope this doesn't sound melodramatic, I'm not seeing any light of the Almighty in this hospital room. No celestial visions, not yet anyway. But out there that day a mysterious aura came forward and settled over us, light that was like time or history, for light exists and doesn't, we can see it and see through it. That aura enfolded me until I couldn't see anything else. Eventually I could see you again. Then I could see you staring into the light of old trees without me, but it wasn't a lonely feeling at all.

I choose that day as my always.

Chapter Seventeen: Lyra

For several days after my mother almost dies, my father and I rarely leave the hospital. Often the ICU waiting room fills with my mother's friends. One afternoon I can barely find a seat but when I do sit down, after embracing several older women I've not seen in many years, I find myself staring at the new man there. The son of the woman with the cane. Electric blue eyes that stare back at me intently. I try to remember if I've ever met him; I think not, he's maybe ten years younger. Quite gorgeous too.

My mother's friends ask about her condition, and I reply to polite inquiries about my life, listen to the women chat about their families or the hot weather. No one introduces me to Mr. Blue Eyes, but he and I continue our staring. He has the same shimmering eyes—iridescent, Monet-milky yet mysteriously translucent—found on Siberian huskies. Everything about him is put together well—his arms aren't too short or too long for his just-right height (long legs encased in silk/linen trousers scream six feet), and his wavy dark hair is silver-flecked in all the right places. Broad shoulders in blue pinpoint.

So I'm fourteen again? Please tell me I'm not sweating.

I've not felt this magnetic charge toward anyone in a long time. Visceral, as though two comets are colliding. Maybe it's true that loss can make one hysterical.

Finally I look down—the staring is conspicuous—and count the pulled threads in the carpet, mauve being the new dull, but I can feel this man—a few seats away but facing me—breathing. I mean it, *breathing.* He does that really well. My peripheral vision works overtime: elegant fingers, no wedding ring. I look back at him and feel a jolt, like I've upended a fifth of Wild Turkey.

Am I really hot and bothered about a complete stranger while my mother is dying? This is right up there with wearing an "I'm with Stupid" T-shirt to the opera.

His mother stands up, leaning on her cane. I go over to say good-bye. She takes my hand, says she'll go in to see my mother briefly, and then they have to be off.

He puts a hand on my shoulder and smiles—even his teeth are in the right order. "I'm sorry your mother is so ill. Please let me know if we can do anything."

The voice of a cello resonating in a deep cavern. I nod at him like I've been hypnotized or dazed by a stun gun or English is not my native language.

Finally I manage, "Thank you. For coming by, for everything."

I didn't know I *could* feel fourteen again.

⚜⚜◯⚜⚜

Dr. Dumaine comes into the waiting room the next morning and sits down heavily, looks at my father and me somberly, runs a veined hand through thin gray hair. Weary, sad eyes. He puts his hands together as in prayer.

"Mr. Copeland, sir. Lyra. We might need to consider Louise's living will." He pauses, says each word slowly. "I'll keep her on life support as long as the family wants. But she's not going to get better. And I can't be sure how much distress she's in. She's worn out, I think."

My father shifts in his armchair, stares at the floor. Others in the waiting room grow silent.

Dr. Dumaine goes on, "Louise and I have had many long talks over the years, and she always told me she never wanted to be kept alive artificially. If the family wishes to exercise her living will, I can make her comfortable with drugs. The infection in her lungs will eventually take her or her heart will stop. You can decide whether to continue the feeding tube."

It dawns on me what this means. "We *cannot* let her starve to death. She felt guilty about eating all her life—she is *not* going that way."

Dr. Dumaine looks so sad that I want to tell him it's all right, that he did his best for years. He holds out a form to my father. "If you want to remove the ventilator, you'll need to sign this."

My father looks off. "This should probably be my daughter's decision."

I whirl toward him. "You're going to make me do this?"

"I won't be around much longer myself."

Dr. Dumaine waits, studies his hands.

Somehow I knew I'd end up on this cliff alone. Having to sign terrible papers to take care of someone runs in our family.

Finally I can help her.

After I sign, I walk into the hall. This was always meant to be my job.

We are no longer restricted to visiting hours. My mother has been moved out of ICU and into a private room. Twice she jerks to one side, and I find a nurse and check to make sure she's getting the painkillers. The nurse tells me she'll likely live for another forty-eight hours, perhaps I should get some rest. I sit and sing to her while my father goes to the cafeteria. He returns and settles into the armchair beside her bed—she's breathing peacefully.

I've no idea why, but I have to go there before she dies.

I take the interstate into the city, exit erratically onto Elmwood Avenue and head down to Bull Street and drive onto the hospital grounds. I park in front of Babcock imprisoned behind its chain-link fence. No cops in evidence as I sit and stare. So much peeling paint on the portico columns bare concrete shows through. A graveyard of a building. I don't want it renovated. Or demolished. I don't want anyone thinking its history can be erased. With it gone, as integral to us as the Lincoln Street house, how would I explain my childhood?

Slipping beneath the chain across the portico staircase, I climb up to confront the plate-glass door. Inside lies a hallway with wooden benches, walls that pale green of all 1950s hospitals, papers scattered on the floor, dirt and debris, an odor of abandonment—*sitting quietly on a wooden bench in that hallway, my mother is bent over crying, her hands shaking.*

I stare through the locked glass door. Was she really there? Would I have had the strength to get through that year?

Inside the hallway an aged oak staircase leads upward; vandals have apparently torn out the carved balustrades, only four remain. The second floor landing is backed by a stained glass window, rainbow squares of light. I photograph the interior stairs and the crumbling portico. Descending to ground level, I pace alongside the north wing, staring at the row after row of barred windows. A window on the fourth floor haunts me—I have the uncanny feeling I've stood in this spot before, staring at that exact window. I take a picture of it. Gazing at the broken windows, the rusted iron bars, I wonder—what did he think when he looked through those bars? That he was in prison? That's what I'd have felt. I have no idea what happened to him here, how bad it was. Was he mistreated, hit, ridiculed? What was the diagnosis? I'll never know—the records are sealed for a hundred years.

Some iron grilles are ornate, almost decorative. I feel like I see people behind the windows, people who're tiny, so many faces, haunted faces, hands reaching through the iron bars, fingers poking through broken glass, wrists bleeding, so many lonely desperate people. I turn and run. When I come to a stop, I lean against a magnolia tree to breathe. Across from me a small dogwood tree has fallen across the fence, taking part of it down. *Face it, look at it.* Impulsively I scramble across the crushed wire, wondering if I'll get caught and arrested for breaking into a nightmare. I head toward a side entrance, sidestepping fallen bricks, stopping to peer through a first-floor window. High ceilings, tongue-and-groove walls painted that same forlorn green, an archway whose entrance is covered by a wire screen door. Locked cage of wire, concrete steps leading upward, shuffling men in loose pajamas herded like animals up the stairs.

The building is shaped like a cross. I've read that all 1800s mental institutions were. I walk through the breezeway into an inner courtyard leading to an exercise field. A nearby door is open, scattered boxes and papers left behind on the floor, as though the building was vacated in a panic, people fleeing for their lives. All the walls are peeling paint, walls like seared flesh. Fallen shards of plaster and layers of white dust. A lone rusted gurney, beyond it a door leading to patient wards. The gurney seems like a stretcher, a man is thrashing about it on it, he's crying not to be taken. My mother is crying even harder. I start toward the door leading to the wards. Filmy light makes a path inside but a voice stops me. "You don't have to go this far." I whirl around as pigeons flutter out of the eves. It sounded like my mother.

For once I listen to her and stride into the quadrangle, into the prison yard. All around me ghosts lean out of barred windows, faces in windows, that's why they won't renovate, too much misery in these brick walls.

My mother saw these faces, it's Christmas—

I think I hear screaming and clap my hands over my ears and lean against a stone wall. Initials have been scratched into it at eye level: "A. Bender 1947," "John Mulhand was here 1971," the anonymous "Please tell my wife to come," dates and names all down the plaster. How many other pleas have been painted over? I stare at a phrase off by itself, near the bottom. Tiny cramped handwriting. A little—is this my imagination— like my own?

I read out loud: *"You don't understand."*

Backing away, I scurry out to the fence and jump across the downed section. I want nothing more than to get away, yet I stop suddenly, turn back to look at the giant deteriorating structure. I re-cross the fence and gaze up at Babcock's cupola. One cupola window, its frame peeling white paint, is half open—*you think anyone got out?* I remember the exhaustive photo album my mother once kept, dozens of family photos. The album simply *stops* in 1957. Not a single picture after that.

I pick up a brick and hurl it at a windowpane, listen to the glass shatter. *I want that beautiful blue house on Lincoln Street.* I don't want other kids laughing at me, I want a father who cares. *Make it not happen.* I pick up another brick and aim for the arched window nearest me. Palladian windows date to sixteenth-century Italy, to Greek and Roman temple architecture, yet found their way to this distant time and place. Suddenly I can imagine how grateful Columbians fleeing the 1865 fire were for the walls and rooms behind those windows. Nothing is sadder, more desolate, than a lovely old building left to die. No matter what it was, the past matters. No one would have built such a hopeful structure, no artisan would have hand-carved the balustrades of a burnished oak staircase, in order to deliberately do harm. The impulse to help gone so wrong that no one will rescue the building, no one will forgive it, no one will acknowledge that *it* is not the story.

I drop the brick. Every story is larger than we think.

I drive back across town. Dark now. A night to make the "good death" many Native Americans pray for? There's a full moon above me—creamy yellow, so low it seems I might touch it if I stood on tiptoe.

I go to my mother's new room. My father is asleep in the armchair beside her bed. She breathes noisily, he's snoring faintly. So here they are—I've lost the cynic in me as I think this—almost sixty years after a Christmas Eve wedding in a small white frame church in Brantley. He's still beside her, she him. Maybe there's something here that I simply don't understand.

I notice Mother's misshapen foot sticking out from beneath the blanket and cover it up.

That night, back at the rancher, wondering if my mother will live until morning, I dream what I dream so often—

I'm on a very windy street, seems like it's in Elmwood Park, pieces of a child's metal swing set are flying about and I have to duck to miss them. I'm going through a long dark tunnel, really a tube, and when I emerge I'm facing the house on Lincoln Street. It's unnaturally tall, the roof disappears into the sky, and the house looks black, like it's been burned.

There's the stone house next door, where the crazy lady told me that in her grandparents' house in Ireland the hearth fire was never allowed to go out, if it did the soul of the house would die. I rush inside our house and cross to the living room, there's the lumpy old sofa. I run to the fireplace, I don't know why I'm running, but I grab onto the mantel and look below. Nothing in the grate but ashes. I drop onto the floor and stir them up, blow on them to try to provoke an ember. Nothing. I jump back up, frantic, and turn and race to the bedroom fireplace and the fire's gone out in there too. I fall to my knees and reach in, nothing but cold ashes. I'm crying hysterically now. I run back to the living room. There's a painting of a fire over the fireplace but still nothing in the grate. My parents have appeared, they're sitting in separate chairs pulled up to the hearth, they're not old or young, just silent, still, they look frozen like statues, and I run over to them but neither gives a flicker of recognition. I know they're alive but they seem dead. I scream—*Don't you know who I am?* Neither answers, neither looks at me. No one can see me, hear me. I run from bedroom to living room over and over to see if either fire can be revived—I have to figure this out—I have to get the fires going I have to have to I must—

A sharp light slashes on and Lincoln Street disappears. I rear up from the bed as though slapped. As in my childhood, my father has flipped on the overhead light, throwing blinding light into my face to wake me. I'm stunned, disoriented.

He tells me my mother is almost gone. I must come now if I want to see her a final time.

He drives crazily through the four a.m. streets, too fast, then too slow, crossing into the other lane twice, nearly running off the road. He tells me a nurse found my mother almost gone; he was in the chair beside her but had fallen asleep, he did everything humanly possible for her. The car lurches sideways.

When we arrive at the hospital, a nurse stands outside my mother's door. She puts an arm around me as my father whips a small camera out of his pocket and barges into my mother's room. Horrified, I see a flash through the cracked doorway.

He emerges and grabs me and whispers—"Don't touch anything. All kinds of bacteria. If she goes, be sure and wash your hands afterward."

I stumble into the room. I can hear him telling the nurse he's been taking care of his wife for years, he hasn't had a day to himself in—

Closing the door on his voice, I walk over and caress my mother's still-thick hair. Her mouth is slightly agape, her breathing shallow, labored. I wish she seemed more peaceful. She's leaving me with the truth: living is hard work.

I lean against her and whisper that I love her.

Chapter Eighteen: Louise

❖

I'm in another room now—how fuzzy I feel—pain medicine? Hurts to breathe but it's quiet, no bustling nurses every hour. No hissing machines. You're crying, Lyra. Don't. I'm relieved to be this near the end. I hope those who say we go home are right. I want to go home. I'm not sure home implies a place, maybe it's a state of being, maybe you get to go back and live in the *before*, that's what I hope for. What I remember most happily doesn't exist anymore: skipping down the street in Brantley humming to myself, passing the open doors of neighbors who're gathered around their radios or telling stories, laughing, the silly ordinary life, that's what I long for. Maybe it'll be 1939 again.

Did I ever tell you I named you for more than the musical instrument, that you're a little-known constellation? I can't recall if I told you or not. A small constellation that's directly overhead during summer; some nights after you left home I used to stand out in the yard and look for it. Your main star—I think it's called Vega, it's among the brightest in the universe. I never realized until now that all your paintings are like stars—you're drawing lines from star to star to form the constellation of your life. I hope and pray you find the pattern that gives you peace.

I have to tell you what you deserve to know. The why. Even if you can't hear me. I want to be like that old woman in *To Kill A Mockingbird*—Lord but I taught that book a thousand times—I can't recall her name, the woman Jem read to who wanted to master her morphine addiction before she died. She defeated her enemy and went out as we come in, clean, uncompromised. Truthful, even if late.

DuBose. I think that was her name.

I want to be Mrs. DuBose.

∽◦◯◦∽

We're driving home from the state hospital under the canopy of colored maple and oak leaves on the day your father was released. You're sitting on Uta's stone fence, watching for us. When you spot the taxicab, you run into our house to get a drawing you've made of your daddy and reappear on the screen porch waving it.

William gets out of the car and stares at the house. I slip my arm through his and say, "Darling, it's so wonderful to have you home."

"The roof looks bad to me. Is it leaking?"

You run through the porch door, stop a few feet from us.

William is pacing back and forth alongside the house, looking at windows, walls. He finally notices you. "How are you, miss? You're bigger."

"Give your daddy a hug, sweetie," I say. You crush yourself against William's middle and show him the drawing; he mumbles something about it, I can't make out what. Then he's back to looking at the house.

Perhaps he's embarrassed. It's not like he's coming home from a nice trip.

Inside, William surveys the rooms and furniture as though he barely remembers them. I follow him around, chatter about dinner. He stops at the living-room fireplace and I babble about how a real fire kept us warmer all winter, that a chimney sweep said the fireplace was safe. William gazes at me silently, and I add that the oil stove is in the garage. He looks over his bookcase in the hallway while I put supper on the table. The books from his seminary locker are in a closet. We'll enjoy tonight and I'll tell him tomorrow. Perhaps he *can* reapply.

"Lyra, William darling, come on, time to eat."

William sits down at the oak table but takes no note of it. "I'll not miss the hospital food, that's for sure."

I don't think he remembers the table. Maybe he doesn't remember much about his breakdown. That would be such a gift.

For the first time in almost a year, we sit together over a meal. I've lit candles, the glow settling softly over my new dress. A stranger peering in our window as that October evening slipped into darkness would have seen an attractive couple and their child, and a warm, lovely supper. William says the roast is good, but he doesn't offer much to the questions I ask: would he like to go to the farm tomorrow, does he have clothes that need to be washed, did I buy the right kind of tobacco? He nods absently and sometimes gazes at the window.

"Maybe we could go to the mountains next weekend," I suggest. "Go to Maggie Valley and see the fall leaves. They must be beautiful by now."

He says maybe so.

⚬⚬◯⚬⚬

After supper William goes into our bedroom and begins unpacking. I flutter around helping and then wash the dishes. An hour later, after a bath, he steps into the kitchen.

"I'd like to speak to you for a moment, Louise." He eyes you drawing at the kitchen table. "In private."

I send you to straighten up your room, and William and I go into the living room. I sit in the green armchair. William paces back and forth across the thin carpet, stops once and stares at the logs I've stacked in the fireplace; his suit is gone, a clean white shirt and pressed khakis in its place. Twice he halts his pacing to stare at me as though waiting for me to say something. I feel confused. "What did you want to talk about?" I smile and add, "We're overjoyed to have you home. Now we can start our lives again."

William walks over and grips my chair arms so tightly his veins bulge out. "Do you have any idea what electric shock feels like? Do you?"

"William, I—" I stare at my hands in my lap. "No, of course I don't."

"It's like your soul is being burned out of your body with a blowtorch."

I feel hit by an electric charge too. Finally he's angry.

He walks back across the room, stands by the hearth. "You have ruined my life."

I rush over and put a hand on his arm, which he shakes off. "We can start over, William. In time everything will be all right again."

His eyes—they're the eyes of Dante's dark wood. "And how will everything be all right? Tell me." He goes and sits down on the sofa, his voice mocking. "Tell me, Louise. Tell me how everything is going to be all right."

"I'm not sure yet." I stare blankly at the floral fiberglass drapes. "But I know we can find our way out of this."

"How do you think people at the seminary will look at me now? A man whose wife threw him in that hospital? Into that *prison*."

"Darling, you were sick. The doctor said that was the only thing that would help you."

"Do you think I got *helped* in that hellhole? Why didn't you just send me back to the war? I guess I'm lucky you didn't order a lobotomy."

William gets up and walks back over to the hearth. He stares at the photograph on the mantel—our engagement picture which I'd recently framed, the two of us on the steps of the Brantley house gazing happily at each other.

I nod at the photo. "Remember that day, darling? Look how you're smiling. It can be that way again. We need time to get our bearings. Remember our life in Summerville? All those Sunday afternoons at Hampton Park?"

He turns and leans into my face. "You've ruined my life in the church. You've taken away my reason for living. How long did you think you could keep me in the dark?"

I step back. *He's known all along.*

"I'm so sorry, William, I'm so sorry about what the seminary did. I had no idea that could happen. I'd do anything if I could change it. Maybe if you reapply—"

"You've ruined our future!" he shouts. "Ruined our lives!" He leans farther toward me, spits out, "What kind of wife are you?"

I open my mouth but no words come out. Tears run down my face.

William orders me to stop crying. "You threw me into Hell," he yells. "I can't hold my head up with decent people anymore. You've ruined my good name. I ought to turn you out, divorce you." He pauses, then says slowly, as though these words have been rehearsed for a long time—

"As long as I live, I will never—*ever*—forgive you for committing me to the state hospital. Never, no matter how long we live."

I stumble to the armchair, bury my face in my hands, rock back and forth.

William grabs the arms and shakes the chair as though he'll never stop. I wait for him to hit me. He never has but when I look up I see the thought in his eyes. I offer my face to his fist. I don't care if he scars me for life if only this can end.

"You're never going to use your precious dining-room table." He leans down. "Did you hear me, Louise?"

I mumble that I will give away the table, it doesn't matter. "I'll do anything to make it better for us."

"No, Louise. It's not what you'll do, it's what you won't be doing. You're finished, just like you've finished me off."

He glares at me and then smiles, a smile so calculated and malicious— *ah, but I've got you*—that I shiver.

"I will never forgive you. And you will never, *ever,* have another child."

Now.

Now as you sit in a hospital watching me breathe in and out, rasping, struggling to stay in the world even as I go out of it, now it's that long night again, when I stare into space—too devastated to speak—as William leaves the room and goes out to the garage to be sure the oil stove is there. I'm paralyzed, whimpering, a wounded animal denied the clean kill. It gets darker and darker and after a while William comes back in and takes a book and sits on the sofa, without speaking to me, and begins to read. As though nothing has happened, as though he's not severed our future. You watch from the doorway, you've almost never seen my hands idle, no sewing, no papers to grade, and when you come into the living room I barely notice you. I guess you knew instinctively that something terrible had happened, but this terrible is different because it's very quiet; maybe that was even more frightening. Your father asks me where did I get the television set and in a toneless whisper I say—"I thought you might like watching it sometime." He says nothing and the silence goes on for an hour or so, how can the world be so noiseless, and after a while William gets up and goes out to look at the roof again. Finally I retreat to the kitchen to finish washing dishes but I do not sing over the suds. I don't think I will ever sing again.

Soon we're all three sitting in the living room once more. Neighbors' voices lilt and fall on the street outside but our family has frozen into stone figures. You sit on the floor and watch TV, your father sits in the old rocker and stares at the paper and then at the TV, I sit on the sofa, untouched mending in my lap, and stare at the TV. The only sound in the room comes from *I Love Lucy*. Lucy is having a tough time getting something done, but she and her friend Ethel are laughing and dancing around their living room anyway. Every now and then I notice our reflections—the three of us—in the glaring television screen. Behind your father's shape is the front window and after a while I can't see the TV screen anymore, just that window and how we're framed in relief on the panes.

That night I sleep on the living-room sofa. After the lights go out, you creep past your sleeping father and tiptoe into the living room and find me there, covered by a thin blanket, my sobs muffled by a pillow. You walk over and put your hand on my shoulder. At first it comforts me and exhaustion pushes me into sleep. You scrunch up and lie down beside me. A few hours later, when I realize you're there, I whisper, "Here, sweetheart, stretch out. Remember that your mother will always love you. Always and forever."

I walk outside in my nightgown, a new one I made for tonight, and sit on the front steps. The darkness is eerily still, not even an insect scrambling about. An oppressive, stifling Southern night, more summer than autumn. Summer that never ends, when life feels arrested, mummified. An hour later I rise and go back inside. I walk into the dining room and sit at the oak table. I don't move until dawn. Sometime after the sun goes up, I go into the kitchen and come back with the butcher knife. In the early morning light I lean over and attack the dining-room table. I stab the beautiful oak, gouging it, scratching deep furrows into the finish. When I pull the knife out, I see several people across from me, three children—one is you, the others are boys, you have brothers like I did—and William is laughing and passing a turkey platter around and there's someone else—a woman wearing an old-fashioned white dress like my great-aunts wore, and she's putting a casserole dish on the table and she smiles at me in a special way—*it's my mother*—and she leans down to kiss the top of your head—

Then there's nothing. They're all gone.

≈ 〜◦◯◦〜 ≈

Night after night, confined to our silent house by shock and confusion, I slept on the living-room sofa. It was never mentioned, night after night after night as calendar pages flipped over and were thrown away, year after year after year. Sometimes your father and I sat staring into space at the kitchen table in silent bewilderment. No matter the year, though, no matter the march of time, our hands did not touch. After a while we barely knew why. No one spoke of the past. No one spoke of leaving. Each of us needed the other in order to sit this lifelong vigil over the death of our dreams.

I will never forgive you.

You will never have another child.

Words that form the sentence of forever. From some words, some events, we don't recover. The enemy camp is peopled with giants—an illness, a war, a hospital, a seminary, the meanness of a time and place.

I always said that some things are there even when you can't see them. And some things aren't there even when it looks like they are. A family, a future. Love. Your father and I, entombed in our desolate vault, united by the defeat of the spirit, buried alive by inertia and fate, became our own elegy, static shadows flickering in a lighted window for half a century.

There's one other thing.

A year after William returned, during a blackening depression, I asked for and got a hysterectomy I did not need. I couldn't bear the weight of hope.

Uta Moazen once said that every life is a vulnerable life, that even the act of breathing—elixir of oxygen taken in, noxious poison expelled—makes possible the day of reversal.

Birth begins the end. A beautiful child in a shroud. Love invites us to the banquet of heartache.

Every life is a brave life.

Lyra's Epilogue

∞

2006

Fall leaves skip across the Brantley graveyard, floating crimson and ocher and coral. This is a modest cemetery, its only stately monument a soaring eight-foot angel commemorating the life of a local suffragette. I like it that my mother's family is buried in her shadow. Across from me honeysuckle vines encircle the wrought-iron fence and remind me of my childhood days here, when I idled down these steamy small-town streets, got a Coca-Cola at the gas station and stuffed salted peanuts through its narrow glass neck, went to the drugstore and the dress shop and said "Hey there" to people who always knew my name. My mother sent me here every summer; it was a gift, my annual respite from listening at the door of parental despair.

The October sun is hearty at midday, but floating loose-cotton clouds provide now-and-again relief. I stare at my real grandmother's grave; a low cement wall outlines the rectangular shape of her coffin. My grandfather's grave, with the grandmother I knew beside him, lies a few feet away, my mother's brothers and their wives nearby. Some cousins. A lot of military insignia carved into stone. One way or another, everyone's come home. Mine is the arrested branch of this family tree, though; our line ends with the child who chose to have no child. My path, where I've placed my faith, has veered sharply from that of my mother.

My mother was a child raptly peering into the sky for airplanes she couldn't see; she had faith in the unseen. Bloodlines are borne of this. I was the child wandering through family ruins on the ground, where the losses were too vivid to ignore. Who knows where chance and choice intersect? I made sure I was *inside* those planes.

The sun dazzles, leaves rustle in the trees. It's a gorgeous day to be buried.

Two years ago, when my mother's heart stopped, my father and I were in the room, both asleep; it was the nurse Darlene who discovered she was gone and woke us. My mother probably liked that—no fuss, the messenger a kind woman she respected, who found the scissors for me to cut a lock of my mother's hair. Two hundred people came to the funeral—Mr. Blue Eyes was a pallbearer, Johnny Truesdale brought his whole family. A formally robed choir, the hymns my mother wanted, a regal procession with the casket covered by an elegant white pall. The pall was laid across the burnished wood coffin by two women who'd known her for forty years; one folded the gold-embroidered cloth with tears streaming from her eyes.

I placed my grandmother's painting of a lone woman in a boat in moonlight on a vestibule table. Beside it sat the eight-by-ten engagement photograph of my parents. As people filed into the sanctuary, I studied the old picture. They're sitting on the brick steps of the Brantley house: my father sports a head full of unruly blond curls, my mother wears a 1940s silk dress with a corsage on her shoulder, her shapely legs crossed, her hand on his thigh. Both smile seductively, gazing at each other raptly, intently.

Once upon a time they really did love each other.

Perhaps our lives are like impressionist paintings. Up close, when we're young, it's chaos—wavy lines, thickened textural masses, shadowy indiscernible forms. The picture only emerges as we stand back, as the gallop of years forces us to see again what we thought we knew. Not that all the questions ever get answered. But as I gaze at my parents in love, I wonder: If you start like that, in the innocence of that time and place, do you ever stop hoping love will return?

I remember something Uta Moazen once said: *A long life takes courage.*

Despite my protests that she should go to Brantley, my father insisted we bury my mother in Columbia, in the plot they purchased in their sixties. It was right next to woodlands so at least she'll hear the birds sing, I told myself that day, and if the dead walk she'll have a nice stroll under the pines. As earth was spilled across her coffin, my father leaned over to hide the single tear on his cheek. After the receiving line in the church, he and I walked back out to the gravesite. The funeral home had now lowered the casket and the family funeral spray, miniature red roses amid white baby's breath, lay in state over my mother's heart.

As we stand there, I wish my father would tell me about their early days together, tell me how much he loved her. *Please, just once say you love me too.*

"Daddy—"

He looks at me. "You still doing that painting? You haven't sold anything in years, have you? I didn't think that would amount to much."

He walks away.

I feel shot by a stun-gun. *Did he really say what I heard?* He did. I clamber after him to tell him to go to hell, but family friends waylay me to offer condolences. After they drive off, my father announces, "I won't be buried in this cemetery myself. I have other plans."

A sparse wind blows through the trees, the pines creak, the hot sun blares down. I plan to bury him in a landfill.

"You're going to leave Mother alone? Wasn't this cemetery *your* idea? For the two of you to be here together?"

He looks at me with irritation. "I'm going to sell the house as soon as I can. The paintings are yours, of course. And your mother's jewelry. I know you wanted that table my father made, some other furniture. A man from the church tells me they'll bring a good price from an antique dealer. I could just sell them and send you the money."

"The table your father made with his own hands—don't you want your *child* to have it?"

"I need to get this done now. I'd appreciate it if you'd take down those photos your mother put on the den wall."

"Must you do this so *soon*? She just died." My baby pictures, graduating from high school, leaving for Europe, getting married. Will he keep any at all? I'm sure not.

When we reach his car, I say, "I want my grandfather's desk. And those journals you offered me."

"You can have the journals, but I promised that desk to your mother's cousin from Atlanta. She called yesterday, she said she'd always wanted that desk from Brantley."

I slam my hand against the car door. *What is it with him and furniture?*

"Louise would want her cousin to get that desk," he says. "I promised her the dining-room table too. Her feelings might be hurt if I don't give it to her."

"And *my* feelings? Have you ever cared what I feel?"

He stomps away, turns around. "I gave you and your mother a good life, you had food to eat and a roof over your head."

My blood pressure clears a mountain and I'm set to attack in full force—I've been oiling these weapons for years. "Do you have any idea what kind of father you've been?"

"You're mad with somebody else and taking it out on me. And I don't appreciate it!"

Suddenly it hits me: I need a new language. I need concepts that haven't yet been invented to describe what's been missing here. And even if I find words that differentiate love from obligation, he's not going to get it. I start laughing—I've been doing what my mother always did, acting like if I just say the right thing he'll snap out of it and take me out for an ice-cream cone.

He looks like he doesn't know what to do. Finally he says, "You've had that same laugh since you were a little girl—you laughed all the time at Christmas. You always did love Christmas."

I stare at him in surprise—he did notice *something*.

He says he needs to get home, that he's got twenty things to do. Long and lanky in his pinstriped suit, he slides into his 1992 Oldsmobile; still incensed about Pearl Harbor, he says he'll die before driving a "foreign" car. He tells me my rental car is going to cost a fortune and probably isn't safe.

"In my next life I'm going to be a rich man," he adds. "I'll get a Cadillac and you can borrow it to move off that Rocky Mountain you live on. Not enough air to breathe, you probably have TB. You could end up in an iron lung."

Even he's smiling at this cheery pronouncement. He cranks up the Oldsmobile and waves at me hesitantly. I'm certain he wonders how he ended up with progeny; I'm certain that is the exact word he would use.

As he drives off, I picture him in the rancher's backyard watering my mother's flowers, as I saw him do on a recent trip home. He's standing in the twilight whistling to himself, the hose pressure so high it's drowning the camellia bushes. I stand at a window watching, wondering what he feels, what he thinks about evening after evening as he attends living things. And maims them. Something about him catches in my throat—a loneliness. Only he's not lonely, I am. He's ironically protected by what he does not feel. He looks up toward the window where I stand but doesn't see me. He whistles and waters on and I remain invisible.

When I return to my mother's grave the day after the funeral, I bring wind chimes and hang them in a nearby tree. I want her to have music. Staring at the inert ground, I also yell what I've never said—*I didn't deserve the guilt for your unhappiness, you should have stood up for me, for yourself, I needed—*

The melody played by the chimes stops my tirade; somewhere in the Low Country mingled body tissue still rests deep in Carolina soil. *I will always miss you.*

The next day my father finds the wind chimes. He decides the wind might blow them free to damage nearby tombstones, so he secures them to the tree trunk with baling wire. He ties them so tightly they can't make a sound.

I go back and cut the wire.

He comes back, rebales the chimes.

I go and cut the wire again.

After my parents' house was sold, my father simply disappeared. He always wanted to travel so perhaps he's out there wandering about. Before he went AWOL, he sent me the paintings and jewelry and the blackened silver coffeepot from China Grove. A few months later, care of an attorney, I also received a package and letter from him:

> *This is the lawyer who'll contact you when I'm gone. I've used money left over from the farm, those investments I made, to hire a fellow to regularly clean my family's cemetery there. The cemetery still belongs to me, I wasn't about to let anyone steal my ancestry. I've bequeathed the property to the American Legion. I had to burn my journals—I realized it wouldn't be safe to have anyone read the things I wrote. They could come after me. Or sue you.*

The note is signed "Love, Dad."

I shake my head—did I really think the end would differ from the rest?

Inside the box, carefully folded, almost lying in state, is a World War II army uniform in perfect condition, scratchy dark khaki wool a half-century old, dry-cleaned and protected from moths for decades. I hold the waist-length Eisenhower jacket up and notice how slim he was at twenty; written in ink by hand on the lining are his name and a number. A Second Infantry Division badge and three sergeant's stripes on each sleeve. Above one chest pocket a ribboned bar is decorated with three metal stars: the stars may signify campaigns—the Invasion, the Battle of the Bulge, I don't know what the other would be. There's a brass rifle pin for combat experience, a cobalt blue bar I'll later learn is a Presidential Unit Citation.

Beneath the uniform, in a rectangular leather box, is the Bronze Star Medal, a five-point star with a tiny five-point star in the center. The fourth highest award for bravery hangs suspended from a red ribbon. *My father.*

I pin the medal to the jacket, thinking how much a war that ended before my birth cost all of us. Staring at the smaller star within the larger, I caress the rough fabric and imagine what might have been.

Paint-box leaves—the hues of heaven—flutter into the open grave in the Brantley cemetery. I stare at the two coral maple leaves that will go into the dark cavern of eternity with my mother. As I've begun painting again, painting the ruins of old houses in particular, I've wondered if we're more haunted by the things that happen to us or by the things that don't, by what our parents do or by the things they don't do. Either way, we can never take the full measure of their experience. What I know for sure is that one person's tragic life can mercilessly draw blood from others.

The hearse pulls in slowly. It wasn't easy, getting a judge to declare a living parent missing so I could become next of kin for the other. Various cousins have come and we stand for the short service; a woman from the church where my parents were married sings "Somebody's Callin' My Name." My mother's sheet music of that song was so worn it had to have been important to her. I gaze around the family plot. If my father ever surfaces, I'll bury him here too. There's only room at my mother's feet but it's a nice spot, right behind the Brantley suffragette—that'll probably keep him awake until the resurrection.

As a woman sings over my mother's new grave and yellow leaves drift onto the freshly-turned earth, I recall the day she stopped me from burying the colored leaves I loved. When the singing fades, my mother's pecan casket, made of the same trees that guard Lincoln Street, goes down into the earth again. Home finally, to rest at the right hand of her mother.

⚭⚬⊝⚬⚭

After my mother's second burial, I drive fifteen miles to the outskirts of another small forgotten town and pull into a dilapidated dirt driveway nearly blockaded by a jungle of overgrown vines and trees. I get out of the car and carefully pick my way across the yard filled with broken bricks, rampant weeds, fallen limbs. I reach the green iron park bench cemented to a concrete slab—to keep vandals from stealing it—and sit down and stare at the house. When I had the bench installed, the Charleston delivery men looked at me like I was from another planet.

I sit down and study the flint gray shell of the wooden house built in the late 1800s. The roof is partially caved in and only a few steps to the wide front porch remain; I once took a chance and climbed them but couldn't go farther because the porch floor is missing, as are the railings and every single balustrade. Although the front door remains, there's no floor inside the house either. Scavengers probably pulled up twenty-foot heart pine boards decades ago. The fireplace chimney has toppled over, and a large magnolia tree sprouts through the gaping roof. Decorative tendrils of Spanish moss everywhere. Our ghostly Southern air-plant that feeds on rain and dust and never harms the trees it embraces.

Overgrown tree limbs cast cooling shadows over me on the bench, but sunlight floods the house's interior, stripes the century-old dark beams that supported the missing floors. The light slides like warm liquid across the magnolia's leaves, the white blooms velvety, iridescent. The air is loamy, thick with the promises of nature. Copperheads may be lurking in the piles of broken boards and bricks behind the house, but in the old trees warbling songbirds carry on a different life.

My painter grandmother grew up in this house. My mother once brought me here: the family who owned the house had discovered several paintings in the attic and offered them to us. Stretchers so old they looked historic, supporting images undoubtedly painted by a teenager. To my mother's delight, the owners let us wander about. The twenty acres behind the house sported tall rows of corn; now they're a geography of weeds and brambles. Even so, sometimes what I see there are long symmetrical rows of loblolly pine trees.

For days after he sent it to me, I kept my father's uniform draped over a chair by a window, as though he were visiting and might enjoy the view of the Rockies. Eventually this seemed demented, so I got out the box and began refolding the heavy wool jacket. When I got to the pants, I felt something in the right front pocket and reached in and pulled out several hundred-dollar bills. I reached in again and came out with others. Had to be over two thousand dollars. Very old-looking bills. Did he hide this money here years ago and later forgot about it?

I picked up one of the bills and stared at Grover Cleveland's face.

Good Lord. It's a thousand-dollar bill. Is it real?

I stared at the other bills spilling across my father's uniform. All the same. I counted them one by one. A quarter of a million dollars.

The world is kinder for those who can love unselfishly, and more colorful, more intriguing, for the idiosyncratic, the truly unforgettable who range among us. I gaze again at the tumbling-down structure from my mother's family purchased with my father's money. It feels like a place to come home to, a place where I *belong.* Symbols matter, and a ruin is not always a ruin. The house is too gone to be saved, true; I know my cousins wonder what I'll do with a worthless old place in the middle of nowhere. Maybe I should buy a Checker cab to sit in the driveway. Likely I'll just visit here now and again. Do a painting of the house. Walk about and see what I see. Plant a pine tree or two. I'll have to show up from time to time to check on my ancestral holdings.

What would Mr. Blue Eyes say to a picnic at my old home place?

When I get to Columbia two hours later, before heading to the airport I drive across town to Lincoln Street and park at the renovated house we never owned. I sit and watch our lives coalesce in the air above the house and descend into the willing earth beneath it. Now we're down there with the man-killing elephant, the carousel ladies, the wounded men in gray, the white-haired old lady with one arm. We rest in the comforting arms of our dearest possession, our history.

I wave to the barefoot young woman in a flowered dress—she's smiling and swinging her child in a circle.

Acknowledgments

My gratitude to the following organizations for their financial support of my work: the McKnight Foundation, the Jerome Foundation, the Helene Wurlitzer Foundation of New Mexico, the Hawthornden Castle International Retreat for Writers in Scotland. Also to Lenoir Rhyne University, the Loft Literary Center, and the St. Mar Arts Group.

Individuals who made significant contributions to this book, directly or indirectly, are: Natalie Goldberg, Ellen Hawley, Constance Kunin, Brian McDermott, Rose Munns, and Rebecca Schneider. My thanks to one and all.

To my father, my appreciation and admiration for his steadfastness, generosity, stellar wit, and an originality beyond compare.

My love to Robert Bush and to Jill Nichols Dineen, the compatriots of a lifetime.

And certainly not least: Kudos to Kieran the Retriever for his sage advice and excellent company. That dog ferries sunlight in his soul.

This book is indebted to the history of the grandparents I never knew, William Martin Lightsey and Henrietta Elizabeth Copeland. Love to all my Lightsey kin, bred in the bone *raconteurs* who never let a good yarn depend on fact or lack for truth.

So many people who cross a writer's path affect who that writer becomes. A special few have been: the wonderful teachers in the Carolinas who first ignited my imagination, the New Yorker in love with Virginia Woolf, the dyslexic who made me understand reading, the bookseller who showed me St. Thomas, the fabulous mask-maker in New Orleans, the Canadian pianist whose music (and high comedy) inspired me, the British poet and our hike to the Rosslyn Chapel, the Tennessee redhead who died too young, the Taos native who let me open the acequia gates when the spring run-off came down, my Twin Cities writing students who showed up at a public lecture I gave dressed as "Southern Belles" (complete with mammoth hats) and sat in the front row.

Thank you to those who listened to the stories in this book, and to all my gratitude for so many luminous moments.

Linda Lightsey Rice
Minneapolis, 2012

About the Author

Linda Lightsey Rice is the author of the novel *Southern Exposure,* originally published by Doubleday, which was nominated for the PEN Hemingway Award, was a featured selection of The Literary Guild, and was compared by *Kirkus Reviews* and other publications to William Faulkner's *Sanctuary.* An excerpt from *Southern Exposure* recently appeared in *The American South* anthology published in Germany.

The author was a 2004 recipient of the McKnight Foundation Fellowship in Creative Prose. A former newspaper reporter who also worked in the New York publishing industry, she has received artistic awards from the Jerome Foundation, Virginia Commonwealth University, the South Carolina Humanities Commission, the Loft Literary Center, the Helene Wurlitzer Foundation of New Mexico, and the Hawthornden Castle International Retreat for Writers in Scotland.

She has taught creative writing at the University of Tennessee, Lenoir Rhyne University, St. Catherine University, and the Chautauqua Institution. She taught master classes in the novel at the Loft Literary Center in Minneapolis, where she won a teaching award and led several programs for promising young writers.

A native of South Carolina, Linda Lightsey Rice has also lived in New York, Virginia, North Carolina, Ohio, New Orleans, New Mexico, and Ireland. She currently resides in Minneapolis and in Tennessee.

Southern Exposure remains available in paperback and as an eBook. For information about the author's upcoming projects or events, please visit *www.lindalightseyrice.com*.

18482756R00156

Made in the USA
Lexington, KY
07 November 2012